HOUSE *of* BELONGING

ALSO BY ANDREA THOME

THE HESSE CREEK SERIES
Walland
Seeds of Intention

HOUSE *of* BELONGING

ANDREA THOME

hesse
creek

media

This is a work of fiction. Names, characters, organizations, places, events, and incidents are either products of the author's imagination or are used fictitiously.

Published by Hesse Creek Media, Chicago
www.andreathome.com

Edited and Designed by Girl Friday Productions
www.girlfridayproductions.com

Editorial: Stefanie Hargreaves, Michelle Hope Anderson
Interior Design: Rachel Marek
Cover Design: Paul Barrett
Image Credits: Cover photographs © Andrea Thome

ISBN-13: 978-0-9978504-4-4
e-ISBN: 978-0-9978504-9-9

Library of Congress Control Number: 2017919827

First Edition

Printed in the United States of America

*"There is nothing I would not do
for those who are really my friends.
I have no notion of loving people by
halves, it is not my nature."*
—Jane Austen

*For my friends. You're the second family
I've created for myself, and I adore you.*

CHAPTER
ONE

She'd sworn she wouldn't look, but when the moment arrived, Laina Ming couldn't help herself.

It felt like intruding on something she had no business witnessing, but Laina was confident she wasn't the only one who felt like an interloper that day because of the way his emotions were so plainly and openly etched across his face. The groom's expression had run the gamut from carefree to nervous, to the look he wore now as his gaze finally settled on his bride. Laina felt a tightness in her throat as she watched from her seat. He was so dashing in his shirt and bow tie, with trousers held up by suspenders, a dusting of russet whiskers covering his face. But it was the raw emotion behind his smile that caused Laina to swallow hard in an effort to rid herself of the lump in her throat.

She turned her attention toward the object of the man's affection. The bride's tall, slender frame was draped elegantly in the most perfect strapless pale-yellow dress with an attached lace collar that accentuated her collarbone. A mane of chestnut-colored hair floated gently in the breeze behind her. She wore a crown of tiny white flowers, and as she drew closer, Laina could see tears rolling down her cheeks, in contrast to the brilliant smile on her face.

Everyone gathered that evening at Walland House in Aspen, Colorado, was enchanted. They knew what Laina had come to learn over the past year. Willow Armstrong and Garrett Oliver were kindred spirits, and two of the most likable people you'd ever want to meet. It was impossible not to root for this couple's happiness.

Laina had met them both the previous summer, thanks to an introduction by India and Wyatt Hinch, mutual acquaintances who were visiting from Tennessee. Laina had only been living in Aspen for a few months at that time, and had literally bumped into India coming out of a yoga class downtown one morning. They'd met a few years before when Laina had been a guest chef at the resort in Tennessee where India and Wyatt still lived and worked. They hadn't really kept in touch, though, so they were delighted to have run into each other so unexpectedly in Aspen. Before she knew it, Laina had agreed to cater the upcoming wedding of India's dear friends and coworkers.

The music ended, and Willow was standing next to Garrett at the edge of the forest, their hands clasped together. The energy between them was palpable as they stood surrounded by the glow of twinkle lights that tightly wrapped the trunk of the old oak tree serving as their altar. It was no surprise to anyone when Garrett leaned over immediately for a soft kiss, drawing an admonishment from the minister.

"Who gives this woman in marriage to this impatient young man?" Finn winked at Garrett, glad for the moment of levity. The old farmer needed the opportunity to get a handle on his own emotions. He'd been stunned when they'd asked him to officiate their wedding, and even wondered if they'd been kidding. Garrett had come to feel like a second son to Finn, and was something of a brother to Finn's own adopted son, Wyatt. Finn's wife, Susan, had helped him become a minister online, and now here he was, a bona fide preacher man.

Finn raised his eyebrows expectantly at Wyatt, waiting for an answer to his question before he moved on.

"I do," said Wyatt, clasping Garrett on the shoulder and giving Willow a kiss on the cheek before stepping to the side to stand in line with the only other groomsman.

Wyatt glanced across the altar at his own wife, who was standing up for Willow, along with their good friend Violet. Both women had tears in their eyes, and the expression on India's face reminded Wyatt once again why he was so grateful she was his partner in life.

Laina watched the exchange between them, trying to ignore the feeling of envy that bubbled up every time she was around these people. Shaking her head slightly in an effort to clear the unwelcome thought, her eyes shifted inadvertently to the other groomsman standing next to Wyatt. He was the only one in the entire congregation who wasn't focused on the bride and groom.

Instead, he was staring right back at Laina, with a corner of his mouth turned up in a slight smile.

Damn.

Laina knew he'd be there; after all, Logan Matthews *was* Willow's brother. She'd met Logan before she'd met Willow and Garrett, both introductions made by the hand of India. Their first encounter had been during the Food and Wine Classic the previous summer, after Laina had finished up her presentation on the kitchen garden. It had been obvious to Laina that India thought she and Logan would be a good match, but Laina had made it clear to Logan on several occasions since that she wasn't interested, despite his continued attempts at flirting with her.

Laina had come to Aspen to begin again after abruptly ending an unhealthy relationship. The last thing she'd wanted was to wing walk into another situation like the one she'd left behind in New York. She recognized a charmer when she saw one, and she'd had enough of that type of man to last her a lifetime. It occurred to her that Logan was doing it again now, and it was unsettling. Enough so that she felt herself involuntarily frown at him before she could resist. She lowered her gaze, paying her program more attention than it deserved, but not before she'd registered his response.

Is he laughing at me? Why did I give him the pleasure of a reaction at all?

Laina was certain Logan wasn't used to being ignored, but that was exactly what she'd done whenever she'd seen him in town over the past year, and it's what she planned to do again that night. If she could just get through the reception, she knew she'd be much too preoccupied in the coming weeks and months to give him another thought. Besides, Laina was aware that Logan's job at Walland House was time-consuming and would keep him out of her chili, literally and figuratively.

Willow and Garrett had informed her that their new resort, Walland House, had been so well received that they were forgoing their honeymoon until late October. That signaled the start of the shoulder season, which began at the end of autumn and lasted for the few quiet weeks before the popular ski season kicked off around Thanksgiving. Besides, the Aspen Food and Wine Classic was just a couple of weeks away, and they were all entering their busiest time of the year as a result. The Classic was the largest and most prestigious of its kind, a huge draw for the Aspen Valley each summer. Hordes of foodies showed up to mix and mingle with the top names in the food and wine industry. There wasn't much time to think about anything else during the hectic June weekend.

Laina was shaken from her thoughts by a murmur from the young woman seated next to her.

"Isn't he adorable? How that man has managed to remain single is beyond me." The petite blonde gave her a sidelong glance before continuing. "Maybe by the end of the night he won't be. Rumor has it—he didn't bring a date."

Laina followed the woman's gaze straight back to Logan, who was now watching as the bride and groom sealed their vows with a kiss. He was still wearing the same lopsided grin, however, almost as if he could feel Laina's eyes on him.

Before Laina could answer the woman, everyone rose to their feet to cheer the bride and groom as they made their way back down the aisle, hand in hand. The sun had set, casting a warm glow over the wedding guests as they spilled out of the rows of white wooden folding chairs and headed for the crushed gravel path that would lead them to the reception area. A dance floor was set up nearby, next to the aspen grove that separated the resort from Willow and Garrett's own property next door.

Dinner would take place just steps from the main lodge of Walland House, where Laina's staff had been busy during the ceremony putting the final touches on trays of appetizers. Even now, servers dressed in dark denim pants and gingham shirts headed out the door, silver trays in hand.

Laina could hear the music starting up as she stepped into the kitchen, and she glanced out the window as she slipped into her chef's jacket. She smiled when she saw Violet's husband, Rex, on the steel guitar, kicking the evening off with a bluegrass rendition of a popular wedding song by Train. She was happy to see that guests were helping themselves to the drinks being offered out of the back of two vintage pickup trucks parked near the clearing. One held galvanized buckets of beer and wine nestled in ice while the other had everything needed to make mixed drinks in little glass mason jars.

The wedding celebration continued, and the edible creations that spilled forth from the kitchen were absolute showstoppers. Laina had just put the finishing touches on the nests of chocolate egg truffles that would go home with guests after the reception when she felt a playful slap on her rear end.

"I can't believe you pulled it off."

Donovan Laird was Laina's sous-chef and best friend. They'd met years ago at the Natural Gourmet Institute in New York where they'd both been students, and after an awkward attempt at dating, they'd been brutally honest with each other about their lack of chemistry. They'd been two peas in a pod ever since. Van was six years older than Laina, and he'd always been a stabilizing force in her life, despite remaining a bit of a mystery. He didn't share much about his family, but that was OK with Laina. He'd become her confidant and closest friend over the years, and she trusted Van with her life. Laina couldn't imagine having anyone else by her side, especially as she prepared to open her new restaurant in Aspen.

Convincing Van to move to Colorado with her hadn't been hard. He'd recently broken up with a girlfriend and had been looking for a reason to do the same with a particularly temperamental chef he was no longer inspired to work for. Van was an excellent chef, even though he'd started his culinary career later than most. Still, Laina wondered sometimes if his heart was truly in it. She hoped that this new opportunity in Aspen would provide him the creative freedom she knew he'd always craved.

Laina smiled at her dear friend, wiping the chocolate-avocado mousse left on her hands with a nearby dish towel before unbuttoning her chef's coat and shrugging out of it to reveal the simple black dress she'd worn to the wedding.

"Come on, Van, you doubted me? You know better than to do that." Laina kissed him on his whiskered cheek, and was rewarded with a dimpled smile. Van was one of the most handsome men Laina had ever met, and his faint Scottish accent was the clincher. It was a minor miracle that he had maintained such a total lack of self-awareness for someone so good-looking. Even tonight, in his own black chef's jacket, and with his lucky bandanna wrapped around his forehead, he was striking. His hard work alongside Laina and the rest of the kitchen crew over the last fourteen hours had done nothing to diminish that fact. Laina hadn't been surprised at all by the number of female guests who'd stopped by the kitchen to catch a glimpse of her captivating friend at work.

Van leaned his large frame against the counter now, handing her a brew that he'd swiped from the Sub-Zero refrigerator as they watched the rest of their team clean up the remaining pots and pans. Laina and Van clinked bottles, each of them taking a long drag from their icy-cold beers. They could hear the laughter and music as guests enjoyed the post-dinner dancing and drinks, the alcohol having loosened everyone up just enough to consider themselves excellent dancers.

Van bumped Laina with his hip to get her attention and pushed away from the counter, unbuttoning his coat and slipping it off to reveal his usual all-black work ensemble of a T-shirt and jeans.

"Come on. They've got this covered." He gestured toward the rest of their young staff, busy tidying up the kitchen. "You know full well that India will come looking for you if you don't get out there and enjoy a little bit of this party. You promised her you would, and I promised her I'd make you."

Van finished off his beer in one long swallow, setting the bottle down with a thud on the counter next to Laina. Ignoring the protest in her eyes, he nodded toward the beer in her hand. "You'd better finish that if you're planning to, because we're hitting the dance floor."

Outside, the party was in full swing. The evening was warm for early summer, and the dance floor was hopping. The band had finished up a while ago, and now the tunes were cranking thanks to the DJ who had been hired for the late-night crowd.

India's husband, Wyatt, was headed toward the house when he saw Laina and Van emerge from the kitchen. "You've got good timing. My wife just sent me in after the two of you. I'm glad I won't be returning empty-handed."

The trio chatted for a few moments about the rave reviews guests had given the food and the impending opening of Laina's new restaurant. But when the conversation shifted to the NBA playoffs, Laina saw her opportunity to escape, and she quietly slipped away while the men talked.

The setting was pure magic. Hundreds of icicle lights hung from the tree branches overhead, and tables held flickering lanterns surrounded by mason jars overflowing with delicate flowers.

This wedding was Willow and Garrett personified. Laina watched for a moment as the couple danced together to an upbeat Bruno Mars song. She couldn't help but grin when Garrett picked his bride up and swung her around before letting her slide slowly down into his embrace for a kiss that made their friends blush.

Laina turned to fix herself a vodka and soda, and as she was squeezing a lemon wedge she felt someone ease up next to her. She knew who it was before she turned to face him.

"You know, you really *should* open a restaurant. That was some dinner you served up tonight." Logan smiled at her, that same cheeky look he'd given her during the ceremony. "Just a shame you weren't out here to enjoy it with us."

He reached around her to grab the bottle of vodka to make himself a drink, brushing up against her ever so slightly in the process. The effect was as if someone had run a feather across her bare neck and shoulders, and Laina involuntarily shivered at the intrusion of her personal space.

Logan noticed her stiffen, and he stifled a smile. "Sorry, I just figured I'd need something a little stronger if I was going to get up the courage to ask you to dance. I mean, a guy can only handle so much rejection from one person, so go easy on me if the answer is no."

He'd added ice cubes and a splash of Pellegrino to the vodka in his glass while he spoke, and now he was stirring his drink and trying to gauge her response to his offer while he did so. This was the closest he'd been to her in weeks, so he took the opportunity to study her while he awaited her answer.

Logan felt that, with her flawless skin and jet-black hair, Laina was the most exotic woman he'd ever laid eyes on. Her last name spoke of an Asian heritage, but he knew from a quick Google search that she had Italian roots too. He didn't think she looked like she belonged to either ethnicity. No, she was definitely one of a kind. She studied him curiously with eyes that were somewhere between brown and green. He couldn't decide which.

"Here you are. I knew you'd try to wriggle away when I turned my back." Van had sidled up next to Laina, sliding his left arm around her waist protectively. He reached for a sip of her drink before handing it back to her with a wink.

Laina watched in amusement as Logan's face fell just for a moment before he regained his composure.

Van wasn't through with him yet. "Who's this, Laina?" He looked squarely at Logan. "Friend of the bride or groom?"

Logan steeled himself with a sip of his drink before extending his right hand in greeting. "Logan Matthews. I'm a friend to both actually, but I'm also the brother of the bride. And you are . . . ?"

Logan knew exactly who this man was. Chef Donovan Laird had been the talk of his dinner table, at least among the ladies, but Logan wasn't going to give the man the pleasure of divulging that awareness. He'd heard his sister and India giggling about the handsome Scot and pondering whether there was anything going on between him and their mysterious girlfriend. Apparently, there was.

Van just laughed, extending his own hand to meet Logan's. "I'm Van. Nice to meet you. Your sister and brother-in-law are good people."

Van turned his attention back to Laina. "Now, you promised me a dance, lass, and a dance we'll have."

He nodded at Logan, who mumbled something unintelligible as Van ushered Laina out toward the pulsating mob of revelers. They hit the floor in time for an Ed Sheeran song that Laina loved, so they jumped right in.

Laina leaned forward to shout over the music into Van's ear. "You enjoyed that, didn't you?" She pulled back to watch the grin bloom across Van's handsome face, and there was her answer.

He moved closer to respond. "I predicted that coming a mile away. I've seen the way he looks at you, and I know you've been doing your best to get him to bugger off since last summer. So I thought I'd help drive the point home."

They laughed together, enjoying the freedom of cutting loose after such a long and stressful night of cooking. From all outward appearances, anyone would have thought they were a couple, thanks to their comfortable way with each other.

Logan was still watching from the edge of the dance floor, wondering how he'd read her so wrong. He knew Laina had been doing her best to avoid him, but he also thought he'd felt chemistry when she'd caught him staring at her during the ceremony. He hadn't been able to help himself.

No one had ever captured his attention the way Laina had. Sure, the thrill of the chase was exciting, but he'd been intrigued by something else about her from day one.

Now, as she danced with abandon, her eyes closed and arms up over her head, he thought she was more beautiful than ever. Her dark hair was cut into an edgy midlength style that perfectly framed her chiseled features.

As she swayed to the beat, her hair swept across her face, inciting Logan to curse under his breath: *Damned Scottish accent; it wasn't that cool.*

Laina was fully aware that Logan was still watching her, and she was mildly annoyed with herself for feeling pleased by his attention. She was about to tell Van that she felt bad for torturing the poor guy when she saw the blonde who'd been admiring Logan during the ceremony glide up next to him and start flirting. Before long, Logan took the woman's hand and led her to the dance floor, just as the music slowed down. When Laina saw him draw the woman up against his chest, it wasn't relief that she felt.

Grabbing Van by the hand, she steered him back toward the lodge kitchen, ready to wrap things up for the night and put this reception behind her. She intended to focus on why she'd come to Aspen in the first place. She had a restaurant to open and a new chapter of her life to begin. There was no time for distractions.

CHAPTER
TWO

It was well past midnight by the time they had finished packing up all their equipment. Laina made sure the staff had been paid, and Van had already left to drop their equipment back at the restaurant before heading home for the night. Laina was about to shut the lights off in the kitchen when the bride and groom surprised her by rounding the corner. Willow was barefoot and had the bottom of her dress tossed over one arm, her other hand joined with Garrett's.

"Oh, Laina! Thank God you're still here. Everything was amazing. Thank you for helping to make our reception so special." She paused, biting her lip. "There's just one thing; we must have burned so many calories dancing—we're starving! Is there anything left we can grab to take home with us?" She grinned up at her husband's adoring face. "We were hoping for a carpet picnic in front of the fire before we call it a night. It's sort of our thing."

Laina laughed and turned back toward the refrigerator to remove a stack of Tupperware filled with leftovers that she'd stashed inside earlier. Placing the containers on the counter in front of the newlyweds, she couldn't help basking in their glow for a moment. "I don't think my food made much difference, but I appreciate the compliment. It was a beautiful night, and you two deserve every bit of happiness. I'm honored to have been a small part of your story."

Willow stepped forward to give Laina a quick hug. "I'm glad to see you managed to have a good time while you were at it." Pausing, she smiled shyly. "Van seems like a lot of fun. I'm sure it was nice to have him here . . . working with you."

Laina could tell that Willow was fishing for information about her status with Van, and she was about to fess up when she thought better of it. Willow *was* Logan's sister. Better to be vague. "Van's great. I couldn't have done it without him. We've known each other for a really long time, which makes it easy to be together."

It was the truth, even if it was a little misleading.

They chatted for a few more minutes before saying their goodbyes. Once Willow and Garrett had gone, Laina grabbed her backpack and the velvet bag that contained her knife set, then turned out the lights and locked the door on her way out. She never left anyone else in charge of her Japanese steel knives, even Van. They were her prized possession, and she felt naked without them.

The air was pleasantly cool out on the porch, and she paused for a moment to savor the quiet. There was nothing quite like a Rocky Mountain evening, particularly out here, away from town. She was still adjusting to it, after having spent the better part of the last decade in New York City. It had taken her months to get used to falling asleep without the bleating horns of the taxis and other city chatter outside her window. These days, the only sounds she heard as she drifted off at night were the crickets and the frogs. And the white noise emitting from the little machine on her dresser. Old habits died hard.

Laina smiled at the scene before her, the trees still dripping with twinkle lights that no one had bothered to turn off. It really was like a scene from a movie. She was about to walk to her car when a noise from the other side of the clearing stopped her cold. She shrank back into the shadows of the porch to get a better look.

Logan had tried not to lead Kiera on, but the woman didn't seem to be too good at reading signals. Sure, it had been nice to have the distraction after his most recent rejection by Laina, and Kiera had been lots of fun out on the dance floor. She wasn't much of a conversationalist, though, and, consequently, Logan had been ready to call it a night hours ago. He was still smarting a bit from having to watch Laina with Van, who, much to Logan's displeasure, appeared to be the most charismatic man in the universe. Unfortunately, Kiera had cornered him, and before he'd known it, they were the last two guests left at the reception. He'd waited patiently with her for her Uber to arrive, which had mercifully just pulled up the driveway to collect her.

Logan opened the car door to usher Kiera inside when she surprised him by stepping closer to him, throwing her arms around his neck, and planting a kiss full of longing and invitation on him. He would have pulled away, but he was acutely aware that Laina had just appeared on the front porch, and from the way she'd stayed hidden in the shadows of the eaves, it was clear that she didn't want him to know she was there.

Logan allowed himself the indulgence of enjoying Kiera's attention, just long enough to needle Laina a bit, and to confirm what he'd already known. There wasn't any chemistry with Kiera, at least as far as he was concerned. Laina didn't need to know that, though, so he took his time exploring Kiera's eager mouth. He finally broke the kiss after a few moments before saying good night. Kiera looked sweetly at him, still blissfully unaware that he didn't return her affections.

Logan hated himself a little for misleading her, so he inwardly promised that, spark or not, he'd take Kiera out to dinner sometime as penance. The Uber pulled away, leaving Logan standing alone in the yard. He watched from the darkness as Laina rushed silently off the porch in the opposite direction and emerged into the clearing where she'd parked her own car. As the engine purred to life, he marveled once again at this woman who'd managed to captivate him so completely. *Why is she leaving alone instead of with the Scot? And what kind of girl drives a car like that?* He watched the fading taillights of her vintage Alfa Romeo Spider as they wound down the lane and out of sight. Logan knew one thing. He wasn't finished trying to find out the answers to those questions and a whole lot of others.

It was probably too cold to have the top down, but Laina had wanted to get the hell out of there before Logan realized it was her. She shivered now as her small car flew across the winding pavement of Maroon Creek Road, the intoxicating smell from the surrounding canopy of pine trees filling her senses as she made her way back down the hill toward town.

She didn't understand why it had bothered her to see Logan with another woman. She wasn't interested in him.

She didn't have the time or energy necessary to get to know a man like that. It wasn't the first time she'd seen him with other women either. He was one of the most eligible men in town, after all, and she'd heard rumors that he'd dated his way through a good sampling of the local single women. The way he'd flirted with her again tonight, she wasn't surprised than none of those relationships had stuck.

Damn it, though, he does have charisma.

For a moment, before Van had joined them, she'd almost considered taking him up on his offer to dance. She shivered, remembering her desire to know what he smelled like. Reflecting on that carelessness now, she wondered what had gotten into her. She had enough to worry about. Her restaurant was set to open, and the Food and Wine Classic was hot on the heels of that.

Blowing out a breath, she forced herself to go over the mental checklist that was omnipresent in her thoughts these days. Tomorrow was Sunday, but that didn't mean she'd be resting. Van had agreed to meet her at nine, which meant little sleep tonight as the finalized bar order needed to be completed so everything would be stocked and ready for their debut and the start of the Classic.

Laina had opened restaurants before, both of them in New York, but neither of them was as important to her as this place. In the early days of her career, it had been all about the food. The dishes she created were nothing short of exquisite. She'd busted her tail right out of culinary school, single-mindedly working to become one of just a handful of female chefs to eventually earn two Michelin stars. When it finally happened, though, Laina was so stressed out, she was too numb to be able to enjoy the accolades. Of course her personal life had been spiraling out of control at the very same time too, but she couldn't be reminded of that right now.

Nothing was going to steal her bliss. She was living in the moment, and if her move to the mountains and the countless hours she'd spent building her yoga practice had taught her anything, it was to stay present. This restaurant would be different. She would bare her soul in a way she'd never known she'd always wanted. The concept was an exploration of detachment: from the decor, to the menu, to the food and the way in which it would be served. Laina and Van wouldn't be the only executive chefs in residence either. She had big plans for that aspect of the place. She would never again be beholden to investors and their predictable ideas. It didn't have to make sense to anyone else. It made sense to her. The concept could change every evening if she wanted it to. It felt really good to be doing something entirely her way for a change.

The gravel crunched under her tires as she pulled the car into her driveway and put it in park. She still smiled every time she came home. The small farmhouse hadn't been much to look at when she'd first seen it, but it sat on enough land for her to be able to have her own kitchen garden, and she'd had plenty of vision left to convince herself to sign on the dotted line. Because she'd been smart about the sale of her first two restaurants, she also had plenty of money left over with which to get the neglected old house up to snuff. She'd spent hours painting it inside and out, and sanded the floors back to life until they looked better than they ever had, at least according to her real estate agent, who'd already sold the property two previous times.

Laina had chosen to splurge and go fully retro in the kitchen, including black-and-white-checkered flooring and a massive Big Chill refrigerator in a color called "Pink Lemonade." This house suited her. It was quirky and fun, and it always thrilled her to walk past the suspended porch swing and her hanging ferns to open the wooden Dutch front door.

She flipped the light switch and laughed at the sight staring back at her from the foyer mirror. Her hair looked like she'd run it through with a blender, and her eyeliner was smudged at the outside corners from when she'd teared up during the chilly ride home. Another perk of living alone. She could look as terrible as she wanted to, and no one would be the wiser.

She tossed her shoes onto the bench at the foot of the stairs and bent to pick up the pile of mail that was scattered on the floor under the slot in the front door. It was mostly contractor bills, with a couple of trade magazines mixed in, but there was one letter that caught her attention. It was post-marked New York, but there was no return address on the envelope. Laina lumped it all together, the letter on top, and made her way down the hall to the kitchen. After setting the entire pile on the table, she filled her teapot with water and lit the stove to boil it, then sliced a lemon in half, squeezing the juice into her empty mug to wait.

She had a bad feeling about the letter. She'd left New York with virtually no strings attached, and she couldn't imagine how anyone had tracked her down to send a note through snail mail. She kept in touch with friends and colleagues mostly through text and e-mail these days, enjoying the peace and quiet of the new life she'd created for herself.

The whistle of the kettle brought her back, and she grabbed the handle with a hot pad, pouring the bubbling water over the lemon juice. She warmed her hands on the mug, letting the steam drift up and around her face before taking a sip. She should wait until morning to read the letter. It had been such a great day, and the wedding reception had been a huge success. It would be a shame to ruin her natural high.

Staring at the envelope for a moment longer, she decided she'd never sleep for wondering, so, setting the mug back down, she grabbed the letter and slid her finger under the flap to tear it open. As she unfolded the paper inside, a scrap of newspaper fluttered to the floor before she could catch it. She picked it up and scanned the contents of the article. Grasping the edge of the table as she read, her knees almost buckled underneath her. Both papers slipped from her hand and came to rest on the floor in front of the fridge. Laina barely made it around the corner and into the powder room before vomiting up the entire contents of her stomach.

Van had been knocking loudly, surprised that Laina had slept in so late. She was normally an early riser, which was unusual for a chef, but then she was an unusual woman. Her car was parked in the driveway, so she'd obviously made it home safely the night before. Van turned back down off the porch, trying to figure out which window might be unlocked, when he noticed her off in the distance. She'd been out for a run, which wasn't uncommon, but with the long day and late night they'd had, Van was impressed she'd found the energy to rip off her daily five-miler. She lived across from the North Star Nature Preserve, so she had miles of trails at her disposal. As she drew closer to Van, she slowed her gait, stopping just short of where he stood, bending in half to stretch her lower back and hamstrings.

"Morning, sunshine. Someone's up with the roosters." Van waited for her to respond, but she just stayed that way, bent in half, taking deep breaths in and out while she stretched. Finally, she rose, looking more beautiful than anyone should after exercise. Van shook his head, perplexed by her sour demeanor.

"Tough run, lass?" Van studied his friend, aware that she had something on her mind. He didn't press her, though. He knew better. If she wanted to talk, she would. If not now, she would when she was ready.

Laina reached into her car, grabbing a water bottle she'd stashed there in the cup holder on the way out. Taking a long drink, she felt her heartbeat start to return to normal, grateful for the gift of exercise. She'd managed to scrape herself up off the bathroom floor the night before, and after reading and rereading the article and letter, she'd folded both back up and stuck them inside the drawer next to the fridge until she could manage to process the information. She wasn't ready to talk about it with Van, though, or anyone else, for that matter, so she'd forced herself to go for a run to clear her head, as she often did. Five miles later, she wasn't exactly good as new, but at least she could cope now in a way she wasn't capable of just an hour ago.

"We've got a lot to accomplish today. I guess I'm just starting to feel the pressure a bit. Figured a run might help me get my thoughts together, and it worked. Come on. I'm ready to get the bar stocked. At least on paper."

They spent the next couple of hours on her front porch swing going over the vodkas, gins, tequilas, bourbons, and whiskeys they'd be carrying, along with a few specialty beverages for nondrinkers, including a locally brewed kombucha. There was a lot of information, and it required plenty of back-and-forth to make sure they had everything covered. Only once they'd closed the book on the needs of the bar was Laina able to relax a bit. Rolling her neck around, she reached her arms up over her head for a much-needed stretch, but instead of feeling relief, the bottled emotions unexpectedly bubbled up, manifesting in a sob that escaped her lips before she could stop it.

Van had been gathering up their paperwork, preparing to leave when the sound caught his attention, his gaze snapping back to Laina. There was a moment when it seemed like the world stood still, with no air flowing at all. Finally, Laina removed the hand she'd clapped over her mouth to utter in a choked voice the name that she'd sworn she'd never speak again.

"It's Patrick."

She didn't have to say anything else. Van dropped the papers he'd been holding and rushed across the porch to pull her into his arms.

CHAPTER
THREE

In the eighteen months since he'd moved to Aspen, Logan had managed to carve out a perfectly comfortable existence for himself. In many ways, it really hadn't been that big of a change. His was a simple life, much like the one he'd left behind in Colorado Springs in order to be nearer to his half sister and her new husband. He'd loved his job as an Expert Ranger for the Pikes Peak Ranger District, but aside from work and a few friends, there wasn't really anything tying him to that area. Finding out he had a sister and having Willow so readily invite him into her world were the best things that had ever happened to Logan. Getting a brother-in-law like Garrett was an unexpected bonus, and the two men had grown close over the past year and a half.

Willow and Garrett were the only family he had now, and his relationship with them was one that he cherished. You didn't go through something as traumatic as they had and not come out the other side monumentally changed by the experience. It had been seventeen months since the accident that had almost cost Willow her life, precipitating the need for Logan to donate a part of his liver to her. They'd both healed physically and become not only closer siblings but also best friends during the months-long process. There wasn't anything he wouldn't do for his sister, and the feeling was mutual.

Logan hadn't spoken to his own mother in over a year, but he'd received a few letters, which he'd thrown into a drawer unopened. He didn't know what she could say to change what had happened; she'd essentially vanished from his life when she realized her relationship with her son wasn't going to be a lucrative one for her anymore. *If she only knew.* He shuddered at the possibility of her realizing her error and shook his head to chase the thought away. He wanted nothing to do with her.

Willow had inherited a great deal of money from their late father, and despite Logan's repeated attempts at refusal, she'd insisted on splitting the windfall with him, right down the middle. Even *after* he'd splurged and bought himself a small horse ranch just north of Walland House, Logan still had enough money to ensure that he'd never have to work another day in his life. That wasn't his style, though. He'd wisely invested the rest of his cash, and had come up with a game plan for all his newfound free time.

He'd been thrilled when Willow and Garrett had embraced his idea of letting their guests use his horses for rides on the Walland House property and in the surrounding national forest. Logan's outdoor survival training made him the perfect person to oversee the program, and it also positioned him to occasionally lead trail rides himself. He'd struck an earlier deal with Susan and Finn, the owners of the flagship resort back in Tennessee, to plan and execute unique outdoor adventures for their Aspen guests who might be interested in such opportunities.

Temperatures were only in the fifties that Sunday morning, but the sun was hot, and he'd worked up a sweat grooming his horse Diamond after their early-morning ride. Logan set the dandy brush on the edge of the stall, peeling his shirt off and tossing it over the paddock door. The crisp morning air cooled him just enough that he could comfortably set about cleaning and storing the rest of his tack. He'd just finished lifting his saddle back onto the rack when he heard a low whistle coming from the vicinity of his office across the hall.

"I know a few ladies in town who'd pay big bucks for a snapshot of what's going on right here."

Logan grinned, shaking his head at the imposing salt-and-pepper-haired man dressed in head-to-toe denim who was standing there twirling the end of his thick mustache with his oversized hand. "Very funny, old man. Do me a favor—don't just stand there in your redneck tuxedo. Make yourself useful. Reach over on my desk and hand me a dry shirt from the stack sitting there."

Buck Randolph was Logan's foreman and one of the first friends he'd made after he moved to Aspen last spring. He'd met the experienced rancher while having a beer at a tavern in town, and after a couple of hours, they'd become buddies. In time, Buck had become a bit of a wingman for Logan. His weathered good looks attracted more mature women; Logan tended to date their daughters. A month after Logan finalized the purchase of his ranch, he asked Buck about partnering with him to run his new stables.

Logan had worked plenty of summer jobs with horses as a kid back in Pennsylvania, so he felt very comfortable around the animals, but he didn't know anything about the real business of a working stable. Buck had sold his own outfit a few years earlier after his wife, Annie, had died, and he'd moved into town to simplify his life. It was divine timing for each of them. Logan needed a steady hand, and Buck needed some excitement in his life. They'd hired a couple of local ranch hands, and together they'd started to make something of the place.

Buck reached into the office and picked up an old U2 shirt from the top of the pile on Logan's desk and wadded it up to throw to his young friend. Catching it with one hand, Logan unfolded the faded cotton tee and slid it over his head in one quick motion.

Buck helped himself to a ceramic mug sitting on a sideboard and filled it with the coffee still warming in the adjacent tack room. "Saw we had a trail ride on the books for this morning, and figured that, after your late night, you might want one of the crew to take the lead. Unfortunately, they all had late nights too, it seems, so those folks are stuck with the likes of me today, I guess." He took a sip from his mug. "Unless you'd rather take them?"

Logan poured himself a cup of coffee, his third of the morning, in the hopes that this one might finally do the trick. He hadn't slept much the night before, replaying the events of the reception in his mind over and over. By the time he'd fallen asleep, his alarm had rudely reminded him it was time to get back up again.

He'd wanted to be sure to wake up early so he'd have time to take Diamond out alone, not wanting his new horse to fall out of the routine he'd worked hard for weeks to establish. Diamond was a rescue horse, and the old boy had trust issues. It was Logan's business to change the stately animal's mind, one day at a time. He knew he was close to a breakthrough, and he wasn't going to let a hangover jeopardize that.

In truth, he hadn't had much to drink at the reception. He enjoyed the occasional beer or glass of wine, but he'd seen during his lifetime how alcohol could ruin people, so he steered clear of that particular vice for the most part. It wasn't too much alcohol that had his brain cloudy at the moment, though.

It was her.

He'd be damned if he could figure out how she'd managed to infect his thoughts so completely. He knew himself well enough to realize it wasn't just the thrill of the chase, although that was a pastime he rather enjoyed. Flirting was fun, and more importantly, it was usually fruitful and harmless because, if he did it right, no one could get that close to him. His mother's example hadn't given him much regard for the machinations of the fairer sex.

But Laina was different from most of the women he'd ever met. For one thing, it impressed him how much time and effort she'd been putting into getting her business up and running. He'd heard bits and pieces from India and Wyatt about her plans for the new restaurant, which was completely eco-friendly and had been built from the ground up. It was located right on the banks of the Roaring Fork River, and the side of the building that faced the water was nothing but glass. It was quite an investment she'd made, and the place looked and sounded like it would be vastly different than anything else in town.

"Where'd that mind of yours get to?" Buck was watching Logan's face as he waited for a response to his question. The boy had something on his mind, and it wasn't the trail ride.

"Sorry, I'm a little tired, is all. I stayed late last night to make sure everyone made it home safe." He stretched, then continued. "You go ahead and lead the group if you would, and I'll go see what else is in the works for the next couple of weeks at Walland House. I told Wyatt I'd swing by the house to meet them around ten, and it's nine forty-five now."

People were starting to wander over from Walland House for the trail ride when Logan made his way out to his old Ford Bronco, greeting them as they passed by. Most of the riders were friends of Willow and Garrett's who'd traveled in from all over the country for the wedding. Logan chuckled when he saw that the majority of them looked like they'd rather still be in bed instead of preparing to ride horses the morning after the big party. He knew from experience that a couple of hours spent in the mountain air and sunshine would be just the thing to set them right again.

Logan rolled down his window, letting his arm rest on the door as he set off for the West End. India and Wyatt were staying over there, in the house that Susan and Finn had purchased a year and a half ago when Walland House was still just an idea.

Maroon Creek Road was already filled with runners and walkers, out enjoying the beautiful morning. As he made his way around the traffic circle, it occurred to Logan that summer had seemingly arrived just in time for Willow and Garrett's wedding weekend. He was so happy for both of them, and found himself tapping along with the Keith Urban song playing on the radio, keeping time on the steering wheel. Wildflowers dotted the landscape, and as he pulled into the drive, he noticed several neighbors out working in their yards, planting flowers and hanging baskets full of brightly colored blooms from their porches.

"There he is." Finn was standing in the doorway waiting for him, having traded his fancy "wedding duds," as he'd called them, for his favorite old overalls.

All was right with the world again.

"Morning, Finn. Hope I'm not late. I squeezed in a quick ride on a horse I'm working with, and time got away from me." The two men shook hands, Finn grasping Logan on the arm in friendship.

"Just 'cause I was up with the sun doesn't mean everyone else has to be. You're right on time. I reckon India and Wyatt'll be right down. I fed the kids pancakes a while ago, so I know everyone's awake."

They heard a car pull up behind them in the drive and saw Violet and Rex, along with their almost-seven-year-old daughter, Sadie, who had already slammed her door and was making a beeline for Finn.

He stooped down just in time for a big hug from his favorite girl. "Hey, sugar, what took you so long? Those babies are needing someone to show them how to play, and Susie and I just put a brand-new sandbox in the backyard, so you'd better get to it."

Sadie squealed with delight and took off through the front door in search of India and Wyatt's eighteen-month-old twins, Dylan and Marley.

Violet was coming up the steps, holding Sadie's two-year-old brother, Evan. "Wait for Evan, Sadie!" She rolled her eyes as she kissed both Finn and Logan on the cheek. "The bloom is off the rose when it comes to her own brother. He's old news. The twins are the headliners now."

Violet went ahead to get the kids settled in the backyard, while her husband, Rex, made his way up the porch steps.

"What's shakin', fellas? Some party last night, huh? We were just questioning the wisdom of this morning meeting on the way over, but I guess with the kiddos on board, we'd have been up anyway. Evan never got the memo about sleeping in on vacation."

They chatted for a few minutes before Susan gathered everyone in the kitchen so they could go over the schedule of activities for the next two weeks leading up to the Food and Wine Classic. Walland House was one of the title sponsors for the first time this year, and they wanted to make sure the decisions they made were going to be impactful.

They'd already made a splash with event organizers by agreeing to sponsor the VIP Grow for Good tent, where a select crowd, who had paid several thousand dollars more a ticket, could rub elbows with the biggest names in the culinary world, all while helping to support and raise awareness about sustainable agriculture.

The group chatted about putting together a couple of auction items, including an overnight Luxury Survivor experience that Logan had offered to lead. Everything fell into place beautifully, as it always did when the team worked together. They enjoyed each other and respected one another, which is what had made Walland House such a successful brand, even in its infancy. People loved the feeling that they were coming to stay at someone's home, but guests were usually more thrilled to discover they could still have the opulence and privacy that Walland House provided once they got there.

Before they knew it, two hours had flown by, and they'd just wrapped up the brunch that Susan had prepared for them when India proposed one final idea.

"I've saved the best for last," she said with a twinkle in her eye. "What about asking Laina Ming to host a small, exclusive event for our guests and some of the Grow for Good folks at her restaurant on the night before the Classic begins? For charity, of course? We can let her select which one. In fact, let's auction off the Luxury Survivor item at her event!"

Logan swore India was avoiding his gaze, despite the fact that his head had snapped around at the mention of Laina's name.

"I know it would be expensive to buy her out for an evening, especially since she's about to be the hottest ticket in town, but I think there is a certain panache in having our brand tied to hers so early on. She's positioned to be quite a local influencer. Thoughts?"

She looked around at all of them, and Logan knew she was working hard to put forth her best poker face. She had tried unsuccessfully to set them up last summer, after all, and he knew by now that India wasn't the kind of person who quit without a fight. He figured he should pull her aside and dissuade her from trying to pair him with Laina, but something gave him pause. It could be a lucrative brand partnership for everyone, and if he was thinking with his business hat on, he didn't want to stand in the way of that.

Susan was the first to answer. "I think it's a lovely idea. She was wonderful when we hosted her at the resort back east a few years ago, and that was when she was just beginning to crest. I've seen the new restaurant, and I think it fits in beautifully with our aesthetic. Let's at least see if she's interested. India, can you stop by today and ask her? I would, but we're leaving within the hour for the airport. We've had this quick trip to Santa Fe planned since we knew we'd be here for the kids' wedding."

India smiled. "I wish I could, but we have a family photo shoot up at Maroon Bells at three, and I'll be lucky if I have my crew ready in time. It's already almost twelve thirty!"

She paused, innocently shifting her gaze over to Logan. "You've met her a couple of times, Logan, and I saw you chatting with her last night. Would you mind approaching her with the idea? It doesn't have to be anything formal. Just swing by the restaurant and let her know we're . . . *interested*."

She looked at him sweetly, waiting for his response.

He wouldn't dare let her know he was rattled by the suggestion. "Sure. I guess I can run by before I head back to the ranch. Buck has things covered. I'll make sure she knows to follow up with you in the next day or so with her answer."

There. Take that, India. He could play it cool.

Violet choked back a laugh, covering her hand with her mouth when India shot her a look.

Rex glanced at his wife before turning his attention back to Logan. "I don't know what you did to capture the imagination of these two, but, brother, I'm gonna be the first to wish you the best of luck with"—he waved his hand in a circular motion among the three of them—"this whole thing you've got going on." Rex shook his head before standing up to carry his plate to the sink.

Wyatt laughed and slapped Logan on the back. "He's not lying, man. You're in the crosshairs now. And there's no way out. Take it from me."

Wyatt took two large strides toward India, who had risen to her feet and was staring back at her husband with a mock offended look on her face. Wyatt grabbed his wife by the shoulders, her mouth open to protest, and dipped her backward for a long, slow kiss that made Violet and Rex hoot and holler.

Finn grinned at Susan, who smiled back at him before rising to escort Logan as he beat a path toward the front door. "Don't mind them, Logan. You know by now that Wyatt and Rex like to have someone to pick on. India clearly trusts you, as we all do. She knows that you're the right person to approach Laina with this idea. It's nothing more than that."

She kissed him on the cheek, patting his arm as he opened the door to leave. "Now go use some of that Logan Matthews charm that seems to work so well on the female population here in our little mountain town."

Logan swore he saw Susan wink at Finn as she turned back around.

What the hell did I just agree to?

CHAPTER
FOUR

Laina had chosen the land for her restaurant for a few reasons. It was a little off the beaten path, tucked quietly down a dead-end street that butted up to the Roaring Fork River. It was also on the east end of town, close to her house and just around the corner from Van's place. She liked knowing that if the mood struck her, it was easy to jump in the car—or even go for a quick run—and get to work in just a few minutes. There'd been evenings she'd found herself alone in the middle of the night, sitting at one of the tables, contemplating how the hell she'd ended up in Aspen in the first place. She did some of her best thinking when everyone else was asleep, and since her restaurant hadn't yet been wired for phone service, it was a quiet place she could go to brainstorm. When any little doubts about her master plan crept in, as they sometimes did, she found it easier to convince herself to forge ahead when she was physically immersed in the space.

As she waited for Van, she absentmindedly ran her hand back and forth over the smooth surface of the enormous butcher-block portion of the countertop she'd insisted on. She could imagine the sound of her knives as they clacked against the Brazilian wood, chopping the organic vegetables that had become a hallmark of her cooking. She'd been classically trained as a plant-based chef, and her other restaurants had been vegetarian and vegan, respectively. But she planned to have a little more diversity on this menu, in the hopes that she could lure people in with the idea of fish and meat, and persuade them to return because her plant-based creations were so inspired. She wasn't the kind of chef who insisted people eat one way and like it. She offered options, and knew customers would end up ordering exactly what they were supposed to experience.

Looking around, she felt her affinity for and personal impact on this space were palpable, from the seamless glass that made up the entire back wall of the restaurant, to the soft-gray color of the walls and the irregular slate floor. It was the creative opposite of her home, all modern and sleek, which pleased her. She'd always professed to her friends that if she could have dozens of houses, each in a different style, it still wouldn't be enough to express all her favorite design aesthetics.

Laina glanced at the clock, glad she'd told Van to meet her here at one. That meant she had a little more than thirty minutes to get her head back in the game. She shuddered when she thought about the letter she knew she had to write later, pushing the thought away to be dealt with in her more productive late-night hours.

She reached for one of the small ceramic cups on the glass shelf along the back wall and set about making herself an espresso, using her new favorite toy. The gleaming La

Marzocco machine had set her back over $20,000, but it had been well worth it. Nothing ruined a great meal like a terrible cup of coffee at the end of it, and she'd not have a subpar cup of anything served to her customers. The Italians knew how to make an espresso.

The machine finished its important work, leaving a perfect, steaming shot of espresso before her. Laina plucked the cup from the stainless-steel contraption and was about to take a sip when she caught sight of someone out of the corner of her eye.

"I said hello, but that noisy machine of yours must have drowned me out." Logan was standing just inside the doorway of the restaurant, his hands in the air, proclaiming his intrusion harmless.

Laina smiled before she could help herself. "It's a beautiful sound, no? Like a tiny symphony of gears brewing up the most perfect cup of goodness a girl could ask for." She took a sip, trying to figure out what to do next. *What is he doing here?*

"Well, I might not have put it that way, but that's why you're a chef and I'm a cowboy. Besides, the mugs I drink my coffee out of are a whole lot bigger than that toy you've got there." His lone dimple revealed itself as he smiled, watching her enjoy her drink.

Laina raised her eyebrows. This man needed an education about the joys of imported Italian coffee. She'd bite. Turning around, she reached up to grab a second cup, placed it on the shelf of the machine, and conjured it to life again.

Logan watched her as she worked. She was wearing a sleeveless black shirt and fitted jeans, and he could see the delicately sculpted muscles of her shoulders flexing as she pulled the different levers and knobs on the machine, thumping the old grounds out of the small basket to make room for a new fresh scoop. He could see that her skin was tan, a little pink even, as if she'd spent some time in the sun that morning.

She turned back around, her face unreadable but her eyes sparkling, as she silently handed him the delicate cup.

Logan laughed, taking it awkwardly into his large hands and lifting it to his mouth for a sip. He'd had espresso before, so he was prepared for the bitter brew to assault his taste buds, but the flavor surprised him. It was strong, yes, but it was almost creamy in its consistency. He finished it in one quick gulp before offering the cup back to Laina, who was smiling at his reaction.

"It's small but mighty. You'd likely need three cups of your cowboy coffee to match wits with this little guy." She dangled the tiny espresso mug from her fingers as she spoke. It was easier to focus on the beverage than the chemistry that was still there between them in the room, crackling with expectation.

Laina cleared her throat. "So, what brings you in?" She broke up the energy by stepping behind the bar to rinse out their cups, setting them upside down on a towel to dry.

Logan filled the empty void that led behind the bar with his large frame, casually bracing himself with his hands on either side of the countertop. Laina had to work hard not to let her eyes travel the length of him, but with just a cursory look, she'd noticed how spectacular he was in his jeans and T-shirt. Of course it was a U2 shirt. She'd always had a thing for The Edge.

"That coffee was worth the trip for sure, but I'm here on behalf of Walland House, actually."

Laina smiled, relaxing a little. It was business. She was good at that. She gestured toward the nearest seats, and they settled in across from each other, the table a welcome safe zone between them.

"Please. Tell me what I can do for my friends at Walland House."

Logan detailed the idea that the team had discussed that morning, encouraged by Laina's reaction as he spoke. He'd thought she'd be more reluctant to agree to such a huge undertaking with all that she had going on in advance of her opening, but she surprised him with her enthusiasm.

"Honestly, this is such a great opportunity for me. I love the idea of the first event in this space being a sort of organic experience." Laina leaned in toward him. "I'll let you in on a little secret; that's what I'm envisioning for this place. I'd really like it to be a space for other chefs to host their own temporary pop-up restaurants. Everyone assumes that because I designed and built the space, it's intended to be my signature restaurant, but that's not exactly what I have in mind. Sure, I plan to be the executive chef here for the foreseeable future, but I want to have options. I want to travel. As much as I love it, I don't want to be tied to this place."

Logan was surprised by her admission. "So you're not convinced you'll stay in Aspen long-term?" Suddenly, time felt a lot more of the essence.

Laina sighed, folding her hands in front of her on the table. "I'm not saying that at all. I love it here. But I want this restaurant to be a fresh concept, and it can only remain that way if I periodically host different culinary minds, giving me time to go back to the drawing board creatively myself. Travel is a great way to become a better chef. Also, it's gotten so expensive to open a restaurant these days; it's nearly impossible to do in New York City anymore. That's the reason *Food and Wine* magazine recently decided to move their headquarters down south, and a part of the reason I moved here. The industry is constantly evolving, and we have to keep up with the changing landscape. Hosting other chefs is a nice way for me to give back to the culinary community too."

She'd gotten up during the conversation to grab them two bottles of water from under the counter, returning to her seat and handing one to Logan. "So many chefs use pop-ups to test new concepts, or build their culinary reputation, and I have the opportunity to help them do that with this space."

Taking a sip of water, she continued. "Back to your idea of hosting the opening event of the Classic for Walland House. It's so perfect, because I also want this restaurant to be a vehicle for fund-raising."

She paused, her eyes lighting up with possibility. Logan was completely captivated by her energy. He could listen to her talk like this, full of passion, all day long.

"I'd like the proceeds from this inaugural event to benefit Grow for Good. I'm all about supporting local farms and encouraging sustainable agriculture, and I think that vibes with the philosophy over at Walland House too. What do you think?"

Her face was open and excited, and he hadn't thought she could be more beautiful than she'd been the previous night on the dance floor, but he was dead wrong. He struggled to focus on the reason he'd come. "I think India and Susan will be thrilled you're interested, and they'll agree to pretty much anything you'd ask of them in return."

He debated whether to pose the question, but he couldn't stop himself. "Do you need to check with Van before you give me a final answer? That's cool if so. I mean, he's your partner, right?" *Subtle, Logan.*

Laina stifled her grin. *He is fishing.* She couldn't let the poor guy go on thinking she and Van were a couple, could she? She was considering the idea when she spotted Van outside on the sidewalk talking to a tall brunette. It was pretty clear from their interaction that he was getting her phone number.

Logan followed her stare, turning to look over his shoulder. It took only a moment for it to dawn on him what was happening, and he looked back at her with a knowing grin on his face, only to see that Laina had slid out of the booth and was headed toward the front of the restaurant.

The door opened with a soft whoosh, and Van walked in, his sunglasses covering his eyes and a huge smile on his face as he spoke.

"Finally. I've been giving that lass the glad eye for weeks." He kissed Laina on the cheek, dropping his messenger bag on the floor next to the hostess stand. "I had to put in some serious hours of yoga to make it happen too. I've practically mastered my downward dog!"

It was then that Van spotted Logan rising from the booth where he'd been listening. It was too late to throw it into reverse, though, and Van could tell by Laina's expression she was irritated with him.

"No reason to give me the boss eyes, lass. I didn't know you had company." Van turned his attention to Logan, nodding hello. "Well . . . Logan, isn't it? Aren't you the bad penny, turning up all over the place?"

Logan bit his tongue as he stood up. The look on Van's face was teasing, and the accent made the irritating Scot seem harmless, but Logan knew that it was time to go.

"Van, good to see you again." Logan turned his attention back to Laina. "I'll be sure to let India know you're interested, and we'll reach out to finalize the details in the next couple of days." He crooked his eyebrow at her. "Thanks for the espresso. Kind of makes me want to invest in one of those machines. The effect was . . . memorable."

He ducked out the front door before she could fully read his expression, but she'd sworn he looked a little mischievous when he said that. She was totally charmed, in spite of herself.

Van had quietly watched the exchange, and he was about to throw out a sarcastic comment when the look on Laina's face stopped him. She seemed almost . . . hopeful. He didn't want to take that away from her after the morning they'd had, so he quickly changed his approach. "Sorry I'm a little late. What was that about? What is it *exactly* that you're interested in?"

Laina spent the next few minutes recapping her conversation with Logan, excitedly filling Van in on her early ideas for the Walland House event. He was just as intrigued as she was by the possibilities, and before long, they were knee-deep in legal pads filled with notes and to-do lists for the rest of the week.

The afternoon blew by in a whirl of deliveries, unpacking boxes, and interviews for the final few waitstaff positions. Most of the jobs had already been filled in the initial call for applicants by career waiters in town who were eager to get in on the ground floor of this rumored-to-be hottest ticket in town. Laina left Van in charge of filling the remaining positions while she went about setting up the back of the house. Actually, that was just a turn of phrase, because this particular kitchen was a completely open space, set in the middle of the restaurant. There was a hidden ramp down to a storage area where extra supplies and everything else that she wished to remain out of sight would be stowed. It gave the unique appearance of a floating kitchen, with dining tables all around it. Between the breathtaking views of the river and surrounding forest, and the open kitchen, there truly wasn't a bad seat in the house. Laina wanted diners to feel like they were part of the creative process, from beginning to end.

It was nearly eight by the time she and Van had finished their respective tasks, and the light had changed, indicating sunset was near. Laina was grateful that her opening was happening on one of the longest days of the year, ensuring the views would be optimal for as long as possible.

They locked up and decided a quick beer wasn't a terrible idea before calling it a night. It was still just warm enough to enjoy drinks alfresco, so they walked over to the Ajax Tavern in the hopes there would be an outside table available, and they were in luck. Laina dug her sunglasses out of her purse and sat facing the plaza, enjoying the final moments of the sun on her face before it dipped and finally disappeared over the west side of Dean Street, rewarding them with a brilliant display of pinks and purples.

The chef heard Laina and Van were outside and sent out a complimentary charcuterie board and some of the tavern's famous truffle fries, so they lingered for a while, enjoying the delicious gifts and chatting about their plans for the coming week. They had just requested their check when Van raised his hand to wave at someone headed their way. Laina turned to see India and Wyatt strolling toward them, having just come from inside the restaurant. Wyatt was smiling widely, but India had a strange look on her face that Laina couldn't quite decipher. India looked mildly uncomfortable, turning to glance over her shoulder before giving Wyatt's hand an almost imperceptible tug as she addressed Laina and Van.

"Hey, guys, are you finished? We were just about to wander around town. Take a walk with us! Isn't the sky incredible? Why don't we have these oil painting sunsets in Tennessee? I mean, they're beautiful at home too, but this is something special. Come on . . . let's stroll together and catch up."

Laina was about to tell her that they hadn't yet paid their bill when she glanced across the table and saw Van's jaw tense up as he stared at something over her shoulder. She followed his gaze, peering behind her. Across the patio, at a table tucked away in the far corner, were Logan and the blonde from the wedding. Laina felt a stab of something she couldn't identify and didn't want to, and was about to turn back around when Logan caught her eye and blanched. As if she'd slapped him, he physically sat back in his chair, defeated by the sight of her.

Laina faced her friends once again. "A long walk is exactly what I need after this ridiculous day I've had. Let me just run inside and say thank you, and use the restroom quickly. I'll be right out."

She stood and rushed inside, unaware that Logan had gotten up from his table to follow her.

India watched the whole scene, shaking her head with a frustrated smile. "Come on, guys. Let's walk ahead a bit. I have a feeling Laina might need a few minutes before she joins us. I swear, I adore Logan, but that man has got to learn to get out of his own way."

CHAPTER
FIVE

Laina made a beeline for the ladies' room, chiding herself for feeling like she needed a few moments to regain her composure before she thanked the chef. She had no reason to be as rattled as she was. She'd seen Logan with the blonde after the wedding, and from the looks of things, it had been the beginning of something and not the end. She let the water run warm before washing her hands, and took her time applying her nude lip gloss. With a deep breath, she turned and swung the door open wide, stepping out into the dark hallway, only to stop short at the sight of Logan nervously waiting for her.

He pushed away from the wall and stood in front of Laina. Reaching out, he touched her arm before speaking, but dropped his hand as soon as he'd made contact, as if he'd rethought the intrusion. "Laina, I just wanted to be clear about what you saw. I was here with India and Wyatt, having dinner and talking about our conversation this afternoon, when Kiera showed up and asked me to have a drink with her. I felt bad about having led her on last night, so I agreed to one glass of wine. It's not a date or anything."

He would have continued, but Laina held up her hand to stop him.

"Please, you don't owe me any explanation. I was sitting with—Kiera, is it?—at the wedding, and I know she was really into you. I can see now that she doesn't waste any time. What is it they say? The squeaky wheel gets the oil . . . or wine, in this case, I guess?"

Laina forced a smile and prayed he'd step aside so she could leave with her dignity intact. She was pissed that she'd allowed herself to be vulnerable that afternoon with him, particularly in light of everything she was already dealing with at the moment. But she must have misjudged his attentions; it wouldn't be the first time she'd done that with a man. It had just seemed so easy between them.

Logan didn't move away. Instead, he stepped toward her, just enough to make her instinctively lean backward. They were tucked into a nook at the end of the hallway, leaving the bathroom doors clear for other customers. It was dark, and Logan was backlit by the light flooding in from the dining room, but she could hear the regret in his voice.

"Listen. Is there any reason at all that I should keep holding out hope that one of these days you'll finally give me a chance? Is that totally out of the realm of possibility?"

Laina paused, considering the question.

Logan sighed in frustration, looking over his shoulder to make sure they were alone.

"I guess what I'm trying to say is, I've been trying to find a way to date you, but apparently, I suck at it. First India tried to help me last year, and you clearly weren't having any of that approach. Then, I thought maybe you and Van were a couple and that I should leave you alone, but after today, over those toy cups of coffee, I got my hopes up again. I just spent my entire meal getting unsolicited advice from India and Wyatt about how to stop stepping all over myself and finally get you to agree to go out with me, and then you show up and see me with Kiera and think I'm some playboy again. So when you finally agree to give me a chance . . . which I'm hoping will be now . . . well, we've certainly taken the long way around to a first date. Maybe that means it's gonna be a really good one?"

Laina could feel that energy between them again, in a way that was almost tangible, and it scared her. Her eyes had adjusted to the dark now, and she could see that he'd changed into a pair of dark jeans and a crisp white T-shirt that made his tan face more prominent. But there was something about the way he was watching her expectantly, his eyes soft despite the wrinkle of worry he wore between them. Laina fought the urge to reach out and smooth the emotion away with her fingertips. She had to give him credit for his honesty. She just wasn't sure she had the time or energy to start something new with Logan, or with anyone for that matter. She instinctively knew a relationship with this man wouldn't be light and airy. Standing eye to eye with him, she opened her mouth to speak, but couldn't bring herself to say no.

So she punted. "Logan, I'm flattered. Really, I know you must have a long line of women who would jump at the opportunity to go out with you. I suspect you could charm the devil himself if given the chance." She sighed, trying to find the right words. "I just have so much happening right now, with the opening of the restaurant and now this Walland House event to plan. Could we agree to revisit the idea of a first date when Food and Wine is over with? If you ask me again after my opening, I promise I'll be ready with a straight answer."

It would also give me time to deal with the other issue.

She watched him digest the information, and reconcile it for himself.

"OK, so it's not a no, which is more than I'd hoped for coming in here, if I'm being honest." He smiled at her and cocked his head sideways. "Is this a bad time to tell you that I'm in charge of coordinating the Walland House event with you? You can thank India for that. She's not exactly subtle when she's matchmaking. But I promise to keep things strictly business between now and the Classic. Scout's honor." He held out his hand to her, and Laina accepted with a grin and a shake of her head.

They were still smiling as they walked back out onto the patio together where Logan said goodbye before returning to Kiera, and Laina paused, looking around for India, Wyatt, and Van.

They'd been watching for her from near the base of the gondola a few yards away, and Van waved to get Laina's attention. As she headed over to join them, Van heard India whisper something to her husband, and then Wyatt's warning to Van rang clear.

"Never, ever doubt my wife's skills. Those two are done for."

Laina caught up with them, and they spent the next hour strolling the streets of town, chatting with India and Wyatt about their vision for the Walland House dinner. Laina loved talking about food when she was inspired, and sharing her vision about how she wanted this event to shape up. Together, the group of friends collaborated as they walked, and by the time they'd arrived back at Main Street to prepare to go their separate ways, Laina could envision the concept firmly in her mind's eye.

India said, "Why don't we leave the rest of the details to you? I can tell we're all on the same page, and after seeing what you did with the wedding, I'm excited to experience how you'll surprise me with this party. Let's meet again a week from tomorrow, so we'll have a few days of wiggle room in case anyone decides to make adjustments before the event. Although, I can assure you, I highly doubt there will be any changes on our part. Unless Logan decides to be a stickler."

India smiled at Laina, leaning in to hug her friend good-bye. "He's a great guy, Laina. And now that we all know the two of *you* aren't a couple"—she thumbed her hand at Van knowingly—"Logan's not going to take no for an answer. I hope you'll accept our word for it." She looked to Wyatt, who nodded his head in agreement. "He's not what you're expecting. At least consider giving him a shot."

Laina struggled for a response, glad when Van jumped in to save her. Or not. "I always say, the best way to get over heartbreak is to leap back in with both feet, lass." Van offered Laina his arm, which she took, waving goodbye to India and Wyatt over her shoulder as they parted ways.

As soon as they turned on Spring Street near where Laina had parked her car earlier that day, she gently nudged Van away. "Some friend you are. 'I always say'? Please! I thought you were going to cover for me, tell them I have too much to deal with right now to mix in a guy. Which is true, you know!"

Van stopped her, laying his hands on top of Laina's shoulders as he spoke. "Laina, I don't want you to take this the wrong way. You are too goddamned serious. And more than a little bit dramatic."

He gestured toward her all-black ensemble, her uniform when she was working in the restaurant, but, more often than not, she gravitated toward the color in her everyday wardrobe choices too. "Do you really need to dress like Lara Croft in *Tomb Raider* every day? With that bonny little haircut and ripped physique, I'm not surprised you've piqued Logan's interest. I have got to hand it to him; he's not easily deterred, and from what Wyatt and India told me, he's a good solid bloke. Believe me. I drilled them for information while you were inside that restaurant. They didn't give me any reason to discourage you from at least getting to know the man better. No one is suggesting marriage."

Laina shuddered at the thought. She'd stopped allowing herself to dream about marriage a long time ago, and she wasn't about to let the efforts of a dewy-eyed cowboy revive the idea. No matter how hot he was and how bad her traitorous body wanted to know what it felt like to be up against his. She plucked Van's hands off her shoulders so they could continue walking together.

"I already told him I'd consider a date once all of this Food and Wine stuff is over with." She made a face at Van's feigned-shock reaction and continued. "But I have some other things I have to resolve first." Her features were tortured as she spoke. "I owe Patrick's family an explanation, Van. I know I have to reach out. But I'm having a hard time trying to come up with what to say to them, because there is a huge part of me that is so relieved. That makes me feel like a horrible person. Shouldn't grief be the overwhelming emotion here?"

Van shook his head. "Laina, you've been grieving since you met Patrick. Grieving what you knew you could never have with him because he wasn't capable of being what you needed him to be. He was sick the day you met, and it's impossible to build something strong on that kind of foundation. There can't be more bad days than good; you know that. The real death was when you finally got the courage to break it off. The death of what might have been. I've seen you finally start to look to the sun again over this past year, even if a bit reluctantly. Colorado has been good for you. Don't step back into the shadows now. Go for it. Live. Love. Get your heart broken, if you must, but don't just exist anymore."

Laina had tears streaming down her face listening to Van tell her everything her heart already knew. Van wasn't finished, though.

"Go home tonight and call them, or write to them, or whatever it is you feel you need to do. Get rip-roaring drunk or smoke some grass and cry your eyes out. But let this be the bookend to it all. That doesn't mean you can't still feel sad when you remember Patrick, but give yourself permission to move on, Laina. What's the alternative? He made a choice, and now so must you. Choose life."

Van leaned over and kissed her on the forehead, leaving her next to her car as he turned to walk to his place the next block over.

That night, Laina took Van's advice. She poured herself two fingers of whiskey neat when she got home and sipped the drink as she made her way upstairs to change, flipping on the light switch that controlled her bedside lamps. Setting her drink down on the nightstand, she reached back to unhook her bra, sliding it off one arm, then pulling the other end of the garment through the opposite arm of her shirt. She changed into her favorite old pair of sweatpants from high school. It was a miracle they hadn't disintegrated by now, after all the times she'd washed them over the years. They felt like coming home, and that's what she needed right now.

Reaching for her drink, she finished it in one gulp, put the crystal glass down on the dresser with a thump, and crawled into her bed. She leaned over and reached into her nightstand for a few of the creamy sheets of stationery and her favorite pen. She usually only used this special paper for her recipes and ideas for the restaurant, but tonight she had something else in mind. Laina leaned back into the stack of pillows she'd assembled, pulling the billowing white duvet up over her lap. She used the back of her laptop as a desk as she started to write.

Pausing, she reached back into the drawer and pulled her journal out. Opening it, she shuffled the pages until she got to the one where she'd tucked the old picture inside. Patrick looked so happy in the photograph, which was why it was the only thing she'd decided to keep from their time together. They were at Burning Man, sitting happily side by side on a colorful blanket in the middle of a sea of humanity: Laina in her tiny faded cutoffs and black tank, and Patrick in his red board shorts, shirtless and wearing his old baseball hat backward. She loved this photograph for so many reasons; it reminded her of a time when she'd felt lighter and unencumbered by all the responsibilities she had now. But there was one reason she loved it most of all. It was the only photograph she had in which Patrick wasn't holding a drink. In fact, it was the only three-day period of time in their relationship when he'd been sober for that many consecutive days. Patrick had loved Laina. But he'd loved drugs and alcohol more.

Dear Mr. and Mrs. Robertson,
I received word today of Patrick's passing, and the news took my breath away. I'm grateful to Jeremy for mailing me the newspaper clipping along with his letter. I can't imagine your pain, and I wanted to tell you how sorry I am. Patrick was more than just a

boyfriend to me. He was my best friend, and my confident, and he inspired me in ways that I hope will continue to be woven throughout my work for a long time to come. There are some who say that the souls with the brightest lights burn out the fastest. We are blessed to have them for a short time only, and we have to make sure we soak up every moment and make them count. I hope you know I tried to do that during my precious time with your son. Our relationship, although not destined to be a lifelong one, was sacred to me, and even after we stopped talking last summer, I continued to love him and to mourn our partnership, and I still do so, even as I write this. I'll never forget Patrick, and I just wanted you to know that I'm one of so many people on whom he had a profound impact.

I'm in Colorado now, making a life for myself. I'm opening a new restaurant in a couple of weeks, so I hope if you're ever in the area, you'll please stop by and say hello. I've enclosed a card with all of my contact information. Please give my love to Jane and Fiona—and Jeremy of course. I can't imagine how hard it is for them to have lost their brother. Patrick loved them all so much, just as he loved the two of you. I know how important you all were to him, and how he must have tried so hard to stay. It's a fickle beast, dependency. Never quite sure who to let go and who to devour. Patrick must have been irresistible, as he was to so many who *met him. I'm devastated that he couldn't find his way free.*

My deepest sympathies to each of you,
Laina Ming

Laina expelled the breath she hadn't realized she'd been holding, and stared at the loose sheets of paper in her lap. She hoped her words didn't make things more painful for them, and she'd hesitated about whether to mention Jeremy at all, but she couldn't write the letter without offering her condolences to all of them. Patrick's relationship with his brother had been complicated to say the least, but despite all that had happened, Laina knew he loved Jeremy in the way brothers who had strained relationships did. Besides, she wasn't sure his parents were fully aware of all that had happened between them, so it was best to act under the assumption that they weren't privy to every gory detail.

She knew Patrick wouldn't have dragged them into the hurt if he were capable of another way. He had his faults, but even at his most intoxicated, he always attempted to protect his family from pain with a ferocity she'd admired. She wished she could say the same about Jeremy, who was much more likely to throw a match over his shoulder as he walked away. Patrick's brother had accused Laina of doing the very same thing when she'd finally left, but all these months later, she knew she'd been right not to look back. It had been between Jeremy and Patrick at that point, and even if she'd have stayed, it wouldn't have made a difference. Patrick was an addict, and he was in too deep. She didn't have a life preserver sturdy enough. Laina prayed that he and his brother had found a way to make things right before his death.

Folding the letter in half, she set it on the nightstand and reached over to turn off the lights. As she drifted off to sleep, she felt a peace she hadn't felt in a long time. Laina couldn't quite remember the details, but when she woke the next morning, she sensed that in her dreams, she'd made a conscious decision to turn her face back toward the sun.

CHAPTER
SIX

Over the next two weeks, the town of Aspen transformed into a place where it became hopeless to try to drive a car, and where grand white tents covered almost every green space available, ready to house the various events of the Food and Wine Classic. It was impossible to find a landscape company in the county that wasn't booked solid. Most were occupied with stuffing flower boxes and planters full of colorful creations outside of the shops and hotels on Durant Street. The Aspen Chamber and elected officials wanted to ensure that anyone who needed one more reason to fall in love with the mountain enclave wasn't disappointed. The city was perfectly polished and ready for its close-up.

Logan spent most of his days working with Buck to make sure they had their horses ready for the sold-out crowds that Willow and Garrett were expecting over at Walland House. They'd also managed to hash out the details of the Luxury

Survivor package. They would be taking four couples on a trail ride up toward Maroon Bells to a private campsite by the river that they'd decked out with luxurious tents and a rustic but fully functioning dining area. Buck had some prior experience as a chuckwagon chef, so they agreed he'd be in charge of the evening's dinner. After a night in the woods and a breakfast by the campfire the next morning at sunrise, the guests would return to Walland House for the remainder of their stay. The campout would take place that Friday evening, the night after it was auctioned off during the special dinner at Laina's restaurant.

Logan and Buck were working side by side the Monday morning before the Classic, setting up the campsite when Logan stood suddenly, reaching for his phone to check the time. *Damn.* It was almost one, and he was supposed to meet with everyone at Laina's restaurant to finalize the dinner details at two.

Wiping his brow, he looked over to where Buck had just finished the stone fire pit they'd begun building that morning. "Looks great, Buck. Let's hope your food tastes as good as this place looks. It's Luxury Survivor; not *Diners, Drive-ins and Dives.*"

Buck snorted, taking a gulp of water to hide his grin before he answered. "You just worry about seeing that those tents are secure. I'll make sure their bellies are full. Don't worry—it's my experience they'll be too tired from the ride up here to expect much. It's kind of like when you take folks snowmobiling and offer them a lukewarm cup of hot chocolate out of a Styrofoam cup at the halfway point. It's the best hot chocolate they've ever tasted when they're freezing their asses off. Same principle here. They'll likely be so saddle sore and sunburned, my brats and beers will taste like gourmet treats."

Logan chuckled and gathered up the tools they'd used to erect the tents, piling them into the back seat of his Bronco. He'd taken the hardtop off that morning in anticipation of the great weather they were expecting all week long. No rain in the forecast, which was great news for everyone. It was more convenient to get the tents set up early in the week and move on to the other items on their massive to-do lists.

"I think we've gotten about all we can get done in advance. The ladies of Walland House are planning to come back up here the morning of the campout to outfit these tents and fancy the place up a bit." He slammed the back door of the truck. "I'll see you tomorrow for that group ride we've got booked at nine."

"Yeah, I love seeing all that red on our books. Idle hands are the devil's workshop, and we sure don't have much time to get into trouble thanks to our schedule. This week anyway." Buck grinned at Logan, slapping his friend's shoulder as he made his way to his own truck. They said goodbye and Logan climbed up into the driver's seat.

The old Bronco flew back down the road, with Logan determined to have enough time to get cleaned up before the group meeting. Fifteen minutes later, he stood in the shower, letting the morning's labor slide off with the scalding water. He debated whether he had time for a shave and decided he didn't, choosing instead to let the pounding hot water beat on his aching shoulders for a little longer. He tried not to let his thoughts wander back to Laina, as they'd so often done since their last encounter, but resistance was futile. He'd been looking forward to this excuse to see her again all week long. His body reacted to the thought of her, reminding him to return to the task at hand.

Shutting off the water, he grabbed a towel, swathing his hips in it, before reaching up to clear a spot on the steamy mirror. He usually didn't let himself get this scruffy, but he'd been so damned busy he hadn't given much attention to his appearance lately. He'd been unable to schedule time for a trim either, so his hair was longer than he normally wore it. He reached under the sink and grabbed the only product he could find, applying a dollop of it to his hair with the hope that it would somehow turn chicken shit into chicken salad. Checking the time again, he cursed, rushing into his closet to steal a fresh white T-shirt off a stack of them, too short on time to make any bold wardrobe choices. Throwing on the T-shirt, clean blue jeans, and his favorite old Vans, he was out the door without a minute to spare. Jumping back into the Bronco, he fired up the engine and headed for Laina's restaurant.

When he turned the corner a short time later and attempted to find a parking spot nearby, Logan could see India and Wyatt walking into the restaurant from a block away. He slowed down and eased the Bronco into the last available space. Grabbing his leather binder off the seat, he hustled out of the truck and started for the restaurant, hesitating briefly when he saw Van waiting for him at the nearest crosswalk. *Right. Van would be here too. The president of my fan club.*

"Morning, lad."

Logan had the strangest feeling that Van knew something he didn't. Maybe it was his tone, or that hint of a smile that hovered on Van's face.

Logan nodded in return. "Van. Beautiful day. You and Laina ready for Thursday night?"

They watched for passing cars, then crossed the street together, pausing short of the door to stand near the large front window outside of Laina's restaurant.

"We're ready for the dinner for sure. Her concepts are going to blow you away. Don't you worry about that." Van hesitated before continuing. "Laina's ready too. She just doesn't know it yet. You'll need to convince her a bit if you're really interested."

Logan started at Van, momentarily stunned into silence. *Laina's ready. Ready. And Van is suddenly on Team Logan?*

As if he could read Logan's mind, Van shook his head. "I'm actually not entirely sure you're worthy of her, but you seem like a tenacious fellow, so I figure you're a good chap for her to dip her toe back into the water with. Just don't break her heart, and take it slow, or you and I will have a beef."

Van's words had very little hang time, landing between them with a thud. It wasn't a threat. It was a statement that had been delivered very matter-of-factly. With the message received, there wasn't the opportunity for further discussion, as the doors of the restaurant swung open and Laina was standing there, inviting them in.

Van entered first, and from the expression on Laina's face, she was not exactly enthusiastic about Van having carved out some alone time with Logan.

Logan's head was still reeling from Van's lukewarm endorsement, so he said the first thing that came to mind when his eyes met Laina's. "Got any more of that fancy coffee? I haven't been able to get you off my mind."

Idiot! What did I just say? Maybe she didn't hear me clearly . . .

He knew from her face, though, that she had.

"I do indeed have coffee. I was making it when I saw the two of you chatting outside the front window. Care to share what that was about?" Her eyes stared back at him, unyielding in their probe. Logan hesitated with his answer, because he could feel Van behind him, their exchange still farm fresh in his mind.

Thankfully, Wyatt and India had finished their brief tour and had walked up to join them. After everyone had exchanged hellos, they gathered around one of the large round tables to hear Laina's vision for the evening. From the moment she began speaking, Logan knew he was in big trouble. Her passion for food and entertaining was captivating, making her even more attractive. Logan had no problem giving her his full attention. He loved the slight rasp of her voice when she spoke.

"First of all, I want to thank you for trusting me with this incredible opportunity. India, I know you're fully aware of how important food is to me, and the fact that the proceeds from this event will go toward promoting sustainable growing practices and local purveyors of food, well, nothing makes me happier." Laina took a deep breath and continued, eager to share her ideas with the group.

"I was thinking that I'd like to present our menu for this special event in the form of poems. Haikus, actually." Glancing around at the group, she explained, "I know it's a bit unconventional, but why not blow their minds? I'd like to try to present them with a culinary experience that they couldn't dream up if they tried."

India was delighted. She'd known that if they only let their friend's creative genius run wild, the results would be remarkable.

Van jumped in, unable to contain his pride. "That's just the beginning. Wait until you see what else Laina has planned. These people are going to leave here with pretty high expectations for the rest of the weekend."

Laina blushed, uncomfortable with the praise. She shared her menu for the different courses, her body language changing as she let herself relax and escape into the fantasy of it all.

Logan was mesmerized. She was so poised, intelligent, deep, mysterious. He could tell by the way she talked about food that she wasn't just a chef. She was an artist. He found himself longing to watch her create, imagining her hands handling the food efficiently with the precision of a surgeon.

He caught himself staring at her slender fingers as she nervously held the pen she'd been using to make notes. Was there any part of her that he didn't desire at this point? Logan shifted uncomfortably in his chair and cleared his throat before noticing that Van was giving him a pointed stare from across the table—as if he'd once again read Logan's mind.

"Did I miss something?" Laina had seen the exchange, and was looking back and forth between Logan and Van with a curious expression.

Wyatt could sense the gnarly vibe between the men, and jumped in to change the subject.

"I think Logan wanted to tell you about the auction item he's put together for the evening. I'm not sure India had a chance to share that with you, but we thought it would be a nice touch, and another way to raise some additional funds. Logan? Did you and Buck get the campsite set up today?"

Logan was grateful to call Wyatt a friend, because he knew he was a damned good one, especially in that moment. "Yep, we finished everything we could today, so now it's just waiting for India, Violet, and Willow to add the finishing touches." He turned to address Laina and Van. "The package is for four couples. We'll take them by horseback on a half-day ride into the mountains up near Maroon Bells, where we've got a group of fancy tents waiting for them. We even hauled in some high-class portable restrooms and hid them just out of sight so they could feel like they were camping, but they won't have to rough it too much."

Laina laughed. "So it's a glamping experience. I get it. I don't think it can be considered camping if you're not worried about bears getting ahold of you while you're doing your business."

Logan chuckled. "We're calling it Luxury Survivor, and I'd have to agree with you. The winners are even going to have their meals cooked for them, chuckwagon style, thanks to Buck. It's been years since he's cooked over an open flame, but he's confident he can throw something edible together."

Van had been watching them interact, and immediately recognized his opportunity when it presented itself. "I've got a better idea. I'm sure Buck is a fine cook, and I wouldn't want him to think I thought otherwise. But cooking for ten people, including himself and you, Logan, well, that's asking a lot of someone who's not a professional."

Van knew the exact moment that Laina realized where he was headed with his train of thought because he could see the smile disappear from her face. It didn't deter him.

"What if we sweeten the deal, and offer up Chef Ming here as the camp cook for the evening? Buck can still make breakfast, but wouldn't it be special if people knew that they'd be enjoying a Michelin star meal made over a campfire? I think they'd pay big bucks, especially after they experience the meal she's going to make for them Thursday night. What do you say, Laina? Are you game? I will gladly take over for you on Friday in the restaurant during your sleepover—or campout. Whatever you're calling it."

She could have grabbed him by the scruff of the neck and dragged him into the kitchen. Laina was well aware of what Van was doing, but he was clever. He knew she wouldn't be able to refuse a chance at potentially doubling what could be made by throwing in her professional services. He was also well aware that, as a result, she would be spending a lot of quality time with a certain cowboy at the table. Just a week before, Van seemed to have softened toward the idea of her giving Logan a chance. Today, though, she hadn't thought Van cared for Logan very much at all, from the looks they'd been exchanging. She'd love to know what had been discussed outside earlier.

India chimed in before Laina had the chance. "Oh, Van, that's a wonderful idea. I think it really puts our auction item over the top, and I'm sure it would go for top dollar." She looked at Laina. "That is, if it works for you, Laina. I promise to make sure you have a private tent with a bed that is every bit as comfortable as the one you sleep in every night. Violet has friends who run a luxury resort in Montana, and they've directed us on how to outfit these tents in supreme fashion. Between Vi, Willow, and myself, we'll make sure you have everything you need for prep and cooking too. Give us the list and leave it to us. So, will you do it?"

Laina loved the idea of a challenge, and this would most definitely fit the bill. If she was being honest, she'd already had a few cool ideas about what she could create fireside that would be special and memorable. With a flourish, she uncapped her pen and flipped to a new sheet of paper, writing *Camping To-Do* at the top in a bold stroke. Looking up, she smiled at the group. "How on earth could I say no?"

Logan had been watching her as she'd worked the thought over in her mind. He was pleased to see that there hadn't been much apprehension; instead, she seemed more than a little excited about the idea. He, too, had a whole new outlook on the adventure. Logan had a feeling that after the initial disappointment wore off, Buck would be grateful to be in charge of just one meal instead of two. Breakfast was well within his comfort zone. Dinner would have been a stretch.

They buttoned up the rest of the details and concluded the meeting, promising to touch base with one another if anyone had additional questions. India and Wyatt had to rush out to make it back home before the twins woke from their afternoon nap, leaving Logan alone with Laina and Van, who quickly found an excuse to head downstairs to check on inventory.

"And then there were two." Laina sighed, hoping Van's hasty exit wasn't as obvious to Logan as she realized it probably was.

Logan grinned, making a mental note to thank Van for everything he'd managed to do that afternoon. *Who'd have thunk it?* Logan was acutely aware that it would be a long while before he and Van would be bros, but this was a start. He was determined to exceed the Scot's expectations. And Laina's too, if she had any.

"I promise to honor what you asked of me. This campout will be strictly business. I want you to feel comfortable and know that I'll be there if you need anything, but only as a coworker and cowpoke." He smiled, his dimple barely visible amid the thick whiskers on his face.

Laina nodded, grateful he'd brought it up. "I appreciate that. I think that we should keep things professional, particularly where guests of both Walland House and the restaurant are concerned. There will be time for things to unfold later, between us, I mean, if and when it comes to that. Obviously, no pressure if things change."

She didn't know what it was about being around Logan that made it so difficult to form coherent thoughts and then verbalize them. He stared at her now, his expression impossible to read, nonetheless causing the flutter in her stomach to tighten and shift ever so slightly to the south.

"No pressure. Of course. I'll see you on Thursday night." He made a move to leave, then turned back around to face her. "I can't wait to see who's going to be accompanying us on our first sleepover. Besides Buck, that is." Logan winked at her, stepping backward out the door without cracking a smile. The door closed behind him and he was gone, walking back down the street and out of sight.

CHAPTER
SEVEN

The morning of any big event in Laina's life for the past ten years had started off one way: yoga. Since she'd been living in Aspen, she'd fully committed to her practice and had managed to find time each day to squeeze in at least a few flows. She and Van had worked steadily all week to ensure that they were ready for the Walland House dinner on Thursday evening. They'd prepared so thoroughly, Laina was comforted knowing that she could walk into the restaurant late morning and have everything ready so that today could just be about the food. It was her favorite way to cook. Eliminate all the minutiae ahead of time and just vibe with the ingredients to create something beautiful.

She turned the corner toward the studio. She loved practicing yoga alone at home, but she also enjoyed mixing in group classes a couple of times a week because the energy was so different. On important days, she always went to class, usually just so she could enjoy a walk and get rid of pre-event jitters. She'd found a favorite studio in town, and that day, her friend Sienna, who was also the owner, would be teaching the class, which made it even better.

After signing in at the front, she slipped off her flip-flops, pushed them under the wooden bench, and headed through the doorway into the dark, warm studio. The room was already almost full, and a dozen or so people were in various forms of stretching on their yoga mats. Making her way to an open spot, she rolled out her own mat and sat down with her legs crossed. Taking a deep breath, Laina closed her eyes and tried to center herself in the quiet moments before class began.

She attempted to use her breath to still her mind, but her thoughts were persistent. It was everything she'd been thinking about the night before while she struggled to fall asleep.

Will the way I wrote the menu make me seem too far out? Had they cut the wicks on the candles? I know we discussed it, but now I can't remember if that little detail got done. It will be a time suck if not. What will Logan think about my food? What will he be wearing? I've never seen him in anything but jeans and a T-shirt in the year I've known him.

She hadn't been able to chase the thoughts of him away all week long. The littlest things would conjure up his image. Every time Van asked her if she wanted a coffee, she'd glance over at her fancy espresso maker and smile, the image of his huge hands holding the tiny cup still so vivid.

She was smiling softly at the memory when she opened her eyes in response to the instructor's voice calling them to practice. Laina's eyes had finally adjusted to the dimly lit space, so when she glanced across from her, she was startled.

How long had Logan been staring at her? He had a smile on his face too. As if he'd somehow known she'd been thinking about him. He raised his hands up as if to say namaste before turning his attention to the instructor. They stood and began in mountain pose, raising their arms upward toward the ceiling to stretch before falling into a standing forward bend.

"Allow your hips and hamstrings to do the work, friends. Open from the hips. Keep the tension out of your lower back by using your breath." The instructor's voice rang soft and clear throughout the studio, guiding everyone in the group stretch.

Laina could hear Logan breathing deeply, and she had to physically restrain herself from looking over in his direction. She'd never seen him in a yoga class before. And there was no way he could've known she'd be there that morning. She rarely came to the studio on Thursdays. Also, he'd been there first. When she sat down, she'd chosen the only open space near the back of the room where she generally liked to sit. *Does he think I specifically chose to sit by him?*

The teacher's voice got her attention. "Remember to remain present in your practice. This is the only moment that counts. Ground yourself to the earth, and feel the beautiful energy we are creating together in this room. Let's transition into a wide-legged downward dog. Feel free to flow down into it, or meet us there any way you'd like. We'll hang out like that for a few minutes."

Just what she needed, a chance to get some blood flow back to her brain and get her head working again. Laina stepped her feet wide and reached her hands out to the floor in front of her, inverting her body so that her head was hanging comfortably between her hands. The stretch across her shoulders and spine felt incredible, and she allowed the weight of her body to rest back in her heels, opening up her always-tight hamstrings. A few deep breaths later, she relaxed into the work and was able to continue the practice with a relatively clear mind.

Yoga had changed her life, even changed how she worked. Before, she'd always cooked with her mind racing two or three steps ahead of what she was doing, always planning, always strategizing about how to manage the clock. Now, as a result of her practice, when she felt herself rushing through the creative process, she'd stop and remind herself to stay present in each methodical step. If she was chopping, she was focused on the dance of the knife against the cutting board, not mindlessly cutting and worrying about layering in other ingredients. She enjoyed the preparation so much more now, and it was reflected in the food. She had yoga to thank for so much in her life.

An hour later, while in Savasana, or corpse pose, she was basking in the glow of having completed her practice when she could feel the room come back to life.

"Join us when you're ready in a cross-legged position with your hands in front of your heart." Sienna, the instructor, waited for everyone to make their way to the pose before continuing. "Thank you for being here today and for your dedication to your practice. Feel the satisfaction that nurturing and caring for your body through your yoga practice provides. Go forward now in love and light, remaining open to any and all possibilities that will become a part of your journey. The light in me recognizes the light in you. Namaste."

There was a chorus of expelled breath and murmurs of namaste as everyone began the process of rising and rolling up their mats. Laina had managed not to look, but she knew that Logan was still sitting across from her. She could *feel* him. Turning her head now, she saw that he'd gotten up and was rolling his mat. He was wearing gray athletic shorts, and he reached to pull a faded white T-shirt back over his head. He'd paused just long enough for her to catch a glimpse of his ripped, sun-kissed abdomen, though, which sported a dusting of blond hair that matched the lightest strands on his head. It made her regret that she hadn't snuck a peek during class after all.

Their eyes met, and Logan rewarded her with that mischievous grin of his once again. Laina just smiled and shook her head, standing to gather her own things.

"I didn't peg you for a yogi. Have you been practicing long?" She clenched her jaw as she watched him run his fingers through his hair, which was wet with exertion.

He was not an ugly man.

"Are you kidding? I come here all the time. I love yoga. It makes you feel so . . . stretched out. Calm too." Logan waited for her to grab her mat so they could leave together. The sun was just peeking up over the east end of Hyman Avenue, lighting up the redbrick street as Logan and Laina stepped outside. Gallery owners were busy sweeping their storefronts, preparing for the influx of visitors for the Classic.

They walked together toward the direction of her house and Logan's truck, which was parked on the next street over. They slowed in front of the Bronco, and Logan turned toward Laina. "Are you excited about tonight? I think it's going to be great."

Laina smiled. "I'm really excited. I had a hard time concentrating on yoga today. So many thoughts racing through my head. But I think we're ready. I'm meeting Van and the staff at ten to get to work."

Logan turned to look at her. "I had a hard time concentrating too. It was hot in there today."

Laina couldn't tell if that was innuendo or not, but she chided herself for blushing. "The hotter the better, in my opinion. That's the point: sweat out those old toxins and leave as a new person."

Logan nodded in agreement, checking the time on his phone. "Can I run you home? It's already nine fifteen."

Laina glanced back at the clock on the street corner by the jewelry store to confirm. "You know what? That would be great, if you don't mind. It will save me some time for sure."

Laina thought the old Bronco suited him. As handsome as he was, Logan didn't strike her as a high-maintenance guy. The truck was simple but cool, just like its driver. The wind felt amazing in her damp hair as they made their way down CO-82 and steered east of town toward her place. Laina closed her eyes and enjoyed the brief ride home, listening to John Mayer's "Edge of Desire" playing on Logan's radio. He seemed to know just where to go, pulling into her drive a few minutes later and parking next to Laina's car.

"Thanks so much for the ride." Laina reached into the back seat where she'd stowed her mat. "I'll see you tonight?"

Logan nodded, watching her intently. "Good luck. Is that the right thing to say to a chef? I guess you probably don't leave much to luck. But it can't hurt to have a little anyway, right?"

Laina's face relaxed into a smile. "I'm prepared, Logan, but I'll take all the luck I can get. See you at dinner."

She could feel his gaze on her as she climbed up her porch steps and unlocked the front door to step inside. The back of her neck was hot with awareness. Turning, she watched him shift into reverse, raising his hand out the open roof in a silent goodbye. She waved back, shutting the front door and leaning back against it for a moment.

She'd had the strangest sensation before she got out of the car that he'd considered leaning in to kiss her, despite the fact that he hadn't moved an inch in her direction. It was his energy. He seemed hungry. For her. Shuddering, she pushed away from the door and headed upstairs to get ready. Time to switch gears. For the next twelve hours, it was going to be all about the food.

After a quick shower, she dressed in a skinny black pencil skirt and a sleeveless black silk blouse. She hesitated before impulsively grabbing an extra pair of shoes for later. She knew she'd have to step out into the dining room at some point to address the dinner patrons, and she decided that the sexy black stilettos would allow her to leave her ugly but practical black clogs behind the scenes. Throwing on a pair of sunglasses, she locked up the house and pulled out of her driveway to head back toward town.

Laina had spent the week fine-tuning the menu and had dropped the final revisions off at the printer a couple of days ago to be picked up on her way to the restaurant that morning. Sitting in her car outside the shop, she opened the box to take a peek. She was pleased with the simple effect of the emerald-green script on the handmade light-brown square slip of paper. She was glad she'd decided to add the aspen leaf at the bottom of each page. She'd have the servers leave them at the place settings prior to each course.

Laina had decided to keep diners wondering, not revealing the descriptions of the courses until just before each dish was served. At the end of the meal, she'd have her waiters deliver small brown envelopes she'd personally signed for guests to store their menus, in order to take them home with them to remember the special evening.

She'd written the descriptions for each of the courses as haikus. The traditional Japanese style of poetry would allow her just enough syllables to express herself without coming across too flowery. Five syllables on the first line, seven on the second, and five on the third. She loved the order of it all. Haikus were also a nod to her own Asian heritage. She'd grown up surrounded by poetry, and her mother had even self-published a book of poems when Laina was in high school. Laina didn't do anything without a great deal of intention. In fact, the last printed card of the evening would reveal the name of the restaurant within the prose. She hoped it would help tell the story of a place that was meant to be a work space for innumerable creative culinary minds to come. It gave her chills when she thought about the big moment.

Laina was about to pull out of her parking spot and leave for the restaurant when she saw her yoga instructor walking toward her. She'd become friendly with Sienna over the past year, and was glad to know that she'd be attending the dinner that evening with her partner, Vivian, who was one of the most sought-after architects in town. It was Vivian who'd collaborated with Laina on the design for her restaurant, and who'd initially suggested her new client try out Sienna's yoga class. They'd all become fast friends, and often had dinner or hiked together when their busy schedules allowed.

"So I was wondering what had prompted Aspen's most eligible bachelor to check out my class this morning, but when you sat down next to him, it became pretty clear it wasn't the Zen he was after. You should have felt the energy he was giving off in your direction! Although, I have to give him props for participation. He's pretty flexible for such a big guy." Sienna lifted her sunglasses off her face, propping them on top of her head. "What's the story, girlfriend?"

Laina knew that Sienna was also very friendly with Willow and Garrett, and since Logan *was* Willow's brother, she decided to play it safe with the girl talk. "Oh no. We're just friends. We've been working together on this Walland House dinner, so we've definitely gotten to know each other a little bit better. But that's all. Besides, he told me he's a regular at the studio. He certainly wasn't there to meet up with me."

Sienna raised her eyebrows and made a face. "I haven't ever had him in any of my classes, but that doesn't mean he hasn't been coming in the afternoons or evenings. Viv and I have had so much going on, I've had to let other teachers sub in for me a lot lately."

Laina worried when she saw the shadow drift across Sienna's features. "I hope it's nothing serious?"

Sienna gave her a tired smile. "Nothing we can't handle. We're getting a game plan together. I'll tell you more about it when we can hike together sometime. Now get out of here. I've kept you long enough. We can't wait for that beautiful meal tonight! I'm on my way for a green juice now. I want to be good and hungry for whatever you're preparing!"

They said goodbye, and Laina pulled away, finally heading for the restaurant. Glancing at her watch as she pulled up, she cursed, annoyed that she'd allowed herself to run thirty minutes late. It was a bad habit, one she'd acquired growing up in ultra-laid-back Southern California. Once she walked through the front door of her restaurant, though, she relaxed.

Van was there, stunningly handsome in head-to-toe black, and he was already in complete command of the kitchen and the staff. The whir of knives chopping and dicing in tandem was soothing, and the intoxicating smell of onions, garlic, and fresh herbs hung in the air. Naturally, Van knew she'd be late, so he had compensated by arriving early to get things under way, allowing Laina to step in seamlessly and begin creating. She walked up to her friend and grabbed his face with both hands, planting a kiss on his cheek, grateful for the millionth time for his friendship.

"How was your yoga, lass? Do you feel like you're blissed out enough to handle all of the stress tonight?" Van got to work clearing a small area of the countertop in order to start flouring eggplant for one of the courses. How he managed to keep his clothes so clean while he worked never ceased to amaze Laina. She'd have been covered in flour if she'd had Van's job, too busy focusing on the food to worry about how clean she kept her chef's jacket.

"How do you know that I went to yoga? Word sure travels fast in this town." Laina finished buttoning up her coat and rolled up her sleeves to wash her hands.

Van looked surprised. "Well, I'm just guessing you went, because you usually do when you've got something important on your plate. Did you decide to skip it today?"

"No, you obviously know me well. I went to class. And guess who was there?"

She waited for Van's response, which he pondered for a moment before providing.

"Gayatri Lima? I don't know . . . that's my best stab."

It wasn't a bad guess. The slinky supermodel was the host of one of the hottest cooking shows on cable, and Laina had read in the local paper that Gayatri had partnered with a large corporate sponsor to host Food and Wine Classic–themed yoga sessions throughout the weekend. Laina remembered that tomorrow's kickoff class was entitled Sunny-Side Up: Sunrise Yoga.

"Nope, but good try. It was Logan. And, like a big dummy, I sat right next to him, which I'm sure he took as encouragement." Laina sighed.

Van choked down the sip of water he'd just taken. "I'll bet he did. I hope so anyway. I'm warming up to the fellow, but if you ever tell him that, I'll deny it."

Laina laughed. "Honestly, Van. The same goes for me. There's something about him; he puts me at ease." She paused, narrowing her eyes. "Just remember: loose lips sink ships. Logan doesn't lack in confidence, so he doesn't need to know that I'm softening. And by softening, I just mean I'm comfortable around him. It's not that I've decided to go on a date with him. I'll figure that out after this crazy weekend. So keep your lips zipped. I'm serious; don't get on my bad side."

Van knew better. "Your secret is safe with me, lass. Now enough of this nonsense. Let's kick ass in this kitchen tonight."

Eight hours later, they were both exhausted, exhilarated, and ready to serve the most exceptional food Aspen had ever tasted.

CHAPTER
EIGHT

Walland House Dinner
first course
oblong melon bite
sweet, wet, juicy, succulent
mouth's satisfaction

The small oval dish was set down before the diners, many of whom had just barely finished oohing and aahing over an amuse-bouche that included a small poached egg with a shaved black truffle on top. The beautiful red melon square had a dash of Celtic sea salt and a drizzle of blueberry oil and was perched on a bed of microgreens. The fresh and cool dish was perfection after the richness of the egg and truffle teaser.

Logan had invited Buck to be his date for the evening. They were seated at a table with India, Wyatt, Willow, Garrett, Susan, Finn, Violet, and Rex. Logan had made sure to stake his claim early, choosing a chair that gave him a prime seat from which to watch Laina work. She had an elegance about her as she moved fluidly amid her staff, and although she and Van had hardly spoken, they appeared to employ a wordless language between them. Logan had hoped she'd come out at the beginning to say a few words, but Laina appeared to be busy in the kitchen and had left that detail to Susan Eden and Finn Janssen, the married figureheads of the Walland House family and brand. Susan took the lead.

"Thank you all for joining us this evening. We are so honored to be part of this intimate group that gets to experience this one-of-a-kind meal served to us in such a remarkable space, and benefiting such an important cause. My family has been fortunate enough to know Chef Laina Ming for the past few years, having had the pleasure of her company as a guest chef for us back in Tennessee. Believe me when I say, you are in for a real treat tonight."

Finn leaned in, still holding Susan's hand while he spoke. "And after we fill your bellies and give you enough wine to loosen those wallets up, we'll be auctioning off an item you're gonna want to get in on. We're calling it Luxury Survivor, and we intend for you to part with a bunch of money if you want a shot at this once-in-a-lifetime experience. Let's see if we can get our friend Logan Matthews up here to tell us a little more about it. He is the man leading the trip, after all. Husbands, when your wives get a look at this guy, they're gonna want you to dig deep, so be ready to spend."

Laughter rippled through the crowd as Logan stood and set his napkin on the back of his chair, ducking his head in embarrassment. Finn had given him notice a few days before that he'd like him to speak, so Logan had taken a few moments earlier in the day to jot down some notes, pulling them out of his jacket pocket as he approached the front of the room.

On his way by the kitchen, he locked eyes with Laina, who flushed as she smiled back at him. She quickly returned to her work, the glimpse of that more private side of her showing only briefly.

Laina had to work hard to refocus on the food, because the way Logan looked in his fitted tan suit was exceptionally distracting.

The next course, a salad that incorporated a brined eggplant with macerated cherries and field greens, was being served as Logan made his way toward the front of the room.

second course
land giveth her gifts
welcome her goodness inside
earth's bounty is love

Logan stood for a moment, enjoying the satisfied expressions worn by those who'd taken their first bite of the sumptuous vegetable dish. He could almost taste it himself as he soaked in their quiet appreciation for Laina's culinary prowess. He glanced down at his notes before tucking them back into his jacket pocket and beginning to speak.

"I was honored when they asked me to plan this special experience for you all, and it looks like the weather is going to be just perfect. Tomorrow afternoon, I'll set off on a horseback adventure with my good friend and coworker, Buck Randolph over there, and eight of you." Logan assessed the crowd, wondering who would be bidding. "We'll ride through some of the most spectacular landscape the West has to offer, and arrive at a campsite that has been a week in the making. The ladies of Walland House have taken over our humble tents and outfitted them to look like something out of *Architectural Digest*.

And you won't be disappointed when it comes to mealtime either."

Logan glanced over at Buck, who gave him a wink and a nod. He'd handled hearing the news that Laina would be taking over the cooking duties with no attitude whatsoever. He admitted that he was better suited to preparing breakfast, and had embraced his duties by combing the Web for unique breakfast recipes intended for camping. Logan was grateful for Buck's easygoing temperament.

"Chef Laina Ming has agreed to come along for the adventure and prepare an incredible meal over an open flame. If tonight's food is any indication, we're a lucky few individuals who'll get to enjoy another meal created by Chef Ming. Let's give her a hand for her extreme generosity in hosting tonight and agreeing to accompany us on this mountain adventure tomorrow."

The restaurant filled with applause while Logan made his way back to his seat, watching as Laina stopped working for a brief moment to raise her hand in acknowledgment of their appreciation.

third course
from the sea we've coaxed
glistening white fish to eat
nourishment divine

The evening sped by, with each dish more remarkable than the next. Logan's favorite so far was the exquisite ono fish nestled into a chayote soft shell and set sail on the most delicious river of broth he'd ever eaten. It was like tasting everything magical the ocean had to offer, composed within one incredibly complex bowl. Logan was sure of one thing: the Aspen food scene, as good as it already was, had just gotten a whole lot better. This was fine dining at its pinnacle, in a restaurant that had been transformed by copious amounts of candlelight into a moody, romantic space. It was dark outside by that time, but the bistro lights that had been strung in the nearby trees lit up the forest outside the large picture windows, making diners feel as if they were eating outdoors in some magical wooded glen.

The final dish was presented, along with the coffee that made Logan think of Laina for the umpteenth time that night. He took a sip of the fragrant brew and reached for his dessert.

conclusion
caramel temptress
salty, luxurious taste
sweet milk for balance

Logan leaned back in his chair to get another look into the kitchen. Laina was shaking hands with her staff as they congratulated each other for successfully completing the evening's service. He tossed the last bite of the salted-caramel doughnut with mescal condensed milk into his mouth, convinced he'd never tasted anything so delicious. As he watched, Laina turned toward the dining room, her eyes seeking and then finding him almost immediately. She looked so genuinely happy, and as she licked her lips nervously and rewarded him with a huge smile, he knew that there was, in fact, something more desirable that he hadn't yet tasted. The thought made him uncomfortable, and so he shifted in his chair, finally deciding to stand.

He was about to push back his chair when the waiters made one final pass, handing each diner a last slip of parchment paper. Logan felt a chill as he read the printed words.

House of Belonging
come together here
love, food, laughter, fellowship
welcome to our home

*thank you for indulging our poetic fancy and
culinary fantasies
please come visit us again in our
House of Belonging
Chef Laina Ming and Chef Donovan Laird

Logan rose and lifted his linen jacket up off the back of the chair where he'd deposited it earlier, sliding it on and buttoning it up. Laina was still watching him, frozen in the midst of the bustle around her in the kitchen, as he moved toward her. Logan saw Van behind her, nodding to him, encouraging him silently before stepping back to take charge of the other chefs.

Logan approached her, watching as she bent over to change her shoes, rising up again a few inches taller. Logan stepped around the pass in the counter, coming face-to-face with Laina.

"Incredible. Really. You must feel such a sense of accomplishment." He wasn't used to having her at that height, the top of her head almost at his chin level. Looking down at her shoes, he could see her gleaming red toenails peeking out from the black leather open-toed stilettos. He looked back up at her with a sideways grin. "So not everything you wear is black?"

She dropped her chin and laughed softly. "No, not everything, although I do prefer to use color sparingly." She reached out to touch the side of his arm. "Thank you, Logan. For your help in facilitating this event and for coordinating on behalf of

Walland House. It was good to be back in the kitchen tonight. Officially, I mean."

She was about to say something else when Wyatt joined them. "India and I were wondering if you two would be willing to stand up front and add some fun commentary while people are bidding on the Luxury Survivor package? Just to make it a little more personal?"

Logan shrugged his shoulders, offering Laina his arm. "I'm game if you are?"

Laina held up her finger to ask for a minute, shrugging out of her apron, and returning with a small fitted black jacket that she slipped on over her skirt and blouse. She was gorgeous and elegant, and she looked like she could have been a guest at the party instead of the chef. The two of them joined the Walland House group at the front of the room, stopping briefly on their way by to say hello and hug Vivian and Sienna, who were chatting with Rex and Violet.

Finn volunteered to be the auctioneer, starting the bidding off at $5,000. Hands shot up at various tables around the room, and the price had risen to $12,500 in under a minute.

"Now folks, twelve grand might sound like a lot if we were just talking about a simple horseback ride and some camping. That's not what this is. Susie and the girls spent all morning up on that mountain fluffing and preening and turning those tents into a five-star resort. Heck, I think it's worth at least fifteen thousand dollars just to have another meal cooked by this gal. What do you say?"

Finn gestured toward Laina, who lowered her eyes demurely, humbly accepting his compliment.

A voice rang out from the back of the room. "I think it's worth double that, actually. We're in at thirty thousand dollars."

The crowd murmured at Vivian's generosity, while Laina stood watching, slack-jawed. Logan grinned, leaning in to whisper in her ear. "I don't know if you've met Vivian. She's a good friend of Willow and Garrett's. She's married to the yoga instructor from this morning."

Laina nodded, answering back in a hushed voice. "I know her all right. She helped design this place. I can't believe that they're interested in this experience, of all people. They don't strike me as campers."

Logan laughed. "Then we'd better make sure that the emphasis is more on glamour and less on camping, because it looks like they are our winners."

Finn was congratulating the women as the crowd rewarded their generosity with robust applause. Laina nudged Logan, indicating that they should make their way toward the winners.

Sienna was beaming when they reached the table, hugging Vivian and wiping tears from her eyes.

"I can't believe you, Viv. I was half kidding when I said we should step out of our comfort zone. I had no idea you'd take me seriously. But I'd be lying if I said I wasn't excited in an 'I'm terrified of the woods at night' kind of way."

Vivian smiled at Sienna, holding both of her wife's hands in her own. "I think this adventure could be just what we need. I'm ready to snap out of this funk we've been in, aren't you?" She looked around, her gaze settling on Violet. "You and Rex up for an adventure?" Then to India she asked, "And you and Wyatt, and of course we'll ask Willow and Garrett. Do you think Susan and Finn would go?" India was laughing at the prospect when Finn walked up to answer for himself.

"Listen, ladies. We're grateful for the invite, but me and Susie, we've done our time. The rest of our nights are gonna

be spent in high-thread-count sheets with a cozy down com-
forter on top of us. Our days on the trail are behind us."

Susan laughed in agreement, offering to step in and run
Walland House for Garrett and Willow, and babysit India's
and Violet's kids in their absence. It was settled.

The group chatted excitedly for a few more minutes,
agreeing to meet by one the following afternoon at Logan's
ranch to saddle up and head out on the trail. That would give
them a couple of hours to ride before arriving at camp, where
Laina would have dinner waiting for them. Buck agreed to
lead the trail riders so that Logan could drive Laina and all
her cooking equipment ahead in his truck. That way, they'd
give Laina ample time to prepare dinner. Logan hung back
by the kitchen with Laina at the end of the night, helping her
take stock of what she'd want to bring the next day, while the
rest of the guests filtered out of the restaurant, ready to call
it a night.

Van found them chatting when he came back up from the
cellar. "I'm headed out, Laina. Is there anything else you need
from me before I go? I've got the menu for tomorrow night,
and I promise I'll get here extra early to make sure everything
is good to go for the soft open. It will be fine. I know you
don't like leaving your baby, but I can handle it. Go, and enjoy
yourself while you're at it." He glanced at Logan. "Need help
loading up?" Van looked at him pointedly.

Logan took the hint. "Sure, why don't you at least come
outside with me and size up how much space I've got in the
Bronco. You know what she wants to bring. That way, if we
need more room, maybe you could make a run up to camp in
the morning for us?"

They left Laina to review her checklist while they headed
outside.

Van slapped Logan on the back, offering his hand in a gesture of friendship. "Well done, lad. Laina looks the most relaxed I've seen her in a long while. And I'm glad the two of you will be surrounded by friendly faces tomorrow. My advice to you? Keep it simple. Caution is her middle name these days, so you'll have to let her take the lead if you want any chance with her." He stopped, evaluating Logan with his steely blue eyes while rubbing the blond hair of his beard. "I don't know why I'm inclined to trust you, but I am. Don't fuck it up, OK?"

Logan nodded soberly, realizing how important Laina was to Van in that moment. He had a newfound respect for Van with the knowledge that they both had Laina's best interests at heart. "I won't. Fuck it up, that is. And I'll be a perfect gentleman, Van. Truth is, I'm not expecting anything from her. We pretty much agreed that we'd wait out the weekend before deciding if we were going to consider anything more between us. Well, she suggested that and I agreed, but if she changes her mind, who am I to argue? She's special, but I don't have to tell you that. I know it too, and I'm not going to hurt her. You have my word."

Van studied Logan, nodding. There was no need to look at the space in the back of the Bronco. They'd both already known it would be more than sufficient, so Van said good night while Logan headed back inside the restaurant.

Laina had switched off the main kitchen lights, and was waiting for him to return before turning off the rest. "Well, are we good on space? I think we can meet here in the morning to load up, if that works for you. Can you be here around eleven thirty?" She paused, thoughtful for a moment. "That would give you enough time to get in a yoga session too."

Logan winced. She must have noticed him limping all evening. "Can I let you in on a little secret? I've never done yoga before in my life. This morning was my first class. I have no idea how you people do it. My hamstrings feel like rubber bands that might snap at any moment. I wanted to cry with relief when you agreed to let me drive you to the campsite tomorrow. I don't think I have it in me to get back on my horse." He paused. "I went to yoga today because Van told me when I saw him on Monday that you'd likely take a class this morning. I guess I just couldn't wait until tonight to see you again."

He wasn't sure how she'd feel about the fact that he'd lied to her earlier, but he figured the sooner he fessed up, the better. He wouldn't tell her a lie again. She was the kind of woman who could handle and would appreciate any truth. He sensed that about her now.

Laina's first instinct was to giggle, because she'd already figured out he wasn't a regular after having talked with Sienna that afternoon. She'd suggested the additional class to flush him out, and he'd passed the test, admitting the truth as she'd hoped he would. But his expression was so open and vulnerable, it was disarming.

Laina closed the gap between them, looking up at his surprised face. His whiskers were shorter than they'd been previously, and it looked like he'd recently gotten a haircut. She reached a hand up to his face impulsively, feeling his pulse quicken to match the pounding heartbeat drumming in her own ears. Laina rubbed her thumb along his jawline, debating whether to say what she was thinking.

She chose not to, instead letting her eyes do the talking. Laina could feel that Logan was holding himself back because his entire body was as still as stone. She could see his suit jacket straining against the tops of his broad shoulders. They stood like that, studying each other, before Logan opened his mouth just slightly, licking his lips and expelling the breath he'd been holding.

"I'm sorry I lied to you, Laina. It won't happen again."

His sincerity was like a drug. Laina rose up on her tiptoes and kissed him softly. The first touch of their lips was just a graze, followed by a lingering second meeting before Laina sighed and rested her forehead against his chest. Even in her heels, Laina was still much shorter than Logan.

After a moment, Logan stepped back and reached down between them, taking her hands in his, lifting one of them to his lips while she watched. "I'm going to say good night while I still have a shred of self-control. We can wait the weekend out. It's probably for the best." He bent down, brushing her hair aside so he could whisper one last thought in her ear before he left.

"But on Monday, Laina, all bets are off."

CHAPTER
NINE

Laina awoke Friday morning to the sound of her chickens calling good morning from the coop. The sky was cornflower blue, the morning air still cool and sleepy. She could see the sliver of the crescent moon as it prepared to sink behind the tree line where a smoky layer of morning mist hovered, waiting to welcome it. Laina stretched her arms overhead into the crush of down pillows built up behind her head. She wanted to enjoy the last few moments of proper back support on a real mattress before she headed out for her big adventure.

Sighing and forcing herself out of bed, she shivered as the cool air brushed across her bare legs. She always wore her favorite old tanks or T-shirts to bed, with nothing else. She liked to feel free when she slept. Last night's selection had been an old top emblazoned with "Save the Whales." All the kids in Southern California had that shirt when she was growing up. Her parents had led several marches on behalf of the giant sea creatures twenty years earlier, which is how Laina had learned the value of standing up for what she believed in. She now had a laundry list of justice issues, courtesy of her liberal upbringing.

Laina kept the stack of old shirts because they held happy memories for her, and she enjoyed choosing a different memory every night before bed. These included her culinary school shirt, her vintage Yankees tee from her very first ball game, and the Hozier shirt from that unseasonably warm spring night at Madison Square Garden with Patrick. They'd gotten crappy takeout afterward and hung out on a bench at the end of Pier 29, laughing and talking until the sun came up behind them. It was early on in their relationship, before his drinking had spiraled out of control.

That was a very happy memory.

It made her sad when she thought about Patrick and all his wasted potential. He was an incredibly talented musician, and when he'd fronted his band, he'd been electric. Patrick's voice had been smoky and soulful, with just enough edge to have a range that meant he could sing anything from reggae to rock and roll. The band played it all, mostly original music written by Patrick and his brother, Jeremy, and they'd been making a solid living for over a decade throughout the East Coast and the Midwest.

Until Patrick's death.

Jeremy.

At some point, Laina needed to have a very uncomfortable conversation with Patrick's brother and bandmate. She wasn't looking forward to it, but she knew it was inevitable.

She showered quickly, packing her overnight essentials, several layers of clothing, and at the last minute, she threw in a swimsuit just in case she was able to sneak in a dip later that evening. Night swimming was something she'd enjoyed since she was a child. Her parents used to take her to the beach for bonfires and camping almost every full moon. Laina wasn't a newcomer to roughing it. She'd slept in some pretty interesting places throughout her lifetime.

She pulled up in front of the restaurant just before eleven and saw that Logan was already there. The Bronco had been washed, its brown paint gleaming in the sun.

Laina hardly noticed.

The tailgate was open, and Logan was inside the rear of the truck on his hands and knees, using straps to secure something. His jeans were stretched so tightly across his rear end, there wasn't room for air in his back pockets. Laina slowed her car long enough to admire the muscles flexing on Logan's back as he yanked tightly on the strap one final time and sat back, satisfied with his work.

Laina shook her head and exhaled. He was exceptional-looking.

She eased her car into the spot next to Logan's, stuffing the keys under the seat so Van could drive it later. He'd promised to drop Laina's car off at her house for her after the restaurant closed. She got out and was about to extract her bag from the back seat when Logan reached in from the other side and grabbed it.

"Here, let me have that." He transferred her duffel bag into the back seat of the Bronco. "Van and I already started loading some of your equipment, but he said there were certain things you'd want to handle yourself."

Laina smiled. "My knives."

Logan's face went deadpan. "That's hot."

After a beat, they burst out laughing together, each of them happy to have the tension broken. They finished loading the truck with Van's help and were on their way before noon.

Laina hated having the air-conditioning on, so she was happy to discover that Logan was a windows-down kind of guy. He'd put the hardtop back on the Bronco today since he'd heard there was a slight chance of rain later that night. The tunes were cranking as they flew up Maroon Creek Road and past Walland House before Logan slowed the truck. Laina had been relaxing with her head back and eyes closed, enjoying the feel of the wind in her hair when she felt the crunch of the gravel drive against their tires.

"Sorry, I wanted to remind Buck to give Willow a gentle horse." Logan threw the truck into park. "I know she thinks she's superwoman, but her body is still recovering, even though it's been eighteen months since the accident."

He jumped out of the truck, jogging toward the barn where Buck had just finished outfitting all the horses for the ride. They chatted for a few moments, and Laina watched from her passenger seat as Logan pointed out a brown-and-white-speckled mare that looked particularly tame. She was touched by his consideration for his sister. As he climbed back into the Bronco, Laina raised her eyebrows and waited for him to meet her gaze.

"Are you referring to the accident where you gave Willow half of your liver in order to save her life? Yeah, I heard about that." Laina sighed. How could she find fault with someone who'd given up half an organ?

Logan huffed, not intentionally showboating his good deed to curry favor with her. "Yeah, well I had the easy part. My body regenerated within the first six months. Willow's had to learn to accept a donor liver from a brother she'd just discovered she had."

Laina was shocked. She thought Willow and Logan had grown up together as full siblings. They'd always seemed close when she observed them together, and their entire group was extraordinarily tight-knit. She was a little anxious about the dynamic of the evening ahead. If it got awkward, she could always sneak away for a swim to allow the friends to have some time alone together.

"What? That's crazy! You mean to tell me you didn't know each other when you were growing up?"

Logan told Laina all about how his mother had hidden her affair with Willow's father for almost three decades. Logan had only discovered who his real father was and met his half sister, Willow, when Logan's mother encouraged him to demand half of Willow's inheritance upon their father's death. Once he'd met and spent time with his sister, he'd refused, instead lying to his mother about the DNA results and claiming Willow wasn't his sister, even though she was, in order to protect her. Willow insisted that Logan take half of the money, which he'd ultimately used to buy the ranch, but his mother would never know that the ranch portion was truly, legally his.

There wasn't anything Logan wouldn't do for his sister and Garrett. They were his family now. He couldn't help but still feel a small amount of empathy for his mother, though. He knew she'd had a painful life, shuttled in and out of foster care as a child. He was grateful that no matter how difficult things had gotten, she'd never given him up to make her own life easier. But she hadn't been warm and fuzzy either. Still, he felt the guilt of denying her every time he tossed one of her unopened letters into the drawer in his kitchen. But he'd finally decided it was what he had to do to protect his own heart. He knew he should throw the whole stack away and move on, but he couldn't bring himself to do it.

"I grew up with different men drifting in and out of my life. Most of them only stayed around long enough to discover that my mother was just dating them for their money. Security was her lover, and without it, she was miserable, always in search of our next lifeboat. She's far from perfect, but as troubled as she is, I know she was only trying to do right by me. No one had ever taught her what to value in life. She was a foster kid from the time she was very young until she aged out of the system. I need to remind myself of that fact sometimes when I feel myself start to resent her manipulative behavior and become bitter."

Laina watched his face, his expression hard to read under his aviator sunglasses. "Do you have a relationship with her now?"

Logan turned and pulled down a grassy lane that had been recently traveled, driving them deeper into the woods. The canopy overhead was dense, instantly making the temperature feel ten degrees cooler. Laina shivered.

"Are you cold?" Logan started unbuttoning the flannel shirt he had thrown on over his T-shirt back at the barn. "I grabbed this as an afterthought. It can get pretty chilly up here in a hurry when the wind changes."

Laina laid her hand on his arm. "I'm fine, it was just a little chill. And if you don't want to talk about your mom, I get it. It's none of my business."

Logan slowed and put the truck in park next to a thick cluster of pine trees, then turned to face Laina. "It's weird, but with you, I feel like there's not much I couldn't talk about. And to answer your question, no. I don't have a relationship with my mom. It's been over eighteen months since we've spoken. She's sent letters, but I haven't read them. Doubt if I ever will." He took a deep breath and then exhaled. "That about sums up the drama in my life. I'm pretty boring, really."

Laina smiled. "So you don't have any other skeletons in your closet? Nothing I need to be warned about, at least while I'm making my decision—whether or not to go out with you?"

Logan shrugged his shoulders and crinkled his eyes, trying hard to think of something. "Honestly? Not really. That's the worst of it. If that doesn't frighten you off, everything else about me is pretty benign."

Laina squared her shoulders to him. "I don't scare easily. My parents raised me to be a fearless, independent free spirit." She spread her arms wide. "Can't you tell? Mom and Dad covered the peace and love aspect, and I"—she gestured down toward her all-black outfit—"I guess I took care of the rock-and-roll part, to balance things out. They're proud of what I do, but I know they'd prefer I was still a totally plant-based chef. They're the ones who encouraged me to go to a vegan culinary school. I'm glad I did, though. I never would have met Van otherwise."

Logan knew she'd been friends with Van for a long time. He'd actually wondered if they'd grown up together. "You went to school in New York, right? I heard Willow and India talking about it one night."

Laina nodded. "Yep, and that's where I opened my first restaurant. My first two places, actually. In the city. That's how I know India and Wyatt. I cooked for them at their resort in Tennessee. Actually, India and I dated the same guy; I was seeing her ex, Jack, when I met her in Tennessee. That was a short-lived relationship. What an ass he turned out to be. Then last summer, I ran into India at a yoga class here in Aspen. I was thrilled to hear they were going to be spending time out here regularly. Shortly after that, India hired me to do Willow and Garrett's wedding—but you know all of that." She realized he was indulging her.

"So tell me something I don't know. Where did you grow up? Any brothers or sisters?"

Laina shook her head. "No brothers or sisters. That I'm aware of anyway. I was adopted when I was a baby. It's not a story that I tell a lot of people, but I was literally given to my parents by my birth mother. She stopped my parents outside of the airport in Kathmandu as they were leaving Nepal and handed me to them to hold while she told them her story. All she said was that she was afraid of what would happen to us if we stayed with my birth father, a Nepalese man she'd been living with but had never married. She was young and he was abusive, and she didn't have the means to keep us both safe. They tried to tell her that they were in the process of departing the country, but she literally ran away from them, leaving me behind crying in their arms and at their complete mercy. They don't know for sure which nationality my birth mother was, but my genetic testing results show a lot of Italian blood, which feels right. Ironically, my adoptive mother is Italian, and my father is Chinese."

Laina looked to see if Logan was listening, and he was. Intently. So she continued. "They had to change their travel plans, and they fought hard for a long time to adopt me. After six months of traveling back and forth to Asia to visit me in the orphanage where I'd been placed, they were finally successful, and were able to bring me home to live with them in Southern California. They felt that we had a spiritual connection from the moment we met. They're big believers in such things. Their trip to Nepal was a meditative retreat, and they still take the same journey every spring, to give thanks to the universe for bringing us together as a family."

Logan shook his head in disbelief. "That might be one of the most amazing stories I've ever heard. So I guess it's safe to say that you believe in fate?" He watched her carefully as she answered.

"Most definitely. But fate can deal you a tricky hand sometimes. It's not always sunshine and rainbows. Sometimes you have some serious crap you have to work through to get to the other side. I thought I had reached my personal zenith a couple of years ago, but then my professional success and the Michelin stars and everything that came along with that was just a mirage. It wasn't my bliss. Here in Aspen, I feel like I'm finally ready to experience some of the good stuff."

Logan studied her, and seemed like he wanted to ask a question, but he hesitated for a moment.

"We should get out of this truck and start setting up your kitchen, or I'm going to present you with a long list of experiences that I think you should be having really soon, and every single one of them includes what I consider to be very good stuff."

The air in the vehicle was charged. They locked eyes and nodded to each other, grabbing the door handles simultaneously before scrambling out of the truck to make themselves busy.

Before long, Laina had her various pots and pans organized on low tables set around the double fire pit. She'd begun dicing chives and garlic that would steam along with the fresh-caught trout she'd picked up from her supplier early that morning. The group had discussed the menu the night before, and decided that they wanted Laina to make simple, easy food so that she could share in the experience with them and not have to be working too hard. Laina knew that just because the recipes she'd chosen were simple, it didn't mean that they'd be any less flavorful. This was a dish she made for herself a couple of times a week. Her number-one priority was using local, clean ingredients. She made it a point to know all her restaurant suppliers personally, so she was aware of where every product came from and how it was produced or grown.

Logan had made himself busy chopping extra wood to have ready in the reserves next to the campsite. Looking over, Laina was momentarily distracted by the sight of him. He'd taken his flannel off as soon as they'd gotten out of the truck, and now he was shirtless, the ax rising and falling with a thud at the same time his muscles contracted, the split logs falling to the earth. A few more swings and he rose, wiping the sweat off his brow with a towel he'd gotten out of the back of his Bronco. He reached down for his T-shirt, slipping it back over his head in one quick motion, then bent over again to collect an armful of firewood.

"Here, let me help you." Laina stood up, rushing to help him stack the wood by the fire, which they hadn't lit yet, but had prepared so it would be easy to start when Laina began cooking.

They collected the rest of the logs before stopping for a water break. The afternoon had warmed up quickly, and there were impressive cumulus clouds building that made Logan think the forecasters may have been right on about the potential for overnight thunderstorms. Luckily the sturdy canvas tents were waterproof, so Logan wasn't worried that anyone would get drenched while they slept.

Logan set his water bottle down on a log, reaching for Laina's hand. "Come on, I want to show you something." She took his hand as he led her down a narrow dirt path through an old grove of aspen trees. They came around the corner into a clearing that surrounded a huge shimmering blue lake. Laina was speechless. There was a small sandy shore before them, but the rest of the lake was engulfed by dense, uninhabited forest, and it appeared to have no other points of entry.

"Wow. This doesn't even look real." Laina reached down to touch the water, it's chill nipping at the tips of her fingers. Cool but not unmanageable. Close to camp. Perfect for a midnight dip.

Logan laughed. "Yeah, it's pretty amazing. The first time Garrett brought me out here to fish, I was blown away. I've seen some beautiful lakes during my time as a ranger, but this one is special. I've yet to see anyone else out here. It's not very accessible, and the owners are pretty private, but they must be fans of Walland House because they let us come out anytime we want. Willow reached out and asked if they would let us use it for this overnight, and they graciously said yes. I've never met them, but they sound really cool. Here, check this out."

Logan crossed to the other side of the small beach, reaching up to untie a tire swing that was secured to a protruding tree branch that hung out over the water. "Want to take it for a spin? You said you were ready to try some of the good stuff."

Is that a challenge in his eye?

Laina couldn't say no. She slipped out of her tennis shoes and peeled off her socks. The skin of her calves was milky white up against the black leggings, and she was acutely aware of her red toenails since he'd commented on them the night before. Logan held the swing still while she climbed on, threading her legs through the center and holding on to the rope at the top.

"OK, ready? One, two—" On three, he gave the tire swing a push, sending Laina flying out over the lake. She laughed with delight as she flew back and forth across the water. As her momentum slowed, it dawned on her that she would eventually end up hanging over the lake, with no way to dismount and remain dry. Looking back at the shore, she could see Logan's body shaking with laughter.

He cupped his hands and yelled out to her, "I wondered when it was going to occur to you that you'll need a ride home!" He doubled over laughing, clearly delighted with himself.

"Logan, if you don't want your dinner served with an extra helping of arsenic tonight, you'd better jump in that canoe and row out here and get me!" She was laughing when she said it, though, having surprised herself for having been *too* in the moment for once. She'd leapt without thinking, and it had felt great. Luckily, Van wasn't around to turn the experience into a metaphor.

Logan flipped over the canoe that was sitting on the shore, kicked off his shoes, and rolled up his jeans before dragging the vessel down into the lake to row out after her. He never took his eyes off her as he dug the paddles into the water on each side of the canoe, sending it gliding across the water in Laina's direction. His movements were purposeful, and they filled her stomach with jitters.

He was coming for her.

Laina started to climb up out of the tire, crouching down on the lip of the swing and wrapping her arms around the body of the tire. Logan positioned the boat underneath her and rose carefully to take her by the waist and help her down into the boat. Laina ended up standing opposite him in the unsteady canoe, close enough to recognize the wicked look in his eye.

"You wouldn't."

"Oh, but I would."

When the rest of the group heard Laina scream, they ran down the path from the campsite where they'd just tied up the horses.

There, in the middle of the lake, were Laina and Logan, clinging to opposite sides of the tipped canoe, their heads thrown back in laughter.

CHAPTER
TEN

"I'm telling you, I trusted him, and he practically threw me in the lake."

Their friends were still laughing an hour later, hearing Laina retell the story. They'd stood on the beach, watching her swim back with the oars, while Logan pulled the canoe behind him. A splashing fight ensued once Laina had the oars in position, with Logan coming out on the losing end and humbly accepting his payback.

They stood around the fire now, the flames crackling and hissing as they licked against the dry logs, sending plumes of smoke up into the canopy of trees. Laina had changed into the only other set of clothing she'd packed for the next day, a pair of blue jeans and a fitted black "Rattle and Hum" T-shirt that had been washed a thousand times. She'd gladly accepted Logan's offer to wear his plaid shirt too, since the air had gotten noticeably cooler after the sun had dipped lower in the sky. Logan had changed too, into a new pair of jeans and a brown pullover sweater.

Laina finished cooking dinner, and they gathered around the fire to eat. The food was simple, fresh, and perfectly seasoned, and everyone raved about the flavors. She'd even prepared some individual tins of blueberry buckle that were sitting on the grill pan suspended over the fire, fragrantly bubbling away. She passed them out so that everyone could enjoy dessert fireside from the comfort of their Adirondack chairs. Wyatt was in charge of drinks, and Laina accepted a hard cider from him, settling back into her own seat with an exhale.

Logan was sitting across from her, watching her through the heat of the fire. Her hair had dried with a slight wave to it, softer and less structured than she usually wore it. She looked relaxed and happy as she chatted with the others about their morning at Food and Wine. Wyatt and India had attended a presentation by a famous Chicago-area chef, and Willow and Garrett had spent the morning networking in the VIP lounge. Organizers had brought in someone to lead a morning meditation session before serving up a gourmet breakfast to platinum cardholders attending the Classic. After a morning surrounded by foodies, Willow's curiosity had been piqued, and she wanted to know more about Laina's own journey into the culinary world.

"What made you decide to be a chef?" Willow was perched on the arm of Garrett's chair, her arm draped casually around his neck. They reeked of that newlywed kind of love.

Laina took a sip of her cider, wiping the sweat off the bottle with her fingers as she spoke. "For me, food triggers memories. Growing up in California, my parents were always reverent about our meals, and they were very particular about where our food came from. It's impossible to be raised with that kind of awareness and not grow up to care about the same things as an adult. When it was time for me to go to school, I thought I might go to art school, actually. I've always been a doodler. But I'd taken a raw foods class with my mom the summer before my senior year in high school and discovered that food was art too. I loved watching how the instructor took care of the food and composed dishes in the most unexpected ways. My mom recognized a flicker of passion, and took it upon herself to research NGI in New York. The rest is history."

Garrett was fascinated. "I appreciate your commitment to working with clean ingredients, and I'm glad we're seeing more and more of that trend. I'm wondering, what made you decide to stray from working strictly with vegan food? I mean, I realize that's kind of what you're known for. I noticed you haven't served us any animal proteins besides fish or eggs these past two evenings. How do you decide where to draw the line?"

Laina loved that they were so interested in talking about food, and that they were presenting her with questions she hadn't considered in quite a while.

"Well, when I was only serving vegan food, which was really just at my first restaurant in New York, I felt like my customers were rather homogenous. Not in a bad way. They were obviously health-conscious, and compassionate. But I wanted to challenge myself a bit. I've always been fascinated by people I don't know. I think it's because strangers adopted me, so I have this natural instinct to try to learn more about the people that are most different from myself."

Logan spoke up for the first time. "Laina, if you're open to it, you could share the story of your adoption with these guys. It really speaks to who you are; you're within the circle of trust here." Logan nodded to her, encouraging her to share her truth, so she did, telling them the story of how she'd ended up with her parents, and opening up more of herself to her new friends in the process.

Vivian and Sienna had been quiet for most of the conversation, sipping their wine while sitting next to Laina, soaking up her story.

When Laina finished, Sienna finally spoke. "Have you ever felt that being adopted made you feel like less than a part of your family than if you'd been raised by your biological parents?" Her expression was so earnest, and she blushed, glancing at Vivian before continuing. "I'm asking for a friend."

Laina smiled and shook her head. "My mom and dad are my parents. My family. I cannot imagine that even if I had the opportunity to meet my birth mother—which I'm not interested in doing—that she'd ever be able to come close to meaning to me what my parents do. Would you mind if I ask why your friend wants to know?"

Sienna looked at Vivian, who nodded slightly at her wife before answering Laina herself. "Sienna and I have been thinking about starting a family, but we aren't sure we'll have an easy time of it if we choose to go the adoption route. Same-sex couples have an uphill battle, and we don't know if we want to go through that at this stage of our lives. Another option would be to find a donor who would help us to start a family of our own, but that's not something you can ask just anyone to do. Most of the candidates we know already have families, or want to have them one day, and are not interested in complicating their future family trees. Believe us. We've asked a few people we thought might be open to the idea, and it didn't pan out. That's why we're revisiting the idea of adoption."

It was quiet for a moment before Logan spoke. "I'd do it for you. Help, I mean. Consider being your donor if you still need one."

Wyatt choked on his beer before regaining his composure. "Sure, Logan, why the hell not? I mean, you gave Willow half of your liver, for crying out loud. I'm starting to feel pretty selfish about not pulling my weight in this group. What about you, Garrett?"

Garrett was looking at his brother-in-law in awe. "Honestly, bro, that is the coolest thing I've ever heard. I know how you've personally struggled with the idea of parenthood because of your own upbringing, so for you to offer to help Sienna and Viv . . . well, that's just incredible." Garrett stood up and bear-hugged Logan, bringing Willow to tears.

Logan had spoken from his heart before he'd thought about the consequences. Occupational hazard of having been a Ranger. Rangers were fixers by nature, and some things would never change. He couldn't imagine what Laina must be thinking, and it wasn't clear from the expression on her face. She was watching Vivian's and Sienna's reactions, who were staring at Logan in complete shock. Sienna had tears streaming down her face as she stood up next to Vivian, who was taking the news a little more stoically.

"Logan, you should really think about this. Obviously, we are so grateful that your instinct is to help us. You have no idea how far that goes in making us feel hopeful again, even if you decide it's not the right choice for you after giving it some more thought. But please, take time to really consider the big picture. It's a huge decision, and we should all sit down together to talk about how it would look in real life, and what our expectations would be of each other."

Vivian was the practical partner, but Sienna was overcome with emotion. She couldn't speak, walking over to embrace Logan in gratitude.

"I don't know how to thank you, Logan. I had a feeling about you—your energy when you were in my class; your light was bright. But I see now that I completely underestimated you. You're an earth angel. Regardless of what happens, you must know how grateful we are for the hope you've given us that there are still good people left in the world."

Laina felt like she was intruding on a personal moment. She stood and began rounding up the dishes while the rest of the group talked some more. She stashed the nonperishables in the back of Logan's truck and secured the trash and leftover food in the bear box located a few dozen yards from camp before slipping unnoticed down the path toward the lake.

Everyone was exhausted at that point, so they said good night and adjourned to their respective tents to enjoy the luxurious beds and candlelight that awaited them. Logan looked around for Laina but didn't see her. Her tent was still dark, and he didn't think she'd have chosen to go to sleep that early. Curious, he decided to take a walk down to the lake to look for her. She'd mentioned wanting to take a swim while they'd been clinging to the canoe that afternoon.

As he made his way through the darkness, he couldn't help but wonder what Laina thought about his offer to Viv and Sienna. Would it be a deal breaker for her? He'd spoken up without hesitation, but even now, as he ran the idea through his mind, he couldn't come up with a reason not to do it. *What if Laina has some objection?* He hadn't considered her reaction, and he hoped that wasn't a mistake.

Stepping into the clearing at the beach, he didn't spot her right away. The moon was still just a sliver, and it drifted in and out of the clouds that had persisted all evening, thickening dramatically over the past hour. When his eyes adjusted, he noticed the wake that rippled back across the surface of the mist-covered lake, fanning out toward where he stood on the shore, a few yards from where Laina lay on her back out in the water. She was using her arms in a gentle back-and-forth motion to keep herself afloat.

He watched, mesmerized by her serpentine movements as she alternated between floating and swimming, her creamy skin peeking above the surface from time to time. Finally, she swam back in his direction, turning away at the last minute to stand and gaze out across the lake. She leaned her head back to look up at the sky as her fingers trailed lazily across the top of the water. Logan was fixated on her, contemplating his next move when he heard her voice.

"Are you just going to stand there, or are you coming in? It feels amazing, but you'd better get moving if you want to swim before the storm rolls in."

Laina stood and glanced over her shoulder, waist-deep in the water. He could see now that she was wearing a small black bikini, showing off the efforts of her yoga practice.

He didn't have to consider the offer for long. Kicking off his shoes, he reached down to unbutton his jeans and slipped them off in a hurry, revealing his black boxer briefs underneath. He yanked the sweater over his head, dropping it onto the heap of his other discarded clothing as he strode with purpose down into the chilly water next to her.

When he got there, Logan stood beside her, looking up at the clouds that were swirling around the moon, doing their best to eclipse it. He wasn't sure what to say. So he waited for her to take the lead.

"You amaze me, you know?" Laina was still looking up at the sky as she spoke, even though she could feel Logan's eyes on her.

"Is there anything you wouldn't do to help others? I know you'll try to tell me that it's what you were trained to do as a Ranger. I've heard you say that in reference to the situation with Willow. But this is different. These women aren't your family, and you didn't even hesitate to offer to help them." She looked at him now, trailing her hands in lazy circles on top of the water. "Why? And be honest with me. Why would a man who is uncertain about fatherhood himself be so ready and willing to help someone else he barely knows have a child?"

Logan studied her face in the darkness before answering. "I never said that I don't want a family of my own. I just wouldn't want any child to grow up in the kind of household I did. You have to understand. The way I was raised . . . it wasn't a happy home. I'm not one to blame my issues on my mother, but I kind of feel like she'd have been better off without me to worry about. Not everyone is fit to be a parent. So yes, sometimes I doubt myself. Wonder if I would be a decent father. But Sienna and Viv? The way they talked about what they were willing to go through to have a kid? It just resonated with me. I go by feel. In my life, if I feel it, I jump in with both feet."

He turned to face her now, stepping closer, lessening the void between them. "Like this. I'm feeling this. But I promised you I'd wait, and I will, if that's still what you want."

Logan could see the breath rise and fall in her chest, shallow and fast as he stepped closer still. They were almost touching now, but Logan commanded his hands to remain at his sides, no matter what. Van's words rang in his ears. *Let her take the lead.*

"Kiss me." It was only a whisper, but Laina's gentle request was all Logan needed to hear.

He cradled her face in his hands, bridging the final gap between them. With his body pressed against hers, he met Laina's lips with his own. He felt her gasp as he swiped at her bottom lip with the tip of his tongue. He could tell that it had ignited something in her, and suddenly they were one, a tangle of slippery wet limbs, their hands working in an attempt to pull each other closer. It was a good old-fashioned high school make-out session, and they couldn't get enough of each other. When Logan felt like he might never be able to draw a deep breath again, he reluctantly broke the kiss, trailing his mouth along her jawline to nip and suck on the side of her neck.

Dear Lord.

Logan knew a part of him that had been dormant for so long was awakened by her, and he could feel his whole body pulsing. That's when the thunder rolled.

Literally.

Logan couldn't believe it. There'd been a storm raging all right, but it wasn't the one in the heavens he was enraptured by. It took every ounce of any willpower he had to take Laina's hand to lead her out of the lake before the lightning started.

"We should probably grab our clothes and head back to camp." The words were barely out of his mouth when the skies opened up and the rains poured down. They snatched their clothes and shoes from the beach, running hand in hand through the woods. The fire had almost died, and the final few remnants hissed back at the extinguishing power of the storm. Logan paused to say good night to her while she unzipped her tent, but she surprised him by pulling him in after her.

It was dark inside, but the lightning periodically flashed, illuminating the space through the canvas long enough for Laina to locate two towels stacked next to her featherbed. She took one for herself and handed the other to Logan. He gave himself a quick once-over, raising the towel to his head to scrub the water out of his hair, when he felt her hands on him again, pulling him down to his knees to join her on the bed.

They knelt across from each other, Laina reaching out to explore his chest. Her fingers worked over the blond hair scattered there, the effect driving Logan crazy, leaving trails of heat wherever she'd grazed him. He reached for her, devouring her mouth with his, wrapping her into his arms and inviting her down into the softness of the luxurious bedding. She smelled like lemongrass and rainwater, and her skin tingled in response to the touch of his hands on her back. They played together like that for a while, neither of them in a great hurry for anything more. Logan had never known kissing to be so damned erotic.

Finally, it was unclear how much time had passed, but the storm gave way to the quiet patter of intermittent raindrops filtering down through the treetops before stopping altogether. Logan pulled Laina in to him, resting her head in the crook of his arm, his other hand caressing her shoulder. She let her thumb brush back and forth against his soft facial hair, content to lay with him that way.

"For the record, I think what you offered to do for the ladies is incredible. I was speechless when you said it, so I'm sorry if it came off as dismissive." She propped up on her elbow, resting her head on her hand, straining to see his face in the darkness. "I've never known anyone quite like you, Logan. You'll have to forgive me while I try to figure this all out. I didn't see you coming."

Logan smiled, knowing she could feel his expression against the palm of her hand. "I wish I could say the same, but honestly, I've been unable to get you off my mind since last summer when India introduced us. I thought you weren't interested, until Willow and Garrett's wedding, at least. Was I wrong? Was there a spark between us then, or have I just now finally worn you down with my good looks and charm?"

Laina stifled a laugh, very aware that the other tents weren't that far away. "You're not wrong. I did feel a little bad for making you think that Van and I were a couple that night. But then you and Kiera . . ."

Logan put his finger over her lips. "Please, I had eyes for only one woman that night, and it was you. I only took Kiera up on her invitation the next evening at Ajax because I'd felt bad for using her to make you jealous."

Laina sat up, indignant. "Me, jealous? Did you know I was there when you were kissing her goodbye?"

Logan answered her in a way that showed Laina that he wasn't going to be thinking about Kiera or anyone else for a very long time.

CHAPTER
ELEVEN

It was cool in the tent when the light started to filter in the next morning. Laina lay still, listening to the sound of Logan's gentle breathing beside her. She'd woken up with her hand still in his, which had made her smile. They'd lain awake talking for most of the night, when they weren't completely enraptured with one another. Logan had mustered up some wherewithal and had been about to leave a couple of hours earlier, but Laina persuaded him to stay until daylight, which had arrived too quickly for either of their tastes.

Laina sat up, grateful she'd pulled Logan's sweater on in the middle of the night. It smelled like him, and she took a moment to bury her face in the neckline, inhaling his manly scent. The cold front that had rolled through with the storm had produced a crisp morning—so cold, Laina could see her breath puffing out in front of her face as she exhaled. She looked over and watched him sleep for a few moments, still struck by how handsome he was. He seemed so peaceful, she hated to wake him. But they were running out of time. She was reaching over to gently touch his face when his eyes opened.

"Boo."

"Oh my God, Logan! I thought you were sleeping!" She swatted at him playfully as he wrapped her in his arms and pulled her back down into the tangle of bedsheets, nuzzling his face into the side of her neck. "It's almost five. The sun's going to rise in a few minutes. We agreed you'd evacuate before anyone else wakes up. Don't you want to protect my virtue?"

"Not really." Logan sighed. "But I guess it's the right thing to do." He kissed her one last time, his lips even softer than she remembered, before he sat up and threw the covers aside.

"Oh, pretty chilly up in here this morning, huh? Don't suppose you'd be a lamb and give me that sweater back? Or do I have to do the walk of shame across the campsite in my underwear?"

Laina considered the idea for a moment. She wouldn't mind seeing him in those bike shorts again, but she didn't want the man to freeze to death. "Turn around, and I'll take it off."

Logan protested, but only for a moment, turning to face the other way.

When he did, Laina slid the sweater up over her head, then tossed it to him. She scrambled to find her own sweatshirt, throwing it on over a sports bra. When they'd each managed to pull on some jeans, Logan asked her for permission to turn back around.

She had already walked up behind him, wrapping her arms around his waist. "Permission granted."

He turned around, amazed again by Laina's beauty. Not many women could climb into a tent after running through a driving rainstorm, go to sleep with wet hair, and wake up looking incredible, but somehow, she'd managed it.

They nuzzled together for a few moments, whispers exchanged in between kisses, each of them reluctant to break the spell.

"I'd better go." Logan stepped away from her, still holding her hands in his. "Last night was so much fun. Really. You're such an amazing person, Laina. I'm grateful you're giving me a chance."

Laina stood up on her tiptoes to kiss him one more time. OK, two more times. Two-ish. "Yeah, I guess this means it's official. We can give this a try and see what happens. But can I ask you something, Logan?"

She looked up at him, her hazel eyes clear and earnest. He'd decided that her eyes were hazel, after all. Not just brown or green. The perfect combination of the two colors. He wouldn't have been able to refuse her anything in that moment.

"Of course, name it."

"Are you willing to take this slow? I mean, I realize we kind of put the cart before the horse with this little sleepover of ours, but it was innocent enough, right?" She blushed at the memory of a few of the evening's moments that were decidedly *not* innocent.

The look on Logan's face seconded those memories. Their lips joined together again, like two magnets unwilling to part.

Logan spent most of the next five minutes making sure he'd explored every inch of her mouth and neck. Finally, he stepped back and got a grip. "Laina, I'm not going to blow this. If it's slow you want, I can give a turtle a run for its money."

The look on her face was doubtful, but he persisted.

"I know that might be hard for you to believe right now." He punctuated the thought with another kiss, this one more tender and chaste. "But I'll dig deep." He wondered how discreet she wanted to be, though. "Hey, are you OK with our friends knowing that we've decided to date? I want to make sure I play this right."

Another kiss, this time from her, and Logan had his answer. Laina wondered if she'd ever get sick of making out with him. He was really, really, really good at it.

They finally managed to separate from each other, and Logan stepped out of her tent, zipping it closed behind himself. He was turning to make his way down to the lake to take care of his morning business when he heard Buck's voice behind him.

"Well, well, what have we here? Did you lose your way in the woods, son?" Logan turned to see his old friend smiling, standing by the fire and tending a frying pan full of sizzling bacon.

Logan put his finger up to his lips, walking back toward the fire. "Who are you, the town crier? How about a little discretion among friends? Besides, you failed to mention you'd be back before sunrise."

Buck had led the trail ride the day before, as promised, so he'd been there to see Logan and Laina splashing around together in the lake. He knew his young friend was smitten. But Buck had begged off on staying for dinner, making an excuse that he had to get back to his place for the evening with the promise to return in time to cook breakfast today. And here he was, with a second equally fragrant pan of Toad in the Hole cooking beside the bacon.

"What was so important you couldn't join us for dinner last night, Buck? Everything OK with the horses?" Logan was fixing himself a cup of the coffee Buck had brought back in two large thermoses.

"Oh, everything's fine. Actually, since we're keeping each other's secrets: I had a date last night. With a woman I met this spring. We've been seeing each other quietly, because she's a little on the shy side. Moved to town a few months ago from back east, and she's a real beauty. I've told her a lot about you and the ranch, and she's been dying to see it. So I figured last night was the perfect time to show her around without getting in your business. I hope that's OK with you?"

Logan laughed. "You old devil. Of course it's OK. I look forward to meeting her. When she's ready, that is. She must be pretty special if she caught your eye."

The rest of the group started filtering out of their tents, the smell of breakfast a powerful incentive. The only people missing when the food was ready and it was time to eat were Sienna and Vivian, who appeared a few minutes later on the path back from the lake, already dressed in workout gear, hand in hand. Logan wondered if they'd noticed that his tent was still tied open and hadn't been slept in, since it was next to theirs, but he decided that they likely wouldn't care even if they had.

Buck handed each of them a plate, inviting everyone to sit for breakfast. "I was just about to send Logan down the trail after you ladies, but I figured you'd enjoy those last few minutes alone at your lake. It really is spectacular."

The words hung over the group, causing a momentary hush, and it quickly became clear to Buck that he'd spilled a secret when Laina's jaw dropped.

She turned toward Sienna and Vivian. "Wait, this is your land? Why on earth didn't you tell us? And why would you spend so much money to go camping on property you already own?" She was dumbfounded by the information.

Vivian just smiled. "We paid all that money for the company and for the experience—not the location—and, honestly, it's been worth every cent. And, of course, the money went to such a great cause."

Sienna nodded. "Besides, we felt like it was the right time to reveal ourselves as the owners. Willow and Garrett have known for a while, since we've been letting them come out here to the lake from time to time. But it's not much fun having such a special place if you can't share it with *all* of your closest friends."

Sienna turned toward Willow and Garrett. "Thank you for keeping our secret, guys. We've loved having you be the first to enjoy this place with us, and then having you all here last night was the perfect way to bless this land."

Logan got up for another cup of coffee, offering refills all around. "What are you planning on doing with this place? Do you think you'll ever build a house up here?"

Vivian shook her head. "Oh, I doubt it, since it's so far from town. It would be a pain to have utilities brought up, and it's just so beautiful as it is."

Wyatt was inspired. "What about tucking an Airstream in somewhere along the shore? India and I have one that we used to live in while we were building our home in Tennessee. Now that we have the kids, we haven't been able to use it much, but after camping with my girl last night, I'm thinking maybe we should take a trip down memory lane sometime soon." The look Wyatt gave his wife made all of them blush.

India smiled, reaching over to kiss her husband, sighing. "Those were the days."

Rex and Violet smiled, reminded of those early days when India and Wyatt had been falling in love. Rex couldn't help but tease his old friend, reminding Wyatt of a sign they'd hung on the door of the Airstream on their wedding night: "If this Airstream's rocking . . . don't come knocking."

"There's magic for sure in those silver bullets, baby." Rex had them all doubled over in laughter.

Logan turned to Vivian. "I have a buddy back in Colorado Springs who owns an Airstream dealership, and they'll customize them any way you want. If you ever decide to explore the idea, I'll give you his information, or even drive you down to take a look. My old Bronco would be a good candidate to haul it back, no problem."

Vivian laughed at the look Sienna was giving her. "I think my hippie wife is a firm yes on that idea. Text me the info, and we'll take a look at their website. If you're serious about picking it up for us, we might just agree to that. What a perfect solution. We could come out here anytime we wanted and have a place to stay. It's important for us to know that this land will remain as undeveloped as possible, as long as we own it." She smiled at Sienna. "Besides, we hope we'll have someone to pass this all down to someday."

Laina glanced at Logan, who was looking back at her. She gave him the smallest nod, knowing it's what he was waiting for.

"Speaking of offspring, I meant what I said last night, ladies. I'm in. I'll be your donor, if you're open to exploring the idea with me. I promise you I'm not a complete weirdo, and I've got decent teeth. No murderers in the family, that I'm aware of. Even a nice big healthy regenerated liver. What more could you ask for?"

They were all laughing again, and Logan had gotten up to model his frame for them in several different hysterical poses. Sienna and Vivian were convinced.

"We spent the morning discussing your offer, Logan, and we've decided that if you really are serious, there is no one else we could imagine having as a part of our child's life. We sat by the lake and meditated, and we both came to the same conclusion. We know that we can find common ground with you, and we would welcome you to be as much or as little a part of our child's life as you would want to be. We believe we can and will come to that decision organically as this whole process unfolds."

Sienna hugged Logan, kissing both of his cheeks, then stepped back. Once Vivian had hugged him too, and they'd accepted congratulations from the rest of the group, Vivian couldn't help but ask Logan one more time if he was 100 percent sure. He was, and everything about his demeanor reflected that certainty. But he really wanted to assure them.

"I've even checked with this amazing girl that I've just started seeing, and she's on board, which is important. Very important. Maybe the most important thing to me."

Willow was listening to her brother intently. "Hold on, Logan. Tell us more about this amazing girl. And how were you able to check in with her about something you just found out about last night? We don't even have cell service here." Willow looked at Laina, confused.

"Well, sis. You'd love her. She's super smart, has a wicked sense of humor . . . she's a decent cook. Very mysterious. And she's drop-dead gorgeous. You've met her, actually." He waited for his description, coupled with the embarrassed look on Laina's face, to give Willow the clue she'd been missing. Everyone else was smiling at Laina, particularly India and Wyatt, who'd been in the adjacent tent the evening before. Willow finally caught on.

"Oh, thank God! I thought I'd been totally off. Laina! You've finally agreed to go out with my brother? That's so awesome. He really is a good guy, despite the fact that he likes to make me feel like an idiot sometimes for being slow on the uptake." Willow slugged Logan in the arm on her way to give Laina a hug.

Logan whistled to get everyone's attention, throwing his hands up in the air. "Time out, everyone. We're thrilled you're happy for us, but we're only telling you all so you can stop with the meddling. We appreciate everyone exercising their matchmaking muscles, but we can take it from here. We'll see where this goes, and, no matter what, we'll all remain good friends." He walked around toward Laina's side of the circle and stood next to her chair. "And now that we've agreed that I'm going to be a sperm donor, and Viv and Sienna are going to be mommies, and everyone appears to be done with breakfast . . . who's up for a swim?"

He glanced down at Laina with a devilish look in his eye.

"No." She stood up and tried to find her way out of his reach, but failed.

"Yes." Logan grabbed her, threw her over his shoulder, and ran the entire way down to the lake with Laina's squeals ringing in his ears.

It was the first occasion of many that they would all spend out on Bonhomie Lake, which they named together that morning. Sienna suggested it, telling them the word meant a feeling of friendliness among a group of people. They'd all agreed with her that it was just perfect.

CHAPTER

TWELVE

The Aspen Food and Wine Classic had a way of chewing a person up and spitting them out, in the very best way, of course. Everyone had left the campout that Saturday morning with a laundry list of life to get back to, their collective to-do lists destined to keep them apart for the remainder of the Classic.

Throngs of tourists had descended on the small downtown area, and the billowing white tents were now filled with vendors hawking everything from wine and chocolate to whiskey. The Grand Tastings interspersed throughout the day showcased the celebrity chefs who'd come to town to promote their latest cookbooks. Lines of fans holding title pages open to await autographs snaked through the crowds, and by late afternoon, almost everyone in town had been overserved. Aspen was officially comfortably numb. It was the party of the summer where the who's who of the culinary world mingled with well-heeled foodies from near and far.

Laina had returned to the restaurant Saturday afternoon for the dinner service and cooked her ass off, invigorated by their short trip. She created her menu with the idea that the earth had something to give back, a savory story laden with mushrooms, wild onions, fresh fish, and other ingredients inspired by her time at the lake with her friends. The feedback was resoundingly positive, as it usually was when she was able to tap into her heart center and cook from that purest of places.

Van had left her alone, recognizing her need to go within after what had seemingly been a stimulating experience in the woods. He'd had a successful service himself in her absence the evening before, enjoying the freedom that came with the blank slate Laina had gifted him.

She hadn't spoken to Logan in person since just after they'd gotten back from the overnight trip. He'd told her on the ride home that his horses were booked for a solid two days by guests of Walland House. Laina was busy too with final preparations for the weekend at House of Belonging. They'd agreed before saying goodbye that they'd touch base when things settled down a bit. Logan promised to at least text her, though, so they could make an official plan to get together once the Classic was over. He'd just dropped her off and she'd barely gotten to her front door when her phone chimed the first time. She'd read Logan's text and smiled, turning to see his fist pumping in the air out the open window of the Bronco as he drove away, back toward town. She'd laughed, covering her mouth with her hand.

Logan: Damn, you look good from behind.

Laina: Didn't anyone ever tell you not to text and drive?

It had only been twenty-four hours since she'd seen him, but she missed Logan already. Laina stood in her kitchen on Sunday morning scrolling through the rest of the text thread she'd started with him the day before, beginning with that moment on her porch.

> Logan: It's not the phone that has me distracted. Wow.

> Laina: Pay attention to the road, hotshot.

Then, twenty minutes later:

> Logan: I forgot to tell you that I had an amazing time. Or did I say that already?

> Laina: You didn't say it, but I was starting to get the picture when you said goodbye.

> Logan: It wasn't goodbye. It was see you later. Speaking of which . . .

> Laina: Tonight's crazy, but we close earlier on Sunday. Drinks? My porch? Tomorrow after close? Around 10.

> Logan: That's a firm yes for me. Will there be kissing? I'll bring the wine. Red? White?

> Laina: Let's see if you can guess the wine. Your first test! May the force be with you. And there might be a little kissing . . . we'll see.

Logan: Game on. Until tomorrow . . .

Laina stuck her phone in her back pocket and picked up her coffee cup, looking out the window into her garden with a smile. She hadn't heard from him yet today, but she knew she would. It was going to be a good day. She had plans to pick some fresh herbs to use at the restaurant, and then she hoped she could squeeze in a run. Sundays were her favorite. The town was sleepy, except for the other road warriors who also enjoyed the light car traffic on the streets.

She finished her coffee and headed out into the garden, basket and shears in hand. Most days, Laina took her time, letting the food send her in a particular direction for the night's meal. She was on the verge of inspiration when she heard a commotion at the end of her driveway. She looked up just in time to see Van kick-step the end of his skateboard, sending it smoothly up into his grip. He sauntered toward her, his sunglasses hiding his eyes, a newspaper tucked under his arm.

Laina smiled. He was a gorgeous human being, but a little intimidating-looking if someone didn't know him well. He'd taken to wearing his blond goatee and hair a little longer than usual, which, together with his suntanned skin, made his blue eyes even more piercing, when they weren't covered by his shades. Laina remembered how when they'd first met she'd thought part of his appeal was that, even though he had that bad-boy thing working for him, he was a big softie. She discovered that he had the best sense of humor once he'd finally decided to let her in. Looking at him now, it was still amazing to her that their chemistry had presented as more of a friendship. It probably had something to do with the fact that they were a lot alike. Too similar for there to be enough of the kind of electricity needed for a romantic relationship to endure.

Laina kissed Van on the cheek when he leaned in to greet her.

"Have you seen the paper yet?" Van handed it to her, letting his glasses drop down enough to be able to make eye contact with her in his most dastardly way. "It's an extra copy. Page three."

Laina set her basket down, reaching over to borrow the sunglasses from Van's face so she could see well enough, and began to read:

> *There exist already a million and one reasons to visit Aspen, but as of this weekend, the count stands at one million and two. Chef Laina Ming burst onto the scene with a charity dinner for Walland House on Thursday night, raising loads of money for sustainable agriculture in our beloved valley, and keeping diners guessing with a creatively composed meal described only in haiku form. If you've never seen art on a plate, you need to make your way to the banks of the Roaring Fork River where Ming has constructed her glass castle. Look closely, though; the magnificent structure blends in so well with the surroundings, you might miss it if you get distracted by the mystical aromas drifting out of Ming's open kitchen. There isn't a bad seat in the house, so everyone is treated to not one but two culinary geniuses at work. Despite being a California girl, some of Ming's best work was in New York City, where she earned her two Michelin stars, alongside*

Donovan Laird, a renowned chef in his own right. The pair trained together at Natural Gourmet Institute, their education steeped in the plant-based curriculum that also included organic seafood and eggs, which are still components of their present-day styles. Chef Laird took the reins solo in the kitchen on Friday night, cranking out an edgy and well-thought-out menu with big-city flair, while Chef Ming's Saturday-night meal was an homage to local ingredients found in and around Aspen. Rumor has it Chefs Ming and Laird plan to import some of the greatest culinary minds, old and new, to join them in presenting the lucky diners who can score a table with innumerable unforgettable edible experiences. The possibilities are endless. House of Belonging, indeed. ★ ★ ★ ★ ★

Laina took the glasses off, handing them back to Van with a smile. "Five stars! Well, that certainly makes an already-stellar day even better. Wow, and I was told by India not to expect too much in the way of good reviews. This woman is a tough critic. Sure sounds like you won her over, Mr. Edgy."

Van slipped the glasses back onto his face, doing his best aw-shucks impersonation. "I just whipped up a humble little meal in your absence. No big deal."

"Ha, OK. I'm throwing my bullshit flag on that one, Van. You don't do anything halfway, and we both know it. I just wish I'd been there to taste your most recent masterpiece." She picked up the basket, heading toward the garden to collect herbs. "Although I must admit I had a great time with the Walland House crew."

Van reached over to pick a fresh chive, chewing on the end of it while he studied her. Something was different. Laina could be a moody one, but today she seemed a little lighter. Happier. Smitten.

"Really, now. Why don't you tell me all about it? Stole a cookie from the cookie jar, did you? I'm sure you'll try to convince me that the guilty look on your face is just my overactive imagination at work. Am I right?"

Laina was about to answer him when her phone chimed in her back pocket. "Excuse me, nosy Nancy. This might be one of our suppliers."

> Logan: I can't stop thinking about you. And I've decided. There will be kissing. Consider yourself warned.

Laina worked to keep a straight face, but she felt the warmth creep up along her chest and neck, and knew she was busted.

"Not the suppliers, huh? Never mind, Laina. I don't need details. That was enough for me." Van walked to the top of her drive, set his board down on the pavement, and pushed off to head back toward town. He couldn't help himself, yelling to her over his shoulder. "Logan will fill me in when I see him anyway. We're having lunch in twenty minutes."

> Laina: Oh, you've decided about the kissing, huh? We'll see about that. Also—lunch with Van?

> Logan: Yep. We're bffs. You hadn't heard?

Laina: Tell Van to mind his own beeswax!

Logan: Amazing review in the paper. Well deserved. I'll congratulate you properly later.

Laina: Just bring my favorite wine. And no cheating. Asking Van doesn't count. Also— tell him nothing!

Logan: Already bought the wine. Feel good about my choice. I went by feel. That's my game plan for tonight, btw

Laina: See you later.

Laina finished gathering what she needed from the garden, then headed inside. Checking her watch, she figured she had time for a short run. When she got home an hour later, she was dripping in sweat and about to head upstairs for a shower when her landline rang.

Her parents. They were the only ones, besides Van—who was currently on his big lunch date, who had the number.

"Hi, Mom." Laina guessed right, smiling at the sound of her mother's greeting on the other end of the line. They chatted for a few minutes before her dad joined them on the call so Laina could fill them in on the opening and everything else that had happened over the past couple of days. Well, *almost* everything. Her parents had always been so proud of her, but she thought she detected a little extra emotion in her mom's voice this time.

"Is everything OK, Mom? Are you guys still going to be able to come visit next month? I know it was impossible to be here with the opening of your center coming up next weekend. Hey, if the travel is stressing you out, don't worry about it. You'll get here when the timing is right."

"Laina, your mom and I were wondering if you might be able to come home to California for the opening?" Laina smiled at the sound of her dad's voice. "We realize it's not ideal timing for you, with House of Belonging being so new, but it would mean so much to us if you could be here. There is something we'd like to discuss with you."

Laina was chewing on the end of a pencil she'd been using to doodle with while they talked. "OK, now you're scaring me. Can you tell me what you need to talk to me about? Are you guys OK? No one is sick, right?"

"No, honey, it's nothing like that. Dad and I are fine. If you can't make it, we understand. Just think about it and let us know in the next couple of days if you can make it work. Maybe Van could take over for you there? Daddy read me the local review online this morning; it sounds like you two still make a pretty great team, even after all these years. Are you sure there's no hope for anything romantic between you? I sense something different in your energy field. There is love energy around you, Laina. Is it Van?"

Her cell phone chimed again, the excuse Laina needed to stop her mother's intuition in its tracks. "Mom, that might be work. I have to run, but I'll see what I can do to make it next week. I'll let you know in a day or so. Love you both. So much."

Laina exhaled, always unsettled that her mother was so plugged in to her. She wasn't surprised; it had been like that her entire life. But it wasn't always welcomed, and she'd learned how to pull back when she wasn't ready to share something. She didn't want to get her parents' hopes up yet with talk of Logan. She needed to see how things were going to shake out first.

Remembering the chime, she turned her phone over to reveal the text. It was a selfie, taken by Van of himself and Logan at lunch. They were both giving her a thumbs-up.

Great. So much for keeping Van out of their business. She would have loved to have been a fly on the wall at Whitehouse Tavern at that very moment.

> Laina: I'm warning you.
>
> Van: What, I thought you'd like a picture of your two favorite guys?
>
> Laina: You're a rat.
>
> Van: Love you too.

She switched over to her text thread with Logan.

> Laina: Do not be fooled by the accent. He's a predator.
>
> Logan: lol. Don't worry. A harmless lunch. Your name hasn't even come up. And stop stalking me.

Laina laughed, and decided to let them be. Secretly, she was pleased that Van had come to think of Logan as a friend and not foe. They were so different, but also alike in certain ways. They were both guy's guys, although it had always surprised Laina that Van didn't maintain more close male friendships. Men gravitated toward him because he was so cool and easy to talk to, but he kept a wall up, probably because of his upbringing, which he rarely spoke about. As close as she was with Van, and after dozens of late-night conversations about some pretty deep stuff, his family still remained a bit of a mystery. Occasionally, she got snippets of information. He'd told her that he was one of three brothers, but in all the years she'd known Van, she'd never met his family.

And he never spoke about his father.

Laina had met Van a short time after he'd lost his mom to cancer. She knew his family had emigrated from Scotland to a farming community outside of Portland, Oregon, when Van and his brothers were young. Other than that, Van had managed to keep his past under wraps.

Laina was pleased that Logan had been the one who'd finally won Van over. In the two years she'd dated Patrick, Van had never been able to warm up to him. And he'd detested Patrick's brother, Jeremy.

He wasn't the only one.

Laina shuddered, trying to forget that she still hadn't deleted his most recent text.

Jeremy: I need to see you.

She hadn't known how to answer him. Sure, Jeremy would persist, but she couldn't imagine being in the same room with him, and she was well aware that he intended for them to meet face-to-face. Laina couldn't be sure, but she assumed he was still living in New York. She'd made it a point to avoid reading information about his band, which was getting harder and harder to do. In a cruel twist, they'd become even more popular since they'd split with Patrick last year. Laina felt sick when she thought about how Patrick had been so happy pouring his heart and soul into their songwriting. When he and Jeremy wrote together, it was electric. They made each other so much better. In some ways. But like Cain and Abel, ultimately, brother destroyed brother.

She hadn't seen Jeremy since that night. How would it feel to be in front of him again, after they had both lost Patrick for good?

After all, in Jeremy's mind at least—his brother's death was their fault.

Laina rushed upstairs, wishing for a shower hot enough to wash away both the past and her morning run.

CHAPTER
THIRTEEN

Logan was at the point where he wondered if his hamstrings would ever recover. The yoga had been the catalyst, but almost a dozen hours in the saddle over the weekend had sealed the deal. He could feel his muscles barking as he stepped into a fresh pair of jeans one sore leg at a time. He was still trying to cool down from the hot shower he'd taken, so he left his shirt on the bed. He moved into the bathroom to grab his tooth-brush and toothpaste, scrubbing his teeth as he made his way back toward the kitchen. He wanted the wine to be at just the right temperature when he opened it with Laina, but he didn't have a wine fridge, so he'd stuck the cabernet that he'd settled on in the main refrigerator.

He was going by feel.

Logan figured if he let the wine get sufficiently cold, he could take it out a few minutes early, and it would be warmed up to the desired temperature by the time he drove to Laina's.

He chewed on the toothbrush as he reached in to touch the bottle. *Cold enough.* He grabbed the wine and set it on the counter next to his stack of mail.

He'd gotten another letter from his mother that afternoon. Seeing it now, he was unsure why he'd left it in the pile, so he snatched it off the top and threw it into the drawer with the rest. He'd been doing that for months. What could she have to say to him that would change things? He didn't wish her ill, but he'd decided he wasn't interested in having a relationship with her either. It was too painful. Not answering his mother's letters was the clearest way to get his feelings across, and the least hurtful way for him to move forward. He didn't want to rehash it. He wasn't trying to be cruel to her. But he didn't want to look back. He was feeling too hopeful about the future. His mother had no place in it.

His phone lit up, a message from Van.

Van: Don't mistake kindness for weakness.

Logan: From who? You?

Van: Funny. Just remember. Don't fuck this up.

Logan: Roger that.

They'd had a great lunch that afternoon, although Logan had been surprised that Van had invited him in the first place. At first, Van had been friendly and the conversation casual, mostly about Food and Wine and how busy they'd each been. The waitress had just delivered their lunch when Van's tone changed, becoming decidedly more serious.

"So, Logan. All kidding aside, what is your endgame with Laina? You and I both know this is a small town, and it's not a secret that you've dated your way through a decent-size cross section of the women in it. I have a sense about you, though—I think that you might be smart enough to recognize that Laina is different. I care a lot about her. A lot. But I need to know what you're thinking."

Van studied Logan, noticing his consideration. "I'm not wrong about you, am I?"

Logan sat back in his chair, staring at him. "I recognize that she's different, Van. I have from day one, but she's finally just agreed to give me a chance. Also, I'd bet that if you ask any of the women I've dated in this town, you'd be hard-pressed to find one that would tell you things ended badly between us. First of all, I never got in deep with anyone else. When I know it's not right, I move on pretty quickly."

Logan saw Van's eyebrows shoot up and rushed to put his mind at ease. "Even though I've known Laina casually for a year, it's early on, and we've agreed to take things slowly. But if I had to say today, I'd tell you that I have a pretty good feeling about where things are headed. I think Laina does too. This feels very real."

Van knew himself to be a decent judge of character, and Logan's answer confirmed it. Logan was under Laina's spell. Van had recognized it before, most recently with Patrick, and with Jack Sterling prior to that. Logan had known pretty quickly that the relationship with Jack wouldn't be long-term. Jack hadn't been Laina's emotional equal, and Van had silently predicted that the weatherman would be gone the minute the spotlight moved from Laina to the next media darling. Van had been pleasantly surprised, though, when Laina had been the one to end things, and he'd been proud of her for recognizing that she was worthy of more.

Patrick was another story. Van had liked him initially, but that ended when he discovered the substance-abuse problem.

Patrick wasn't a casual user, and he hated Van for being one of the few people who could see through the facade he'd carefully constructed. Patrick had been good at hiding his problem from most people, but Van saw him for what he really was. An addict. He'd experienced it with his father, and he knew the kind of destruction dependency could wreak on important relationships.

Logan was the first person Laina had chosen who Van knew was different enough from her but still complex enough to challenge everything she thought she knew about being in a relationship. There was a time when Van wondered if he and Laina could have found a way to conjure up some of the sexual chemistry that had been missing between them, but he quickly reverted to accepting that Laina was the sister he'd always wanted and never had. It's why he'd felt it necessary for his radar to be spot-on when it came to Logan.

"Good. That's enough for me. I trust Laina's judgment, for the most part, but she's a little vulnerable right now." He paused. "I'll let her share that with you when she's ready, though."

Logan could feel that he shouldn't pry any further. They'd enjoyed the rest of their lunch together, switching back to casual conversation about hiking and fishing and some of their other mutual passions.

It was shortly before ten when Logan had finally cooled down enough to throw a shirt on, checking to make sure he had his keys before he grabbed the wine from his counter on the way out the door. This was one evening he wasn't going to be late for.

Laina knew that the drive from Logan's house to hers would take him no more than ten or fifteen minutes. She'd texted him earlier to tell him to meet her around ten, which meant she only had a few minutes to change out of her work clothes. Probably less, since she'd just come from town herself and knew that it was a pretty quiet night, with all the Food and Wine folks having wrapped up their events earlier that day. Laina was happy to have her sleepy mountain town back, at least for the short-term, until the Ideas Festival at the Aspen Institute kicked off at the end of the month.

She peeled herself out of her black jeans, reaching into her closet for a white pair. She'd been thinking about her outfit during dinner service, deciding that she'd change it up for once. She didn't wear a lot of color, so even the starkness of the white felt like she was making an effort. She'd been a bit chilly on her drive home, so she paired the jeans with a soft heather-gray sweater that slouched off one shoulder.

She heard a car coming, so she switched off her bedroom lamp and peered out one of her front windows. She could see Logan's Bronco pulling into her driveway. She watched as he got out of the driver's side, a bottle of wine tucked under his arm and a bouquet of flowers in his hand. She smiled when he paused to check his reflection in the window, running his free hand through his hair before turning to head for the porch. He wasn't the least bit vain, and Laina took the self-conscious gesture to mean he was aiming to impress her, which gave her a little thrill.

She scrambled down the stairs, getting to the front door just as Logan did. She opened it, struck again by how gorgeous he was. He'd shaved, and his skin was the smoothest she'd ever seen it. He usually wore at least a shadow of whiskers, but Laina wasn't complaining.

His eyes crinkled at the corners when he smiled and stared back at her. "Are you going to invite me in, or are we just going to stand here and gawk at each other?"

Laina laughed, stepping aside to make way for him, accepting the flowers that Logan held out to her. "Wow. I don't remember the last time someone brought me flowers. In fact, you might be the first." She motioned for him to follow her back into the kitchen in search of something to put them in.

Logan found that hard to believe. "No way. You're just trying to make me feel good. I'm not buying your lonely-spinster routine." He set the bottle of wine down between them on the counter as Laina arranged the wildflower bouquet in a large mason jar. Logan was dying to know if he'd passed her test.

"So, I guess this is it. I thought long and hard about what kind of wine you might like. Took a few different things into consideration. First of all, you're mysterious. You're a chef, so your favorite would likely be a wine that is more mature, not some young upstart. And you love the color black; although I see you've thrown me a curveball with your outfit tonight. Not that I'm complaining. This good-girl vibe really works on you."

She was laughing as she reached over to rotate the wine bottle so she could read the label. She was impressed, wondering if he'd asked Van for help after all. "First of all, thank you for the compliment. I'm trying to branch out into some other neutrals." Picking up the wine, she studied it for a moment. "A bold selection—well played. It's actually one of my all-time favorites, so obviously you figured out that I'm a red wine person. Did Van help you?"

Logan feigned offense. "I did this all on my own. A feeling I had. Can I pour you a glass?" He gestured toward the chicken-wire-fronted cabinet that held her dishes before reaching in to pluck two wineglasses from the top shelf. "Where's the corkscrew?"

Laina was reaching into the fridge to pull out the snack plate she'd put together for them earlier. "It's in the top drawer to your left."

Logan pulled it open, his attention caught by a newspaper clipping that sat on top of the scissors, pens, and other household objects housed there. He couldn't help but notice the headline and byline.

> *ROCKER'S DEATH APPARENT SUICIDE*
> *Top chef's former lover found dead by*
> *bandmate brother*

Laina was turning around with a plate in her hand when she saw Logan standing there, looking down at something in the open drawer. Remembering what she'd stashed there, she felt sick. "Sorry. It's one drawer over from that. Here, I'll get it." She set the plate down, rushing over to get the corkscrew herself, but it was too late.

Logan closed the drawer, the instant tension making it obvious that they couldn't avoid talking about what he'd just seen. "Laina, I'm so sorry. I wasn't trying to pry."

Laina was standing next to him, the forgotten corkscrew in her hand. She closed her eyes for a moment to collect herself before looking at him with a sad smile. "It's not something I wanted to lead with, but I wasn't trying to hide it either. My ex-boyfriend's brother recently sent me this article. We broke up last summer, before I moved to Aspen, and I'd been out of touch with them both for over a year. Until the article and his letter arrived."

Logan could see that the information was still painful for her. "Listen, you don't have to tell me any of this. Not if you don't want to. But I'm a pretty good ear if you need one, and an excellent shoulder, if I do say so myself."

He took the corkscrew from her hand, making quick work of the wine bottle. Logan poured two glasses, handing one to Laina, before leaning in toward her to tenderly brush his lips against hers.

"Let's go sit on the porch for a while. We can talk—or not talk. It's up to you."

They settled together on her swing, close to each other but not touching, their feet pushing the swing back and forth slowly in tandem. It was dark since Laina switched off the porch light on their way out. She didn't want Logan to see her while she remembered her time with Patrick and shared painful parts of the story with him.

They'd met at the Music City Food and Wine Festival in Nashville. It wasn't Laina's first time at the event, but that year she wasn't cooking for the public. She'd been hired to cook plant-based food for musicians that wanted the option. There were several bands that played the event, with that year's music curated by Nashville's own Kings of Leon. She'd had her arms full with a pan of beautifully stuffed squash halves and was trying to figure out a way to open the door to the greenroom when she heard his voice for the first time.

"Here, allow me." Laina noticed his sleeve of tattoos first as he reached in front of her for the door, pushing it open. His entire forearm was covered in inked pine trees, from the wrist up. It was a stunning piece of art.

He waited for her to step into the room ahead of him while he held the door.

"So you're the one who's been making all the incredible vegan food? This is the best we've eaten at any venue. Ever. Us plant-based guys usually get stuck with spaghetti and marinara. Not the creative stuff you've been making us. So, thank you. Are you local? Could I persuade you to move to New York City with us?"

Laina laughed and told him he wouldn't have to convince her, that she lived in Manhattan too, having just opened her second restaurant in the city. She didn't mention her Michelin rating. She didn't have to. Patrick was completely enraptured by her, and the feeling was mutual. She'd been single for almost eight months by that time, having ended her relationship with Jack Sterling the previous fall. While Jack had certainly not been the love of her life, the relationship had been all-consuming, and Laina had needed some alone time afterward to remind herself of who she was at her core. Laina figured she'd know when she was ready to move on, and from the moment she met Patrick, it was full speed ahead.

His drinking hadn't been out of control when they'd first started dating, or had it been? Laina still wondered if he'd been just that good at hiding it, as Van had suggested to her when she'd finally realized how serious his problem was just before their breakup. Early on, it was just another part of what made him so attractive. He lived on the edge, never saying no to anything. Experiences. Drinks. Other women. Drugs. Laina wasn't aware of the latter until that last day. It wasn't that he wanted those things more than he wanted Laina. Patrick loved her with a white-hot intensity. When she was with him, she was his sun. But Patrick was trying to fill a hole that was bottomless, attempting to slay demons he'd faced since his childhood. He'd told her and no one else about them. He'd trusted her. She'd promised Patrick that she would never discuss his past with anyone else. It contained Patrick's secrets, the ones that had mercifully died with him.

Laina glanced over at Logan, who'd been listening quietly. He smiled at her, taking her hand and squeezing it encouragingly. She'd come this far. It felt strangely cathartic to talk to him about it. She wondered how he'd feel about the way things had ended, though. She decided there was no turning back.

Patrick's drinking had gotten so bad, it began to affect his writing and singing. He'd been in a very successful band with his brother, Jeremy, and they cowrote most of their songs together. Jeremy had been well aware that his brother had been cheating on Laina, and it frustrated him. He, too, had developed a close relationship with Laina, since he and Patrick lived together when they weren't out on tour. At times, she suspected that Jeremy had deeper feelings for her than he should, but then he'd never done anything in particular to confirm those suspicions. One night, Laina had been alone in Patrick's apartment, having used her key to get in and pack up the few things she'd kept at his place. She'd been verbally assaulted that morning at her restaurant by a woman who'd been so descriptive about certain tattooed parts of Patrick's body, it was obvious she'd had physical relations with him. It was the first time Laina had been confronted with what had, up until that point, only been rumors. She knew his drinking had spiraled into drug use, and that he was likely trying to find other ways to feel numb, but she'd decided that the affair was her match in the powder keg. It solidified something she'd been mulling over: her decision to sell her restaurant to the group, which had been persistently trying to buy it, and move to Aspen. She needed to live in a healthier, less emotionally toxic place, that was as far from New York as she could get. Van finally agreeing to move with her pushed her in the right direction, but it was Patrick's behavior that had ultimately convinced her.

She'd finished a letter she'd written to him, leaving it on the kitchen counter, and had gone back into Patrick's bedroom to pack her final few things when Jeremy showed up in the doorway. Laina looked up at him, tears streaming down her face. She hadn't even realized she'd been crying until she saw Jeremy's face flare with anger first, then sympathy, then something else altogether. He knelt down to where she'd been folding her shirts on the floor and took Laina's face in his hands.

"He doesn't deserve you, Laina. He never did." Jeremy crushed his lips to hers, forcing open her mouth to accept his intrusion. Laina was too shocked to do anything and too numb to push back. She felt like she was outside of herself, watching what was happening with Patrick's brother with a morbid fascination. So this is what it was like to kiss Jeremy? He did have feelings for her after all. She felt her wits start to return after a few moments, and was about to push him away, when Patrick showed up, wasted as usual.

"Fuck."

He stood in the doorway of his bedroom, taking in the scene and getting the wrong idea about what had just taken place between his girlfriend and his brother. Jeremy snickered, standing up to meet his brother face-to-face.

"You fucking horse's ass. You screw up everything you touch. Always have. Don't blame her for choosing the sober brother."

With that, Jeremy stared at his brother a moment longer before pushing past Patrick to leave. Laina heard the door slam, shuddering at the way the sound punctuated the moment. It was the end. Of Laina and Patrick. Of Patrick's relationship with his brother. Of Patrick's will to live, but then Laina didn't know that at the time.

She'd zipped up her bag, telling Patrick she was sorry but that she couldn't do it anymore and then left the apartment in tears. It was the last time she'd see or talk to either of the brothers.

Until Jeremy's letter had arrived, essentially blaming Patrick's overdose on himself and Laina.

CHAPTER
FOURTEEN

Logan could sense that Laina was finished talking, but instead of interrupting the peace, he simply took her hand in his as they continued to rock back and forth on the porch swing. He knew it had to have been incredibly emotional for her to share those painful details with him, but Logan was grateful she'd felt comfortable enough to do so. They sat together in silence for a few moments, letting the story wash over them before Laina spoke again.

"You must think I'm a terrible person. For leaving things the way I did, so unresolved with Patrick. I never corrected the idea he had about what had happened between myself and Jeremy. I thought it would be easier that way, and I didn't want to come between brothers. I knew Jeremy wouldn't admit to Patrick that he'd been the aggressor, so I hoped they'd at least be able to mend their relationship, 'ignorance is bliss' and all of that. In my mind, our differences at that point were irreconcilable. But maybe I *should* have made it clear to Patrick that I didn't cheat with his brother. Maybe Jeremy's right; Patrick wouldn't have felt the need to work so hard to stay numb. I can't help feeling that we are each responsible in some way for his overdose."

Logan squeezed her hand before answering. "Patrick's death was not your fault. It sounds to me like his addiction was ruling his life at that point. You couldn't have helped him if he couldn't manage to help himself. First rule of addiction, Laina."

Logan paused, not sure if he should share his thoughts about Jeremy. "I'm disgusted that his brother saw fit to reach out to you in such a cruel way. He clearly has some guilt over his own behavior, and is looking to lay some of it at your feet. Don't allow him to do that. It's your decision, but you must realize that you have no reason to own any of Jeremy's stuff. Also, I hope to God I never have occasion to meet him."

Laina shuddered at the thought. Jeremy had indicated in his letter a desire to see Laina again at some point, but she didn't think that would be healthy for either of them. Laina hadn't mentioned it to Logan during the course of their talk, and she felt she'd made the right decision. There wouldn't be a meeting between her and Jeremy. Not if she could help it.

She turned to face Logan for the first time, the side of his face dimly lit from the kitchen light they'd left on in her house. "Thank you for listening. I'm sorry to ruin our evening talking about this stuff. Nothing says romance like discussing an ex."

Logan smiled softly, shaking his head. "It's strange. I feel like nothing has been orthodox about you and me. It took us a year of false starts for you to admit how awesome and irresistible I am. Our first date was a sleepover. And we're not even two dates in, and we know each other's deepest, darkest secrets." He looked at Laina pointedly. "Wanna try out some casual conversation, see how that goes?"

Laina laughed. "Well, OK, we could give that a shot." She thought for a moment. "I talked to my parents today. They've been working on opening a wellness center back home in California for the past few years, and it's kind of a big deal. They've asked me to travel home for the big kickoff next weekend. I'm not sure I can manage it, though. I couldn't ask Van to take on that much responsibility at the restaurant so early on."

Logan was impressed. "Wow, that sounds pretty important. When do they want you to come? I'm sure Van would tell you to go. Don't you think?"

Laina nodded. "Of course he would, which is why I hesitate to ask. He would never say no. It's just that they want me there a few days early. They said they need to talk to me about something, which is a little unsettling. And this kickoff event is not going to be small. It's kind of a who's who in the spiritual and alternative medicine world. Black tie. The whole deal. I'm not comfortable at those things, and I don't really want to go alone."

Logan chose his words carefully. "Hear me out. What if you flew home midweek, spent some time with your parents, and maybe I could fly in just to take you to the event? If it's not too soon for me to meet your family? OK—it totally is. But we could tell them I'm just a friend. I think you should go, Laina. I would suggest you take Van, but I know he needs to be here to cover for you, so you're stuck with me as an option, if you decide you want to bring a date."

Laina leaned in to kiss him, stopping him midsentence. This man was constantly impressing her. She was waiting for the other shoe to drop. He couldn't be this thoughtful, this giving. In that moment, she didn't care to consider the alternative.

Logan stood up, pulling Laina into his arms, their lips desperate for more of each other, the heightened emotions of the night fueling their passion. Logan felt her gasp and had to stop himself from doing the same when their tongues met, his hands sliding up her shoulders and into her hair so he could better control the kiss.

Laina couldn't quite get close enough to him, but she wanted to try. Stepping her feet a little wider, she pressed herself against him, forcing a deep groan out of Logan that made her feel a little light-headed. They were frenzied, unable to quench the desire that had been building between them with kisses any longer.

"Come inside with me." Logan led her by the hand to the front door, opening it to let Laina lead the way. Once they were in the living room, he turned toward her before sitting down on the couch and pulling her onto his lap. With Laina's knees straddling him, the two of them sunk down into the comfort of the big soft couch. Logan slid his hands slowly up the back of Laina's sweater, feeling her shiver at his touch. His hands were strong and calloused, and the effect of them on her back made Laina think she might be losing her self-control. She let her own hands reach down to untuck his shirt so that she could reach underneath, giving her hands the opportunity to explore the expanse of his chest and torso. Logan groaned again, shifting in an unsuccessful effort to get comfortable. It was the best version of uncomfortable he'd ever experienced. The fire burned between them, until it was as if they both sensed things were careening toward the point of no return, so they both slowed their pace, and Laina eventually peeled herself away from him, climbing off his lap to settle next to him within the crook of his arm. Logan took a minute to catch his breath.

"So, does that mean you'll let me escort you to the event? Because I want to be clear . . ."

Laina giggled. "I'm not sure you realize what you're in for, but if you're willing to subject yourself to the laser scrutiny of my mother and all of her very intuitive friends, who am I to say no?"

She leaned up to kiss him again, softly this time. "Thank you for listening tonight, Logan. And for your willingness to be so open. You continue to surprise me."

Logan had to stop himself from revisiting that delicious little spot on the side of her neck with his mouth. He licked his lips, the taste of her still there. "I'm just full of surprises. And I can't wait to see you in formal wear. If you look this good in jeans and a sweater, I can only imagine."

They talked a while longer and decided that Logan would fly into LAX the following Friday, the morning of the event. Laina would leave Wednesday morning, so she would only need to ask Van to cover the Wednesday through Saturday dinner service. They could catch an early flight back home from LA on Sunday, and Laina would be back in time to work.

It was well after midnight when Laina stifled a small yawn.

Logan chuckled. "OK, I'm leaving. I know this week is going to be busy, for me too. Call or text when you have time, but don't feel like we need to get together. I'll have you all weekend long. A nice, taking-it-slow kind of weekend." He kissed her one last time just that way. Long and slow.

Laina slept peacefully that night, a smile on her face when her head hit the pillow.

The chime of her cell phone woke Laina just before seven on Monday morning. She smiled when she saw it was Logan.

> Logan: How did you sleep? Without me there, probably not very well.

> Laina: If I recall correctly, the sleep I got next to you was VERY minimal. Last night=dreamless.

> Logan: Can you blame me? Hey, I didn't get a chance to tell you last night. I'm getting together with Viv and Sienna tonight for some baby talk. If all goes well, we'll meet with doc Wed or Thurs. (Can't do Friday. I've got a hot date.)

> Laina: Really? That was fast. How are you feeling about it? The meeting. Not the hot date.

> Logan: Great, actually. At peace. Feels right. V&S will be such great moms.

> Laina: You're incredible. I'll txt later. I'm late to meet the girls for breakfast. I'm sure they'll be plying me for info.

> Logan: That's ok. I'm off to my yoga class anyway. Not.

> Laina: Go easy on those hamstrings.

Laina replayed their evening again on her drive over to meet the girls for breakfast at Element 47 inside of the Little Nell. Over the past year, the four friends had tried to get together anytime India and Violet were in town, and since they were headed back to Tennessee in the morning, Willow had arranged for the group to share one last meal before they had to say goodbye.

Laina was the last to arrive, rushing to her seat after breathlessly leaning down to kiss each of her friends on the cheek.

"Sorry I'm late. You will almost never hear this from me, but I actually overslept. I think this crazy weekend got the best of me." As she put her napkin on her lap and accepted the coffee the waitress offered, she missed the look exchanged among her friends.

Willow had already heard the same excuse earlier that morning. "Hmm, that's the same thing Logan said. I guess he had a late night too, which was his reason for being tardy for fishing this morning with Wyatt and Rex. Weird, because my brother is *never* late." Willow sipped her coffee, watching Laina's face closely for any kind of reaction.

Laina thought they'd at least give her a moment to get her wits about her, but not these ladies. Willow had just dropped the velvet ax on her. She decided she wasn't going to make this too easy for them.

"Huh, must be something in the air." She studied the menu, even though she knew it by heart and would likely choose the buffet anyway. "India, Violet, I'll bet you're ready to get home. I heard Susan and Finn left yesterday for Tennessee? Were they traumatized after having to take care of all of the kids while we were camping?"

India laughed. "Well, they did say something about sched-uling yet another vacation soon—just the two of them. I think we'll probably leave them alone for a while. The kids can be overwhelming when they're all together."

Violet wasn't going to let Laina off the hook. "So, back to the reason you're so tired. A little birdie told us that you had a date with Logan last night. Or have our sources misled us?"

Violet's red hair was lit up from the sun slanting in through the window behind her, enhancing her beauty and making her seem even more formidable than usual to Laina, who wasn't easily intimidated. She'd gotten to know Violet pretty well, and recognized that she was using her presence to her advantage in this situation. Laina thought she'd be better off at this point to just fess up.

"OK, you hens! Yes, we had a drink at my house last night after the restaurant closed. Just a chance to sit and get to know each other a little better."

Violet snickered. "Oh, I don't know. Rex told me you guys got to know each other pretty well at the campout. He was wandering around in the woods in the middle of the night, looking for a place to pee, when he thought he heard a bear. Turns out, the growling was coming from one of our neighbors." Smiling sweetly, she reached for a sugar, tearing open the packet and dumping the contents into her coffee.

Willow's jaw hung open. "Violet! Leave her alone. She'll never have breakfast with us again." Turning toward Laina, she was about to apologize for their bold friend when something caught her eye at the front of the restaurant. "Hey, is that Buck? And was he just here on a breakfast date? How juicy!"

The ladies turned together to see Logan's handsome coworker escorting a thin blonde out of the restaurant. They couldn't see her face, but when Buck turned to thank the hostess, he was grinning from ear to ear.

"He's such a good-looking man. I feel like that's what Wyatt will look like when he's older. So distinguished, and perfectly salt and peppered. And that beard—mmm." India swiveled back around to the surprised faces of her friends. "What? Don't tell me you all haven't thought the same thing. Just because we've already ordered, ladies, doesn't mean we can't take a peek at the menu."

Across town, Logan was getting a similar grilling at the hands of Wyatt, Rex, and Garrett. The morning had started out peacefully enough, with the four friends standing in the gentle current of Maroon Creek, fly-fishing and enjoying the warm and sunny weather. Garrett had caught the first trout of the day, setting off a flurry of friendly competition among the others to do better.

Rex wasn't having much luck, so he decided to shift the focus. "Speaking of a good catch, Chef Laina seems to fit the bill, eh, Logan?"

Logan had his hat pulled down over his eyes, but there wasn't enough room to hide from their inquisition. In truth, he was dying. If he couldn't be with her, he'd settle for talking to his friends about her.

"She's the real deal, fellas. Smart, funny, ridiculously gorgeous. And she's deep. We had a good night last night. That's why I was late this morning." Seeing their surprised faces, he hurriedly added, "I got home late last night. Not this morning. So I overslept. Very innocent. Well, *very* might be a stretch." He turned toward Garrett. "If you tell my sister, I'll have to kill you. That's up to Laina to share with the girls. I don't want to screw this up." He finished attaching a fly to his line, preparing to cast again. "She invited me to go with her to meet her parents in California next weekend. Well, I invited myself, technically, but she said I could come."

Garrett laughed. "Sometimes you have to invite yourself along. I did it with Willow, and look where that got me. You ready to join the brass ring club, buddy?" He wriggled his hand, pointing to the wedding band he wore on his fourth finger.

Logan sighed, surprising himself with the answer. "Honestly? For the first time in my life, I'm not repelled by the idea, which is both exciting and terrifying. It's early enough that the excitement is winning out. For now anyway. But I keep looking over my shoulder, waiting for the fear to creep up on me."

Wyatt shook his head. "When you know, you know. Day one for me with India. There was something about her. It felt like she was made for me. I cannot imagine being single again; there would never be anyone who could fill her shoes."

Rex was watching them all with interest. "Listen, guys. As much as I feel ridiculous in these waders having this conversation, I'll admit that I feel the same way about Vi. She completes me and all of that." He turned to look at Logan. "I can see that you've been sunk, Logan, even if you haven't fully surrendered yet. Don't waste time worrying about the terror. It will always be there, in one form or another. First, you'll worry she's going to realize you're not good enough for her, which let's face it—none of us are good enough for them. Then you'll get married and you'll worry that your life as you once knew it is over. And you'll be right again. Finally, if you're lucky enough to become a father, you'll worry every damned day that your wife and child will have something terrible happen to them, robbing you of everything that you consider important in life. So embrace the fear. It's part of the process, brother. And I'll tell you a little secret: if Laina's the one, she'll be worth every bit of it."

CHAPTER

FIFTEEN

Logan wasn't sure what the protocol was for meeting friends to discuss being their sperm donor. Should he bring flowers? Wine? His medical records? Luckily, he'd recently been in to see his doctor for his yearly checkup, now a requirement after the liver transplant, so he knew he at least had a clean bill of health to offer them.

He settled on wine and flowers, since it felt like a big deal. He was going into this blind. They hadn't discussed any of the logistics, so there was a lot to talk about. He suspected the wine might come in handy when they got to the more personal topics. A quick Google search had given him an idea of what to expect, but he didn't know if their doctor would work the same way.

He parked his Bronco in the driveway, blown away by their location. They had built a beautiful home on Red Mountain, which Vivian had designed herself years ago when she'd sold her first architecture firm. Lucky for them, they'd built before the prices had skyrocketed. It was impossible to find a home on their street now for less than $8 million.

It was early evening in Aspen, so when Logan turned around to admire the jaw-dropping view, the city lights were twinkling before him. He gazed in the direction of the restaurant, wondering how Laina's dinner service was going. It hadn't even been twenty-four hours, and he was already wondering how he'd make it until Friday without seeing her. They'd texted a few times, but both of them had been busy. Logan had spent the rest of the day helping Garrett with some repairs over at Walland House, and Laina was getting everything in order so Van would be prepared to step in during her absence. Since she was taking off in two days for California, he was trying to leave her alone so she could get ready to go.

"It's beautiful up here, isn't it?" Sienna had seen him pull up, so she walked down the front pathway to meet Logan. "It's like living on top of the world." She followed Logan's gaze. "We are so happy that our child will get to grow up here in Aspen. It's such a special place. It feels protected from the world, don't you think? The energy is pure. And we know that our child will have a special connection with nature. Or at least we hope so."

Logan nodded. "I agree. It's strange how different it feels from Colorado Springs, which is where I lived before this. I think it's because it's completely tucked into the mountains. It's not easy to get here. All good things in life take effort, right? If something is worth having, it's worth working for." He turned to look at Sienna. "Are we still talking about Aspen?"

They laughed together as Vivian came down the steps to join them on the driveway. They exchanged hellos, then decided to wander around back to sit outside on the terrace and enjoy the wine Logan had brought them while they talked. Once they were settled, Vivian raised her glass in a toast to the three of them. "To you, Logan, and your generous and selfless offer to help us start our family. You will never know how grateful we are for this gift." They clinked glasses, and Vivian paused before taking a sip. "I'd better enjoy this. My days of having a glass of wine are numbered." She smiled softly at Sienna.

Logan was surprised. "So does that mean you're going to carry the baby? I was wondering about that. I guessed wrong. I thought for sure it would be Sienna."

The women looked at each other before Sienna answered. "I know, as the 'earth mother hippie,' I might seem like the obvious choice. That was our plan, in fact. I would have loved to have had the privilege of carrying our child. Unfortunately, the doctor told us last month when we began exploring this idea that I likely couldn't conceive. Or that it would be much harder for me to get pregnant than it would for Viv." Sadness flickered across her face, but only for a moment. "It's OK, though. Vivian has agreed to do it, and we're in this together."

Vivian studied Logan. "There is a lot to discuss, Logan, and we want to be fully honest with you about everything. A good place to start would be to tell you that because I'm in my early forties, we've been told this pregnancy could be high risk. It could also take us a while to conceive, which means you'll need to be . . . available . . . when ideal conditions are present. I guess we should start there. Do you have issues with either of those things?"

Logan took a big sip of wine. "When you say 'high risk,' do you mean for you or the baby?"

Vivian answered him. "Both of us, actually. I have hereditary high blood pressure, which the doctors say can make things more difficult, but that it's usually manageable with careful monitoring and sometimes late-term bed rest. And as for our baby, well, there are always risks of genetic abnormalities when a woman is over forty." She looked at Sienna, who finished the thought.

"Vivian and I are committed to seeing this pregnancy through, regardless. We won't be doing genetic testing, because no matter what, we want this child. The child that we know is meant for us, irrespective of any potential challenges. We just want you to know the risks and to feel comfortable with them too. This baby will be genetically linked to you too, after all."

Logan was blown away. He hadn't considered all the medical intricacies, but he surprised himself in the moment when he wasn't deterred by them. "Ladies, I have to tell you, I'm here to help you in any way I can. It's not really my place to be weighing in on these kinds of decisions when I'm simply providing the seeds. You guys are the ones who will grow the garden and do all of the work. My job is simple. And yes, I know there's a joke in there somewhere."

They laughed before talking more about the medical nuts and bolts. Logan assured them that he was medically cleared, and let them know that he'd even had a full STD screening as a part of his physical the month before.

"I'm as clean as a clock. There hasn't been anyone new since I received my glowing bill of health, so rest easy. But full disclosure: that could change this weekend."

Vivian and Sienna looked back at him, neither of them surprised. "You're going to California. We know. Laina told me this morning after yoga. We missed you there, by the way." Sienna winked at him.

Logan winced. "Yeah, I have this leg thing going on, so once I get that worked out, I'll see about getting back to class." He smiled. "So she told you I'm meeting her in LA? What else did she say?"

Sienna laughed. "Oh, that's highly confidential, Logan. But I will tell you that she is very much looking forward to spending the weekend with you." She paused. "Speaking of Laina. I know you guys are brand-new, but we want to make sure that you take everything into consideration. Laina assured us that she is comfortable with you being a part of this, so we aren't worried about that. She brought up a valid point, though. Do you want to be a part of our child's life, in any way?" Sienna looked at Vivian before continuing. "Because we've discussed it, and we want you to know that you're welcome to have a relationship with this child if you want one. By the same token, we will not take it personally if you decide not to."

Vivian sighed. "Our attorneys are recommending that we draw up papers that would legally sever your parental rights. We know it's a technicality, but it sounds so cold to us. How do you feel about that?"

Logan thought about it for a moment. "I understand. They are protecting you, which is what lawyers do. I'm comfortable with that. Again, this is your child." He hesitated. "But if you would want the baby to know that I helped him or her join your family, I'm OK with that too. It doesn't feel like something that should be a secret. I'd be honored to have a relationship of some kind with your child. But only inasmuch as you're comfortable with it. Tell me when you want me. For the guy stuff, I guess. Or however you want to frame it. Listen, this kid is so lucky to have the two of you as moms; I don't think you're going to be needing me for help. But if you do, I'll be there for you."

Sienna used her fingers to blot out her tears. "This is a blessed little person we're going to have, you guys." Holding hands with Vivian, she looked at Logan.

"So here's the interesting news. We called the doctor this morning because of where Viv is in her cycle. If you're comfortable with this, we can get some basic legal documents drawn up overnight. If it's not rushing you, we'd actually like to have our first attempt at insemination take place at the end of this week. Which means . . ."

Logan blushed. "Which means you need me to deliver the goods sooner than later? OK. So how's that going to work? I mean, do I have to go into the office with you? Or is this an at-home kind of thing, and then I bring it to you? Or you pick it up? I know—how about another bottle of wine?"

Vivian laughed, refilling his glass. "The doctor would prefer that you come into the office to donate, but first they need to run a few basic blood tests. You could go in tomorrow to do those, and if all goes well, you could go back on Wednesday and Thursday for two separate donations, and then Sienna and I could have our appointment for insemination on Friday. You wouldn't have to be there for that, obviously. Don't worry. They are very discreet, and there is a private room with everything you'll need for . . . motivation."

Logan cleared his throat. "OK, then. Tomorrow, blood work. Wednesday and Thursday, a little public shame. I can handle that. How soon will we know if it worked?"

Sienna sat forward excitedly. "Surprisingly soon, thanks to the accuracy of blood tests. You'll be the first person we tell, we promise." She stood up, holding her arms out for a hug. "What do you say, guys? Let's make a baby together!"

Everything went smoothly with Logan's initial screening, so he scheduled appointments for both Wednesday and Thursday mornings at nine, hoping he could get the donations over with early in the day. He prayed that the office would be quiet at that hour. The last thing he wanted was to get stage fright.

On Wednesday morning, he'd texted back and forth early with Laina, while she was riding in an Uber to the airport to leave for California.

> Logan: Any chance you'd be able to call me around 9 . . . whisper some sweet nothings into my ear for inspiration?

> Laina: I'm sure there will be plenty of material in the office for you to choose from.

> Logan: What? Dirty magazines? Never really been my thing. I prefer mysterious raven-haired beauties with hazel eyes.

> Laina: Well, just think about our upcoming weekend, imagine what it might be like. Worked for me.

> Logan: Wait. Did you just admit you've fantasized about me? That is so hot.

> Laina: I've got to go. Hope everything shakes out ok.

> Logan: That's not funny. But thanks for the visual. I think I'm good to go now.

Logan arrived at the office, where a kind and mercifully older nurse showed him into a small room that housed a recliner and a side table with a computer. There was a rack that held an assortment of books and magazines on the floor, and a box of Kleenex on a small table next to an empty plastic cup. The nurse told him that when he was finished, he should place the cup inside a two-way metal box in the wall and push a button that would illuminate a light on the other side, indicating that she could collect it.

He'd had a joke prepared about whether the nurse would buy him a drink first, but when she'd turned out to be his grandmother's age, he thought better about using comedy to defuse the situation, keeping his nervous chatter to a minimum. When she'd closed the door behind her, Logan walked over to triple-check the lock before turning back around to survey the room.

He picked up a magazine and leafed through it, setting it back down in disinterest. A single click of the mouse showed him that the computer contained a link to a free porn site, which didn't feel like the way he wanted to bring Viv and Sienna's child into the world.

So Logan sat down in the recliner, removed the cap from the cup to have it ready, and unzipped his pants before taking a deep breath and closing his eyes.

Good old-fashioned imagination would have to do the trick this time.

Laina was almost always the first thing he saw when he let his mind wander now, and this time was no different. He conjured up the image of her standing with her back to him in the lake that night of the campout, but in this fantasy, she wasn't wearing her swimsuit. The full moon cast a warm glow on her bare back, and as she heard him approaching, she turned to face him, her arms crossed over her bare chest. *Logan.* She said his name, asking him to join her. He stepped out of his boxer briefs, striding toward where she waited for him in the water. As he drew closer, Laina lowered her hands, revealing her small, perfect breasts, with nipples that instantly hardened at the exposure to the cool air. Logan leaned in to suck on her neck, his hands cupping her, teasing her nipples gently, provoking a gasp from her parted lips. He could hear the thunder in the background, but he was in no hurry to leave the lake.

This was his fantasy, after all. There wouldn't be any damned lightning to ruin things this time.

Where am I? Oh right. Laina moaning. He slid his arms around to her back, letting himself absorb the feeling of her slick, wet skin as he allowed his hands to travel lower, below the water, to the small of her back. Her ass felt incredible in his hands, and he lifted her up, closer to him so that her body met his. Laina's hands wound their way down his chest and torso, into the water, and found him there, hard and ready for . . .

The cup. *Where is the cup!*

Logan had never been so grateful for good aim in his life. If it weren't for some fortuitous quick thinking, he would have had to leave the room completely humiliated because he'd let himself get lost in the fantasy. How would he have explained that to Viv and Sienna?

Tomorrow, he decided, he'd simply make do with the porn.

Logan checked his phone once he was back in his truck and decided to see if he could reach Laina before she left town.

> Logan: Have you taken off yet?

> Laina: Nope. On the plane now, taxiing. Have YOU taken off?

> Logan: Roger that. All I can say is . . . thank God I have a vivid imagination.

> Laina: Anything you want to share?

Logan: I don't want to violate any FCC rules. So no. I'll tell you when I see you.

Laina: Tell me, or show me?

Logan: Stop it. Are you trying to send me back into that office? I might break donor records!

Laina: Ha! Taking off. Talk later? Xoxo

Logan: Be safe. I can't wait to see you.

CHAPTER
SIXTEEN

Laina had moved away from the West Coast right after high school and hadn't lived in California since. She questioned that decision for a moment when she felt the warm, humid air greet her in the Jetway. It was so welcome after living in the dry mountain climate.

It had been a long travel day since she'd been unable to book a nonstop flight with such late notice, instead connecting through Denver. She was starving when she landed, so after she'd picked up her rental car, she made a quick detour to swing by her favorite coffee shop in Santa Monica. She loved the cozy vibe of the place, filled with writers and creative types clicking away on their laptops and iPads. Also, she was craving their famous ginger tea, which they brewed strong enough to clear a person's sinuses in a hurry.

Laina had just gotten back in the rental car when her phone vibrated.

Jeremy: Are you going to be in LA this weekend? We should talk.

Laina was frozen, glad she hadn't yet pulled out of her
parking spot. She looked around to see if he was nearby. How
did Jeremy know she was home? She shivered, unsettled by
the unwelcome intrusion. She wouldn't respond. He'd get the
message. Jeremy wasn't obtuse.

She buckled her belt and headed for the Pacific Coast
Highway, hoping she'd be able to avoid the midday rush.
Summer traffic near the beach was brutal, and it was nearly
impossible to predict which lane to be in. If she chose the left
lane, Laina risked getting stuck behind tourists trying to turn
left into the already-stuffed beach parking lots. In the right
lane, she'd need to be careful not to get whacked by a surfer
hoisting a longboard overhead and hoping they could dash
across four lanes of heavy traffic to get to the beach.

Laina knew this stretch of road, because she'd spent four
years traveling back and forth on it to a private high school in
Santa Monica. She'd graduated from the school's visual arts
program and had seriously contemplated a career as an artist.
It was only when her mother had come to her suggesting she
explore food as art that she'd wavered. Laina had grown up in
California, and she'd known she was ready for something very
different. New York City fit the bill, so three weeks after she'd
graduated, she'd moved across the country and had never
looked back.

She'd decided to rent a Jeep while she was in town, after a
peek at the forecast told her that the weather was going to be
perfectly pleasant. Although, up the coast, the temperature
rarely deviated from the seventies during summer days anyway. It tended to be cool in the mornings and evenings near
the coast, but nothing a light sweater couldn't take care of.

Laina smiled, picturing Logan in the passenger seat next to her. She'd been thinking about him the entire morning, and part of her wished he could have come home with her for the entire trip. He had officially possessed her thoughts, and, as if he'd known she was thinking about him, her phone buzzed again in the cup holder. She tensed up, hoping it wasn't Jeremy. When she slowed at the next light, she glanced at the home screen on her phone.

Logan: Do I need a tux for this weekend?

Laina smiled, relieved. Instead of texting him back, she plugged in her earbuds so she could hear over the wind and dialed his number.

He answered on the first ring. "I know I should let it ring a few times, so I don't seem anxious, but who are we kidding? I'm going to devour you when I see you."

Laina covered her mouth, laughing in delight. "Well, hello to you too! Sorry it's so loud. I have the top down, and I'm actually making decent time, so it might be hard to hear me."

Logan stuttered. "Wait—top down? What now?"

Laina rolled her eyes, still laughing. "Ha-ha. To answer your question, you can absolutely wear a tux, but a nice suit is totally fine too. I'm wearing a long dress, but it's pretty simple. Go with whatever is comfortable."

Logan scoffed. "I'm at the men's store now, and let me tell you . . . none of this stuff is comfortable. But I'll figure it out." She heard him cover the phone with his hand and muffle something to the salesperson. "They want me to ask you what color you're wearing. Can I guess first?"

"Yes, I'm wearing black. Listen, these kinds of events are out of my comfort zone too, so I'm not going to stretch myself too much. Don't worry, though: I'll bring the heat." She smiled, excited to have the chance to dress up for Logan. She'd packed a few other special pieces of clothing too, just in case.

"Oh, I'm not worried one little bit. You could throw a belt around your chef's jacket and look hotter than anyone else who'll show up. I'm proud to have you on my arm. At least for the weekend."

"We'll see if we can't come up with something a little longer term if you can behave yourself." Laina loved flirting with him.

Logan didn't hesitate. "Forget it. I'll take one weekend of misbehavior over a lifetime of goody-goody anytime. So prepare yourself. We're going for it, baby."

They said goodbye, and Laina returned her attention to the road. After a while, she made a left, heading down into the seaside community where her parents had moved ten years before. When she'd lived at home, they'd had a place closer to Santa Monica, but after she'd left for culinary school, her parents had decided they wanted a quieter life, still near the shore. Their current house came with a beach key, which provided access to a private cove popular with surfers because of its relative inaccessibility to the general public. It was impossible to reach when the tides were high, unless you walked down a long and guarded hidden forest pathway with four different locked gates along the way. Having a beach key had been known to raise property values in the neighborhood by up to $250,000. You weren't paying for the key. You were paying for access.

Laina's parents had a very unique setup. Their expansive property trailed down through a couple of acres' worth of impressive gardens, spilling out into the bottom of the path that led directly to the beach, so her father had commissioned a small private shack to be built near the path, making it easy to grab his board on the way down for his morning surf. Laina's parents were the picture of health, the youngest-looking sixtysomethings she'd ever known.

Her father had spent his early life as a studio executive, and had done very well for himself. Her mother had always been interested in health and spirituality, and she had rubbed off on her husband during the course of their marriage. Laina's father committed fully to the lifestyle after they'd adopted Laina all those years ago. They were well connected within the community, and after kicking around the idea of building the wellness center for a long time, they'd finally decided to make the dream a reality a couple of years ago.

They'd purchased a large plot of land up in the nearby mountains, and with the help of some investors, built what was being called the most luxurious facility of its kind in the country. It would house everything from chiropractors to yoga instructors, to a third-generation practitioner of acupuncture who her mother had worked with for years. The cream of the wellness crop would all be working under one roof, or series of roofs, since the property was made up of a cluster of individual cabins and work spaces, tied together by the gardens, lotus pond, and labyrinth at the center.

Laina had consulted on the menus for the two restaurants. Both were vegan, but one only served breakfast and lunch, while the other was a more formal fine-dining venue.

She couldn't wait to get a look at what her parents' final selections would be, hoping they'd show her the menus before the event.

Laina parked in the circle driveway and hopped out of the Jeep, stretching her arms in the air, happy to be home. The front door swung open wide, and her parents rushed out with a flurry of hugs, kisses, and endearments. Laina loved how her mother smelled, like the jasmine essential oil she knew she dabbed on her wrists and neck every morning, and her father's smiling eyes brought tears to Laina's own.

"Mom, Dad. Oh, it's so great to be home. You two look amazing, and of course your flowers are stunning."

Serena and Bo Ming's home was a neighborhood show-piece, and that was saying something in an enclave packed with celebrities. They'd planted thick bushes of white hydrangea that stood poking out of the split-rail fence that bordered the front of their property. The home itself was composed of a combination of mixed materials, the majority of the structure built with distressed barn wood in rustic red, accented with fieldstone. There were plenty of windows too, welcoming the California sunshine into every room.

Her father reached into the back of the Jeep and removed Laina's suitcase, carrying it through the open front door and into the foyer, while Laina and her mother followed him, arm in arm.

"So how was your travel, darling? You look very well." Her mother stopped and turned to study Laina. "Colorado certainly seems to agree with you. Your aura is the most beautiful shade of pink!"

That caught her dad's attention. "Serena, that means she's in love. Even I know that much." Her father set the suitcase at the base of the stairs and turned to look at his daughter. "Yes, I can see it too. Something's different about you since the last time we saw you. You seem lighter. Does it have anything to do with this friend who's joining you this weekend?"

Serena smiled. "Yes, I was curious about that too, but let's let her get settled, Bo. We can talk more at lunch, if Laina wants to."

"I already knew to resist your uncanny psychic ability was futile. I'll fill you guys in, I promise. Do you mind if I grab a quick shower first? I'd like to scrub LAX off of me.

I'll be down in thirty minutes to join you by the pool." She turned to her father. "Were you still planning to surf tonight? I'd love to go with you."

Bo smiled, nodding his head. "I never miss a day, and I'd love to surf with my girl. Already went out this morning, and the waves were good. I'll dig out your summer wet suit and have it standing by when you're ready to escape our questioning. Here, let me take your things out to the guest house. We thought you'd be more comfortable out there this time, since you're having company. Not that we're assuming anything."

Laina spent the next twenty minutes standing under a hot stream of water. She was glad to be home, but her mind kept revisiting the text from Jeremy. *How did he know she was in Southern California? Did that mean that he was here too?* The last thing she wanted was for Jeremy and Logan to cross paths. This weekend, or ever. She'd told Logan what she'd thought he needed to know, only leaving out the details that she didn't consider pertinent to her story with Patrick. Or at least she'd managed to rationalize it that way. But she couldn't go back now and reopen that can of worms. Things were going so well, she just wanted to bask in the glow of these firsts with him.

Laina plugged her phone in to charge, put on a bathing suit and cover-up, and headed back outside to the pool.

One would have thought that Oprah was coming to lunch looking at the spread Serena Ming had prepared for her daughter. (Oprah had been to lunch at their home, incidentally. Several times.) There was a platter of fresh fruits, likely plucked straight out of the garden that morning, along with other colorful dishes overflowing with avocado, quinoa, and at least two different kinds of salads.

"Mom, geez. Do you think I haven't been eating? This all looks amazing." Laina took a few mulberries from a small ceramic bowl, popping them into her mouth one at a time. "I forgot about the mulberry tree. I'd love to have this garden at my house, but most of this stuff wouldn't grow at altitude the way it thrives here." Her parents had avocado and banana trees, along with oranges, apricots, peaches, and over a dozen different kinds of lettuces and vegetables. Another perk of living in the Golden State.

They sat down to lunch, chatting about Laina's opening and her life in Aspen. She told them a little bit about the campout, the part about her having been asked to cook the meal and how the money went to charity. She decided to share with them a little bit about Logan too.

"So, my friend who's coming. Obviously, my pink aura or whatever gave it away. We are dating, but it's new. I've known him for about a year, and our friends have been trying to set us up, but for whatever reason, this just felt like the right time to give it a try."

Bo reached for the pitcher of lemon water, pouring his daughter a glass before speaking. "What does this young man do?"

Laina smiled. "Logan. His name is Logan, and he works with my friends over at Walland House. You met them when you were in Aspen last summer. Garrett and Willow? Actually, Willow is Logan's sister. He owns the horse ranch next door to Walland House, so he leads rides and helps with other special outdoor activities they do."

Serena's fork was suspended midair. "Wait a minute. Is this the brother who saved Willow's life? The Ranger? You told us about that when we met her. Didn't he donate an organ or something?"

Laina nodded. "He did. And speaking of donating things, I guess I should tell you something else. I know you guys are open-minded, so this shouldn't be a big deal, but it does speak to his incredible character. It's one of the things that made me finally decide to open my heart to him." Laina looked at her parents, smiling. "He's helping two friends of ours, Vivian and Sienna. They want to start a family, and Logan has agreed to be their sperm donor."

Bo Ming sat back in his chair. "Well. This fellow certainly sounds . . . interesting. Are these ladies good friends of his? That's not a decision a person comes to lightly."

Laina shook her head. "They weren't particularly close, but you'll see when you meet Logan. It's his nature. He's a giver, and he acts with his heart, not his head. I thought that's what you guys always encourage me to do more of?"

Bo wiped his mouth with his napkin. "Oh yes, we do want that. I think it's wonderful what Logan's doing. You just don't hear that every day."

Laina looked at her mother, who had been silently listening. "Mom, what do you think?"

Selena looked thoughtful. "I'm just wondering what you think? Really? Do you want children someday, Laina? And if so, if you have them with Logan, which I know is jumping ahead a bit, how would this child fit into the picture? Is Logan doing this because he doesn't want children of his own?"

Laina sighed. "We haven't gotten that far. All I know is that I am at the point in my life where I'm finally choosing to be with a person whose first inclination is to help others. Not hurt them. So I'm taking a leap. Everything else will work itself out in due time."

Serena could see her daughter had given it a lot of thought, so she knew not to push. Besides, there was another issue to discuss. "Laina, Dad and I got a phone call last week, and we wanted to talk to you about it." Bo nodded to his wife, encouraging her to go on.

"Honey, Patrick's brother, Jeremy, called us, and told us what had happened. We can't imagine how painful that must have been for you. Jeremy said that he's reached out to you but that he hasn't heard back. Laina, he really is trying to make things right. He's in San Diego this weekend with the band, and he heard about our gala. Now that you've told us about Logan, we see it's not appropriate to invite him, which is what we were going to suggest, but do you think you could take an hour or so while you're here to get closure with him? Hearing where you're at with this new relationship, I think it could be a good thing."

Laina was flabbergasted. She'd shared with her parents the reasons she'd left Patrick last year, because she'd come home to stay with them for a week right after they'd broken up and Laina had needed her mom's ear. They knew everything, which was why it surprised Laina that they thought Jeremy worthy of a second chance. But then again, her parents believed everyone deserved one. Something about clearing Karma. Laina couldn't believe he'd reached out to her folks. That was just like him. Jeremy would do anything to get his way, which made him a liability.

Laina knew there was only one way to put Jeremy behind her. She excused herself, thanking her parents for lunch, and retreated to the guest house to find her phone.

> Laina: I'll meet you. Saturday. Come to my parents' house. One hour, and this ends.

> Jeremy: I'll be there. Thank you, Laina.

> Laina: I'm with someone. Don't get the wrong idea.

> Jeremy: See you Saturday.

Laina couldn't shake feeling that agreeing to see him again was a huge mistake.

CHAPTER
SEVENTEEN

Logan: Landed safe. Walking into baggage claim now. Call you from the cab.

Laina: Look to your right.

It took a moment for the words to register, but when they did, Logan's head snapped up, and Laina watched as his eyes scanned the crowd. When he found her, Logan dropped the two carry-on bags he'd been holding onto the floor on either side of him and walked toward Laina with purpose. He never slowed, wrapping her in his arms and lowering his face to hers, their lips meeting in a hungry crush. The airport noise faded away, and they were lost in each other, people and luggage carts forgotten. After some immeasurable length of time, Laina finally regained her composure.

"Well, more of that please." She kissed him again to punctuate. "But first, you'd better grab those bags you left back there. This is LAX. You don't want them to grow legs."

Logan retreated to grab his things and walked back toward her. "This is all I've got." He held up the garment bag in one hand and a small duffel in the other. "Monkey suit in here, and beauty products in this one."

Laina laughed, taking the garment bag from him so they could hold hands on the way out of the sliding doors. It felt so natural to be with him, and his hand fit so perfectly in hers. She loved how he rubbed the palm of her hand with his thumb as they walked, sending a shiver through her. They'd been texting often over the past couple of days and in the later hours of the evenings. Some of the interactions had started to get a little suggestive. Laina had reread the texts from the night before while she'd been waiting for Logan's plane to land, blushing as she scrolled through their last conversation.

Laina: What are you wearing?

Logan: Isn't that a question I should be asking?

Laina: Sometimes I give "nontraditional" a try.

Logan: Well, I'm currently wearing only my sheets. I'm in bed for the night.

Laina: Somehow I knew you'd be a birthday-suit sleeper.

Logan: Well, to be fair, my onesie and nightcap are at the dry cleaner.

Laina: LOL. God, what a visual.

Logan: :)

Laina: So, are you going to bring any pajamas with you this weekend? My parents have this idea that you're going to be bunking with me in the guest house. Don't worry. There's a pullout sofa.

Logan: Pardon the pun.

Laina: !!

Logan: I guess the question is, do you want me to bring my jammies? I don't want to upset your delicate sensibilities.

Laina: Leave the pj's at home.

Logan: Now you've got my attention.

Laina: Just wait. You haven't seen what I wear to bed.

Logan: I can only imagine. And if I'm being honest, I have imagined that.

Laina: Is it tomorrow yet?

Their banter was so easy, and Laina loved Logan's sense of humor. But once they were safely ensconced in the back of the car she had waiting for them outside of baggage claim, laughter was the furthest thing from their minds. Laina suspected that the fire between them would ignite immediately, so she had closed the frosted glass partition in the Bentley sedan before she got out to meet Logan in order to ensure their privacy on the way up the coast. Her parents had used this luxury car service for years, and they had insisted she take it today to LAX.

Logan climbed in first, practically pulling Laina down after him. She reached back to slam the door behind her, climbing over her seat to straddle him, his face in her hands. She dipped her head down, but instead of kissing him, she leaned forward to whisper into his ear.

"Was this what you had in mind when you mentioned your back-seat fantasy the other night?" She let her tongue flip the tip of his ear before nipping at it gently with her teeth. Logan responded by grasping her hips in an attempt to reposition her over his lap. She could feel his desire, and it fueled her own. Sitting back to look at him, she could see that his eyes were opaque and full of need. It was clear he was doing everything he could to maintain some semblance of control. Laina leaned forward again, using her tongue to part his lips gently, brushing back and forth with soft strokes, curious as to how long he'd be able to resist.

Not long, it turned out. Logan pulled her up against him, and the energy between them quickly turned frenetic. Kissing was just a futile attempt at satisfaction. Laina reached down, deftly unbuttoning the top of Logan's jeans with her fingers. She felt him shudder at her touch as she pulled his shirt up, letting her fingers slowly trail along the skin that lay just underneath his waistband.

Close, but not yet.

Laina wanted to take him to the brink of desire but knew she'd stop short of anything too naughty in the back of a speeding car. This was just a taste of things to come. The thought produced a tightening in her belly, ramping up their passion once again.

They whizzed by cars lined up to turn left into the beach parking lots but never noticed, completely engrossed in each other. Laina recognized the need to slow things down, but she was having a hard time commanding her body. She wanted Logan with a ferocity she'd never experienced before with anyone. It was as if he were a magnet, and she couldn't ignore the pull. She already knew how they'd fit together; she could feel him against her now. Another crescendo at that thought, and now Logan's hands were slipping inside the back of her jeans, cupping her and grinding her against him with a new, more urgent rhythm. Laina thought she could stop, but she'd lost all ability to reason with herself, settling into a frenzied pace that almost sent them both over the edge.

In the end, Laina had traveled solo, but watching her face while she peaked was enough for Logan. Almost. He had big plans for the weekend. And they had nothing to do with speeding cars or rushing through anything at all.

🍓

They arrived at her parents' house a short time later, having finally managed to pull themselves apart and put Laina back together. The ladies had an appointment to get mani-pedis at noon, so Laina reluctantly left Logan behind with her father.

"Don't worry, darling. Logan's in good hands with your father. I heard him say he waxed an extra board this morning." Serena winked at her daughter, both of them hiding their laughter at Logan's terrified expression.

"Uh, I haven't surfed in a long time. I mean, I used to get out a little bit with my buddies at the Jersey Shore, but that was years ago."

Bo Ming slapped Logan on the back good-naturedly. "Son, I think the ladies are just having a little fun at your expense." Logan looked relieved, but only momentarily, until Laina's dad decided to finish his thought. "It's the perfect day to get out there. The waves are just right. You'll do just fine. Come on. I'll show you to the guest house so you can get changed, and we'll meet by the pool to head down to the shore in ten minutes. A few minutes in the water will do us good before we climb into our formal wear for the evening. Make sure to wear sunscreen."

Logan looked over his shoulder, mouthing the words "help me" to the ladies as Laina's father led him away. Laina and her mother giggled all the way to the salon. They were settled into their pedicure chairs when her mom asked Laina about Logan.

"You really like him, don't you, Carina?" Her mother had used the Italian endearment with Laina since she was a child. *Beloved.* It was one of the little things that Laina cherished most about her mom. She wished sometimes that she could take all her parents' little affectionate words and stitch them together to make a quilt she could wrap around herself in their absence. Being with them made her dread having to say goodbye again. They would always feel like home to her.

"I really like him, Mom. A lot. There's no point in hiding it from you. Logan has surprised me from our first date. I've yet to find his weakness, though, and I'm starting to believe he doesn't have one. But he must, right?"

Serena smiled. "No one is perfect, Laina, but some people are closer to it than others. Like your father. He's put up with me for all of these years, never batting an eye when I dragged him off to a sound healing workshop or a class on sacred geometry. He's open to experiencing life, and even though Logan was teasing you about being scared to surf earlier, I see that same quality your father possesses in Logan. They say yes more than they say no. That's a wonderful trait, Laina. I hope you can allow yourself to feel worthy of Logan, because you are."

Laina listened, hopeful too that she could feel worthy.

Her mother hesitated before changing the subject. "Have you made a decision about Jeremy? Will you see him while you're in town? And have you told Logan?"

Laina sighed. "Jeremy and I are going to meet tomorrow afternoon. At home, if that's OK with you. I feel more comfortable with it being on my turf. I was hoping Dad could take Logan surfing, provided he makes it through his first attempt this afternoon. I haven't told Logan that Jeremy is here in California, but only because I'm not sure why he's insisting we meet. I plan to tell Logan everything. I just don't want to ruin this evening. For you and Dad, or for us. We've been so looking forward to it."

Her mother agreed that it was probably OK for Laina to table any further Jeremy-related discussions with Logan until after the weekend, but she urged her daughter to fill in the missing details soon.

When they arrived home, the guys were still not back from the beach, so Laina took the spare key off the hook by the back door and headed down the path to look for them.

She'd just stepped through the final gate out onto the beach when she saw Logan catch a good-size wave. The sun was still high overhead, but it had started to dip behind the cliffs that served as the backdrop for the east-facing cove, lighting up the dozen or so surfers in the water. Laina swallowed, mesmerized by Logan as he expertly rode the crest of the wave almost all the way into the shore. He was one of the few who weren't wearing a wet suit, likely because her father hadn't had one big enough to loan him. The muscles in his broad torso contracted as he used his core strength to balance himself on the board. Just before he sank back into the water, he spotted Laina, giving her the "hang loose" sign with his hand. He stood up out of the surf, tucking his board under his arm, and walked toward where she waited on the edge of the beach. Laina thought he looked like an advertisement for virility.

Logan glanced down at Laina's feet, her gleaming white-painted nails covered with a dusting of sand. "White. Nice choice. Is that sand going to ruin your pedicure, though?" Logan set his board down, shaking the water out of his hair with his hands.

Laina shook her head. "First rule of the mani-pedi: always get the toes done first. That way, they're dry when you leave the salon. It's not my first rodeo. Speaking of firsts, let's talk more about your surfing. You're no novice. You look like you've done that a time or two."

Logan grinned. "Well, I told you I had some Ranger buddies who used to drive over to the Jersey Shore to surf any chance they got. I tried it a few times but wasn't very good. Your dad gave me some great pointers, though, and today I feel like I got a whole lot better." He turned to scan the water. "Speaking of your dad, that man is incredible."

They watched together for a few minutes as Laina's dad started paddling his way into the crest of an epic wave. Standing, he was poetry in motion, his body covered in the wet suit that made him look even more physically fit. Bo rode the wave as it barreled across the length of the beach all the way to the shore, stepping gracefully off his board and making his way toward his daughter and Logan.

"Logan did all right today, Laina. You should have seen him. Really comfortable in the sea. Fellow's got my vote."

They gathered up the surfboards and headed back up the path to prepare for the gala, for which they were leaving in just under two hours. Laina had moved her things into a spare bedroom in the main house to get ready so Logan could have the guest house bathroom to himself. She'd also made up the sofa bed. Just to keep him on his toes.

An hour later, Logan was pacing the guest house, waiting for her to return, when Laina knocked softly on the door before entering the room.

She was wearing a black silk dress that looked like it was made out of liquid. It skimmed her body and was somehow defying gravity in the way that it was being held up by two of the thinnest straps Logan had ever seen.

Logan noticed the expanse of a bare leg through a slit that started at the floor and ended near a place that he was desperate to explore. Laina's white toenails gleamed now, peeking out of a sexy pair of black stilettos that made her appear a great deal taller than usual. Logan's gaze traveled back up, finding Laina's eyes twinkling in appreciation of his response to her.

"Well, it's a simple black dress, but it's OK, right?"

Logan cleared his throat. "Simple? No. OK? Definitely not. Laina, you look good enough to eat."

Laina blushed, closing her eyes at the brazen compliment. "You look pretty good yourself. I have to say, I'm not sad that you picked the tux. I was picturing how you'd look in one, and you do not disappoint."

Logan had chosen a black peak-lapel tuxedo with a classic bow tie at the advice of the tailor who said the look was never out of style. He had to admit that he felt good in the garment, and now that he saw Laina, he was glad he'd erred on the formal side. He reached out his hand to her, and she took it, allowing him to twirl her around slowly in admiration.

The back of the dress was even more magnificent, dipping down into a low V, revealing her toned back and shoulders. Logan let out a low whistle.

"My, oh my. You look spectacular, Laina. I'm so proud to be with you." Logan reached down, clicking the remote on the table to turn on the sound system. He'd cued up some music for later but figured it would be OK to play one of the songs now. The wail of a harmonica floated out of the speaker, followed by Bono's telltale voice.

Logan extended his hand to Laina. "May I have this dance?" He didn't wait for her to answer, pulling Laina into his arms, swaying with her to "Trip Through Your Wires." Logan tucked his head down, his chin resting on her forehead as they moved in sync with the music. It was just a simple dance, but it was arguably the most erotic thing they'd experienced together so far. Mostly because Logan could feel his resolve crumbling. It was terrifying to think that he could feel this way for Laina so soon, but he supposed he'd known it would be like this with her all along when she finally decided to open her heart.

If there'd been any shred of doubt remaining, it vanished as they moved together. Logan knew without question that he'd fallen in love with her.

CHAPTER
EIGHTEEN

The gala was being held on the grounds of the wellness center, which was a fifteen-minute drive up into the mountains from the Mings' home. They were about to make the final turn into the property when Laina's father glanced at her in the rearview mirror. "Laina, close your eyes. Your mom and I have a surprise for you."

The car slowed to a stop, and Laina could hear the two front doors open and close, indicating that her parents had gotten out. Logan, who was still sitting with her in the back seat, squeezed her hand.

He waited for the signal from Laina's dad. "OK. Let me help you out of the car. Hold on to me." Laina could feel the finely crushed gravel under her stilettos as she exited the car, her hand over her eyes.

"OK. You can look now."

Laina lowered her hand and opened her eyes. Her parents were standing together a few feet away next to a carved wooden sign surrounded by purple flowers. "Karina Wellness Center." Logan heard Laina gasp and turned in time to see her eyes fill with tears. Laina stepped forward and embraced her parents one at a time.

"I can't believe this. No wonder you've been so secretive about the name. I don't even know what to say." Laina wiped her eyes and stared at the sign in amazement before she turned back to Logan. "*Carina* means 'beloved' in Italian, which is my mother's language, but when it's spelled with a *K*, it's a Nepalese girls' name. It's my middle name, given to me by my parents on the day they were finally able to bring me home." She smiled at her mom, taking Serena's hands into her own. "This means so much to me, Mom. I'm honored that you'd include me in your beautiful center in this most auspicious way."

Logan was touched and even felt a tiny twinge of jealousy. He would have loved to have had this kind of relationship with his mother, or to have even known his father at all, but he was happy for Laina and honored to be a part of such a special moment for their family.

The foursome got back into the car and traveled along the banyan-tree-lined driveway up a sloping hill. At the top, they stopped to check in at the guard gate before driving a little farther, finally parking in front of a cluster of established white buildings that looked like they had recently been restored. Laina's father told them a little about the history of the property as the valet helped them out of the car.

"For almost sixty years, this place was a well-known resort, so these buildings here are original. They were in surprisingly great shape when we took over, but of course your mother wanted to put her spin on things, so while we kept the integrity of the architecture, everything has been completely modernized and updated." He pointed toward the various buildings enveloping the circle drive where they stood. "This is the guest reception house, and that's the restaurant. The building behind you is the oldest we have on the property. It was built in 1835, so we left it exactly as we found it, and we filed to have it listed on the National Register of Historic Places."

Laina turned to examine the old structure more closely. She could see that the roof shingles had been laid directly on the ceiling beams, but because of the California weather, they'd managed to hang on for almost two hundred years that way. It was remarkable, and she was so glad her parents had chosen to leave it intact as a nod to the area's history. They'd even displayed some information about the families who'd previously lived in it and about the resort that had thrived in this spot for so long.

Laina's parents stepped away to greet their other arriving guests, leaving Laina and Logan to mingle on their own for a while. They took two glasses of champagne from a passing tray and strolled around toward the back side of the reception house. Each of the buildings was dripping with flowers. There were thickets of coral honeysuckle growing up the sides of the reception house in vines and luscious overstuffed baskets hanging from the eaves of the restaurant. Windows in both of the structures were framed with California lilacs, and hummingbirds danced from one delicious offering to the next, their collective buzz energizing the early-evening air.

Looking around at the acres of gardens, Logan was impressed. Crushed granite pathways separated the chefs' organic garden from the flower beds, and from their location on the top of the hill, they had a great view of the labyrinth down below. Small white cottages framed the property in the shape of a horseshoe, each with private front gates, adorned with customizable plaques used to declare the last name of the guests in residence.

"This place is impressive. Your parents really spared no expense. I mean, it's obviously been updated, but it also feels like it's been here forever, which is part of the charm of the place." Logan raised his glass to Laina. "Cheers to you, Carina. With a *C*, for beloved." He paused, looking at her. "I think that might stick."

Laina smiled, stepping in to kiss him softly. "I hope so. Come on, I hear the music. We don't want to be late for dinner."

The evening's meal was being held alfresco in a big open field at the rear of the reception house. Logan and Laina were seated near the front next to an oblong reflecting pool filled with floating lotus blossoms. The air smelled like jasmine and eucalyptus, the scents wafting down across the yard from a large grove of nearby trees. The tables were swathed in hemp linens and anchored with low vases packed tightly full of white- and blush-colored hydrangeas. Bistro lights hung in the open space overhead, and a full orchestra was playing classical music while dinner was served.

Logan and Laina were seated with her parents' good friends and their daughter and son-in-law, Sara and Cole, who had driven down for the weekend from their home in Montecito. The four young people gravitated toward one another, chatting during dinner about their lives and work.

Laina and Logan listened hand in hand as her parents gave their remarks, welcoming people to the Karina Wellness Center and encouraging their community to take advantage of all the unique services they offered. The dinner crowd was full of luminaries and people who were special to Bo and Serena Ming, having played a part in their spiritual journey in both large ways and small. The crowd applauded warmly when they'd finished speaking and started heading back to their table to join their friends.

Sara turned to Laina. "So, have you guys been together for a long time?"

Logan leaned forward to answer for her. "Well, I've been after her for about a year, but she's just recently stopped trying to escape my clutches." He smiled sweetly at Laina. "If you can't lick 'em, join 'em, right?"

Laina laughed. The wine she'd been drinking made her feel exceptionally relaxed. She reached under the table and let her hand rest on Logan's knee, squeezing gently. "He's a cutup, isn't he? Don't encourage him."

Sara smiled at them both. "I thought it must be pretty new. It's fun to see the looks the two of you have been exchanging." She glanced at Cole with a mock pout. "Five years of marriage and two babies under the age of four can change things in a hurry, huh, babe?"

Cole leaned over to kiss his wife before extending his hand to her. "In need of some romance, are you? How about a dance, lovely?"

The orchestra had transitioned over from the dinner music and added a male and a female singer. They'd just started to play "Need You Now" by Lady Antebellum, prompting people to leave their tables and pack the dance floor. Sara and Cole excused themselves to join the crowd. Logan was about to suggest he and Laina follow suit, when he felt her hand leave his knee and travel up his thigh, gently trailing her fingers back and forth there. He stiffened, his tuxedo having instantly become much too formfitting. Logan looked over at her in surprise, but she stared straight ahead at the dance floor with just the hint of a smile on her face. She knew exactly what she was doing to him.

Logan tried to steady his breath, but every fiber of his body shifted into primal mode. His voice had taken on a new gruff tone when he spoke to her. "Don't start something we'll have to wait to finish. If you ever want me to be able to stand up from this table again, I'm warning you. Show mercy."

Laina could see the muscles in his jaw twitching, and she knew just how he felt. She'd been unable to concentrate on anything else for most of the evening either, and she'd been aware of the current between them since that afternoon. It was white-hot.

"Come with me."

Laina stood and took Logan's hand, leading him away from the party. They didn't speak as they headed around toward a pathway that snaked along the other side of the property. When they'd reached the gate of one of the guest cottages, Laina slipped a key from her purse, unlocking it and stepping inside to a private patio area tucked under a thick canopy of trees.

Logan reached back to pull the gate closed behind them before turning and pressing Laina against the stone exterior of the cottage, his hand behind her head, their lips meeting impatiently. Laina reached down again, taking hold of him, stroking while they kissed. Logan groaned when she hiked her leg up around his hip, and he reached down with the palm of his free hand to cup her rear end, bringing her closer. He was trying to imagine a gentlemanly way out of the situation when Laina showed him that there was only one viable solution, and they both knew it. She unbuckled Logan's belt, a blush washing over her face at the boldness of her own behavior. It was the point of no return, and Logan pulled back to stare at her. Laina smiled shyly, but her dark eyes were flashing when she nodded.

There was zero hesitation. Logan slid Laina's dress up over her hips, reaching down to make sure she was as primed and ready as he was before he entered her. After he'd removed all shadow of a doubt with his deft fingers, Laina helped Logan guide himself into her, their eyes locked on each other the entire time. Laina inhaled sharply at his first plunge, and then they were immediately lost in the rhythm of the universe. The music floated up over the treetops, and they matched the pace of it, unable to control themselves any longer. They peaked together, and somehow managed not to collapse into a heap on the blue stone patio beneath their feet. Their sweat mingled as they caught their breath, unwilling to part so soon.

Logan murmured her name. "Laina. My God, what have you done to me?" He kissed her, slowly this time. "I'm not sorry. I wanted you so bad. I couldn't help myself, and when you nodded . . ."

Laina placed a finger over his lips, which he kissed while she talked. "I wanted you just as much, Logan. I have to tell you, I've never done anything quite like this in my life. I want you to know that I'm not some animal. You just . . . I don't know. I feel like you're my undoing."

Logan stared at her unflinchingly. "Well, then. I'm glad we got this out of the way. Because when we get back to the guest house, we're going to light some candles, play the music I spent all afternoon queuing up, and I'm going take my time giving proper attention to every single inch of you." His lips tipped into a half grin. "Don't say I didn't warn you."

They reluctantly made their way back down to the party a short time later. The crowd had thinned, and her parents were surrounded by friends when her mother looked up and saw them approaching. She and Bo excused themselves to join Laina and Logan.

"Here you are. Did you have a chance to check out the grounds? We're so thrilled with how everything turned out. Wait until you see the cottages. They're all so different, but each one incredible. The two of you will have to come back sometime and stay here, so you can really get a feel for the place."

Logan beamed at Serena. "Oh, I've got a great feeling about it already, Mrs. Ming. I'll never forget this special evening with Laina, and with the two of you."

Laina's nails were digging into his palm as he spoke, and Logan had to fight hard to avoid wincing in pain.

Laina smiled sweetly at her mother. "It was a beautiful event." She hugged her parents. "Would you guys be terribly disappointed if we called a car to go back to the house? Logan was up early today, and I think all the travel and surfing is catching up to him. He's fading fast."

Laina glanced at him just in time to see Logan's jaw twitch again. *Touché.*

Bo had a better idea. "We completely forgot to tell you. Your mother and I packed an overnight bag so that we could be the first people to stay up here tonight before the resort opens to the public tomorrow. We'll be back home around eleven tomorrow morning, though." He looked pointedly at Laina. "Your mother has an errand she'd like you to run with her, so I thought I might take Logan down to surf one last time before you leave Sunday morning." He turned to Logan for approval.

"Sounds great, Mr. Ming. I'll be ready to go at eleven. Thanks for putting up with me."

Laina's mom looked relieved. "Why don't we keep the car here with us? Sara and Cole are headed down the mountain on the way to their hotel, so they've already offered to swing by and drop you off at the house. We were just about to come and find you when you showed up." Serena motioned to where Sara and Cole stood saying their own goodbyes. Sara caught her eye and gave Serena the thumbs-up, mouthing for Laina and Logan to meet the couple at the valet.

The ride home was short, with sparse traffic on the road at that time of the evening. It was only ten thirty when they arrived back at her parents' house and said good night to Cole and Sara, who had booked a room at a nearby hotel.

It was chilly, and the ocean breeze had intensified, so Laina draped Logan's tuxedo jacket around her shoulders as they walked down her parents' driveway, unlatching a gate on one side of the house that led to the backyard and their guest house. As soon as the gate clicked shut, Laina slipped her shoes off, breaking into a run. Logan was caught off guard, but he did his best to follow her down the unlit pathway.

"You can run, but you can't hide." He stopped short when he got to the backyard. Laina was jumping on an in-ground trampoline that he hadn't noticed earlier.

She'd shrugged out of his jacket and was holding the bottom of her dress up over her arm, and she had a huge grin on her face. "Come on. We've got the place to ourselves tonight. Let's make the most of it. We can play a little first." She reached out her free hand to him, still bouncing around like a little girl.

Logan laughed, slipping off his shoes and bending down to peel his socks off. "I'm not rolling my pants up into some kind of 'manpri' look, though, so don't ask."

They jumped around together for a few minutes and enjoyed feeling like rebels in her parents' yard. Laina giggled. "This is the kind of stuff I should have been doing in high school but never did. I was too much of a good girl."

Logan slowed down when Laina did, the two of them coming to a stop just a foot apart.

Laina reached up to stroke his face, gazing at him wordlessly. "You ready to go inside?" Laina knew he was, but she wanted him to tell her. His answer was a surprise.

"Wait here." Logan leapt off the trampoline, walking toward the guest house. He disappeared inside for a moment, returning with the blanket from the pullout sofa over his arm. "You didn't seriously think for one minute I'd be sleeping on that sofa bed, did you?"

He stepped back onto the trampoline, spreading the blanket down in the middle of it. "Come on, lay with me and look at the stars for a few minutes. Like you said. We don't have to rush. We've got the whole night. I plan to use every precious minute of it." He sat, pulling Laina down gently beside him. They reclined, side by side, and Logan took her hand. He felt Laina shiver, so he carefully wrapped the sides of the blanket around them, creating a cocoon from which to study the night sky.

Logan squeezed her hand. "OK. Three questions. We each get three questions, and the other person has to be totally honest with their answers, no matter what." He turned to look at her. "Deal?"

Laina thought for a moment and then agreed. "OK. But I go first." She decided to tread lightly.

"Favorite flavor of ice cream?"

Logan feigned agony. "Oh man, start out with a killer, why don't you. And I can only pick one?"

"Yep."

"Hmm. Well, I guess I'd have to say Black Cherry."

Laina studied him. "Really? Huh. An unconventional choice, but OK."

"Oh really? Well, what's yours?"

Laina smiled sweetly. "Is that one of your questions?"

Logan guffawed. "Oh, come on. And no, it's not."

Laina sighed. "Well, since you're new at this, I'll let it slide. Double Chocolate. All day long. The chocolatey-er the better."

"Noted. OK. My turn to ask a question." He propped up on one elbow to face her. "This is very important. How you answer this will tell me a lot about you, and it might determine whether or not things end right here on this trampoline." He took a deep breath. "What was your first car?"

Laina burst out laughing. "Wow, no pressure. Well, Logan, I'm not ashamed to tell you that it was a 1982 Camaro. And yes, to answer your follow-up, it was black."

Logan fell back on the trampoline, staring up at the sky. "You're definitely still in the running with that answer. I might need a cigarette after that sexy piece of information."

Laina rolled her eyes. "Well, what was yours? And no, it doesn't count as a question."

"I'm still driving my first car. I've had that Bronco since I graduated from high school. It sat on blocks for a while during my Ranger training, and it's had a face-lift or two in the last dozen years, but I've got no desire to get rid of the old girl. She gets me where I need to go."

Laina was impressed. "OK. Moving on. Where would your dream vacation be?"

Logan didn't hesitate. "Patagonia. I've heard such amazing things about the hiking and terrain down in South America. I had a group of Ranger buddies that went, but at that time, I couldn't afford it. Someday, though." He waited a beat. "You?"

Laina had her answer ready too. "I've always wanted to go to Nepal. Not to search for my mother but to see where I met my parents for the first time. That would be a dream come true for me."

"Alright, my turn. I'd better make this good." Logan rubbed his chin thoughtfully while he pondered. "OK. I'm going there. Where is the most erotic place you've ever had sex?" He watched her take in the question.

Laina sat up and looked at him solemnly. "Honestly? Up against a stone wall at my parents' wellness retreat. You?"

Logan sat up too, resting his arm on his bent knee. "Same. Nothing will ever compare."

Laina had one final question for him. "Are you ready to go inside with me, Logan?"

Logan held out his hand, helping Laina up while he answered. "That one's easy. I've never been more ready for anything."

CHAPTER
NINETEEN

Laina quivered at the touch of his hand against the small of her back as she unlocked the door. Every single one of her nerves was on high alert. She started to turn the lamps on but thought better of it.

"Why don't you light candles, and pour us some wine. Do you mind if I take a quick shower? I think I might have actually broken a little sweat out there on the trampoline."

Logan laughed. "Oh, thank God. We'll all be happier if I can wash up too. I'll use the outside shower. When I'm done, I'll take care of the candles and wine. Don't rush. But full disclosure: you're about to be breaking a sweat again up in here." His face was dead serious. Laina shivered in anticipation.

She showered and washed her hair, taking time to apply coconut oil to her damp skin once she'd finished. She used the back of her hand to clear a spot on the foggy mirror and studied her reflection for a moment. Was she brave enough to wear what she'd brought for him? It wasn't something she'd have normally picked out, but she'd planned on surprising him. Laina didn't want Logan to think she had an aversion to color. Taking a deep breath, she decided to go for it.

Logan had rushed through his own shower, mostly because the cool evening air wasn't doing him any favors. He threw on a pair of black boxer briefs but left his chest bare. He hustled into the living room and switched on the Bose speaker, syncing it to his favorite Pandora station. First up: John Mayer's "Slow Dancing in a Burning Room." He'd figured Laina liked Mayer's music because he'd noticed several of the singer's songs playing in her restaurant during the Walland House event. Slow and sexy was the order of the evening.

Logan figured out how to start the gas fireplace and spent a few minutes lighting the candles scattered around the room. He'd just poured their wine when he heard Laina clear her throat behind him in order to get his attention, so he turned to face her.

Sweet mother of all things holy.

She was standing in the open bedroom doorway, her hands resting on either side of the threshold. She was wearing a one-piece lilac corset-and-pantie combo and nothing else. She smiled at his obvious interest.

"I thought I'd surprise you with a little color. You know, keep you on your toes. I don't want to be too predictable."

Logan blew out a breath. "If there is one thing you aren't, it's predictable." He set his wine back down on the counter. "Get over here. Let me have a closer look at you."

Laina blushed and pushed away from the doorway to move toward him.

Logan knew about her love of running and yoga, but seeing her like that, with the evidence of her hard work all over her exceptionally toned body, Logan could feel his erection giving him away.

As she got closer, Laina swiveled her body to the music, a sexy little maneuver that caused Logan's heartbeat to pound in his own ears. He would have to work extremely hard to take things slow with her. All he wanted to do was take her again right then, just for the pleasure of hearing her voice her satisfaction over and over. They'd had to be quiet back at the party. This time, he wanted to hear her.

Laina stopped in front of Logan, reaching her hands out to touch his chest. "You're so beautiful, Logan. Inside and out. I've fantasized about this night."

She brought her lips to his chest, kissing him just underneath his collarbone. Logan reached out and took her into his arms, spinning her around to sweep the hair off her neck so that he could bite and kiss her there, eliciting some very positive feedback.

"Logan." His name tumbled from her lips in a tortured voice.

It's all he'd waited for. He reached down to scoop her up, carrying her urgently into the bedroom. He'd lit candles there too, and the firelight flickered orange against the white canopy of the bed. Logan set her down gently and watched as she scooted back into the stack of pillows at the headboard.

Laina could feel the desire emanating from his pores. "Should I be afraid?" She smiled weakly, only half kidding.

Logan shook his head. "You never have to be afraid with me. Ever." He leaned over to tenderly kiss one of her ankles, then the other, before putting one of his knees on the end of the bed and beginning to crawl toward her. "You just lay back and get comfortable. This might take a while."

Laina closed her eyes, overcome by the feel of his mouth as he worked his way up her legs, one at a time. The top of her thighs got a little extra attention. Finally, he reached up to unsnap her bodysuit, and she gasped at the feeling of it as it sprang open, exposing her.

Logan had arrived at the fork in the road, so he took it.

Laina was gone. She'd never experienced anything like the attention he thoroughly and completely showed her most sacred places, and Logan marveled at the fact that he could send her over the edge so many times. Finally, Logan couldn't resist her any longer. He sat up, slid out of his underwear, and climbed over her so that they were face-to-face in the candle-lit room.

"You're the most gorgeous woman I've ever laid eyes on, Laina. Being with you is so much more than I'd even imagined." He shivered as her hands found him, his pulsing heat overdue for her. They locked eyes as he entered her, slowly and deliberately this time, until her impatience took over and she rose her hips up to usher him inside. They moved together, the heat building in intensity. The room disappeared around them, and they were suddenly just two people clinging to each other in order to survive the storm.

Logan whispered to her in a ragged voice, "Tell me when you're coming. I want to hear you say it. Tell me, Laina."

Laina's own breath was choppy, her body having been teetering on that precipice between pleasure and frustration. Until Logan's words tipped the scales.

"Now, Logan. Now."

He moaned, his eyes fixed on her, watching the pleasure travel across her features like a wave. Logan pulled out of her before it was too late, shuddering as he spent. He collapsed, careful not to crush her, and rolled to the side, pulling her close to him. The air was thick with passion, and as Logan had predicted, they were both covered in a sheen of sweat. Laina trailed a finger through his chest hair while they floated back down to earth together.

"Wow. Just . . . wow." She was dumbstruck. Laina had never had a lover as thoughtful as Logan. She felt cherished. Cared for. She wasn't sure how to gather up all the complicated feelings she was having into one neat pile so she could name this thing that was growing between them.

Logan kissed the top of her head, his fingers softly stroking her hair. "To quote the great Buffalo Springfield, 'something's happening here.'" His voice had that faraway, dreamy quality to it, and Laina knew he must be exhausted, having been awake for the better part of twenty-four hours.

She leaned over to look at him, but his eyes were already closed. Laina kissed him gently on the lips before snuggling back down into his arms.

"Sleep. You've earned it."

Laina closed her eyes too, the feel of Logan's smile against her hair.

She woke up to the sound of coffee percolating. Sitting up, she wrapped the sheet around her breasts and blinked rapidly to try to clear the film from her eyes. It was early. Laina could tell because one glance out the bedroom window told her that the sea fog that was typical of humid summer mornings along the coast still shrouded the backyard. She looked over at the empty place beside her in bed and smiled. They'd woken up in the middle of the night and made love again, unable to resist each other, and this morning Laina was sore in all the best places. She was about to get up to go look for Logan when he appeared in the doorway, two cups of steaming hot coffee in his hands.

"It's not your fancy stuff, but I tasted it and it's not too bad. I had to sneak into your parents' house to get creamer from the fridge. I was glad the key you used to get in here worked, but I was praying the alarm wouldn't go off. Especially since I'm not dressed for a visit from the authorities."

In fact, he was wearing a towel around his hips and nothing else, but Laina thought he looked perfect. She patted the spot next to her in bed. "Get back in here this minute, and bring me that wonderful beverage." She reached her hands out, wiggling her fingers in anticipation of the warm mug. Logan handed it to her, plopping himself back down on the bed, but only after he'd dropped his towel to the floor, giving her a peek at his beautiful behind.

"Yummy."

Logan looked at her, puzzled.

Laina giggled. "Did I say that out loud?"

Logan leaned over for a kiss. "Good morning. How'd you sleep?"

Laina arranged the pillows in a stack behind her, snuggling back with a sigh. "Great. You?"

Logan took a sip of his coffee. "Best night of my life. But actual sleep? I don't remember that part."

They snuggled together, enjoying their coffee for a little while longer. Finally, Laina knew she'd better get moving so she could prepare herself for what the day had in store. She finished her coffee and leaned over to kiss Logan before heading to the bathroom to get ready.

She turned on the water and waited for it to warm up. Laina was dreading seeing Jeremy and wished she could change her mind now. She was struggling over her decision not to tell Logan, but she couldn't bring herself to ruin the perfect trip they'd been having together. She could tell him later, if she needed to, but she hoped that wouldn't be necessary. If she had her way, it would be the last time she'd ever have to see Jeremy. It was time for them both to get closure.

Laina was stepping into the shower when she felt Logan behind her, his hands on her waist.

"I thought I'd see if you had room for a plus one? I promise to behave myself. I'm as worn out as you are, believe me. I'm just in the market for a hot shower."

Laina turned to look at him. "Of course, I can help you with that. Let's make sure you're good and clean before you go surfing."

She took his hand and led him into the cloud of steam, closing the door behind them. The air was dense with moisture, encircling them in a dreamy cloud of warmth. Laina picked up the bar of soap, rubbing it into a lather in her hands. She soaped up his chest and arms, turning him around to do his back as well. Logan started to turn back around when he felt her hands on him again, this time much lower. He sucked in his breath, palming the walls of the shower as Laina moved around to the front of him, lowering herself down far enough to lavish the most recently overexerted part of him with attention.

Their shower ended only when the water finally ran cold.

It was ten forty-five by the time they'd managed to get dressed and straighten up the guest house a little. Laina's dad was already in the pool, swimming laps when they stepped outside. He noticed them on a flip turn, pausing in the shallow end to say good morning.

"Hi, kids. I was finished but figured I'd do a few bonus laps since you weren't out here yet." He looked at Logan. "What do you say, boss, are you ready to shred? I heard the swell is decent this morning."

Logan slapped his hands, rubbing them together in anticipation. "Let's do it." He turned around to give Laina a kiss goodbye, then stopped himself, remembering where he was. "I'll see you when I get back."

He stood awkwardly, not sure what to do when Laina stepped forward and kissed him.

"Have fun. And be careful out there." She gestured toward her father. "This guy thinks he's invincible. Don't follow his lead too closely."

Bo had gotten out of the pool and had finished drying off, so he and Logan said goodbye and headed toward the beach.

Laina exhaled, looking at her watch. She'd cut that too close. Jeremy would be arriving any minute.

Laina stepped inside the main house and saw a note on the counter from her mother.

Running a few errands to give you some privacy.
I won't be back for a while, and your father will be out with Logan.
Be strong, Carina. Allow yourself this closure.
Xoxo, Mom

Laina sat down at the kitchen table and waited. She had no idea how their conversation would go, but she knew she would be glad to have it all behind her after today. At quarter after eleven, she checked her phone to see if she'd missed a text saying he'd be late, and by eleven thirty, she was frustrated and angry with herself for inviting him in the first place. Laina felt anxiety start to creep in, hoping that Jeremy wouldn't want to linger and risk running into Logan. Finally, at a quarter to twelve, the phone rang, and she looked out the front window to see someone on a motorcycle at the gate.

Of course. She buzzed him through, rushing to the front door and out into the driveway to meet him.

Jeremy parked the bike in front of her, killed the engine, and climbed off. He was wearing jeans and a black T-shirt, same as always. He lifted his helmet off, running his fingers through his hair, which he was wearing longer on the top and closely cropped on the sides. His arms rippled with the tattoos he was known for, and his beard was fuller than Laina remembered. Jeremy was taller and more muscular than his brother had been, mostly a side effect of Patrick's hard living and a by-product of Jeremy's love of himself.

"Laina."

"Jeremy. You wanted to talk?"

Jeremy smiled at her, but it came off more like a sneer. His eyes were cold. Accusing. "Spare me the niceties. I see you aren't even going to invite me in."

Laina scoffed. "I would have, but I was expecting you almost an hour ago. I have plans this afternoon, so we're going to have to make this quick. I don't know what there is left to say, really." She paused, her soft heart getting the best of her. "I'm sorry about Patrick, Jeremy. I was sick when I got your letter. He deserved a better ending to his story."

Jeremy studied her closely. "Really? Because I thought you didn't give two shits about my brother. I mean, you left that day and never looked back. That was a coldhearted move, Laina. Leaving me there to clean up your mess."

She was disgusted with herself for having forgotten what Jeremy was like. "My mess? You know what? The most compassionate thing I could have done for Patrick at that point was to disappear from his life. I knew we were over, and don't be flattered; it was certainly not because of you. Patrick had demons that I tried to help him overcome, but the cheating was the final straw. By leaving, I was trying to get out of the way and give the two of you a chance. If I'd stayed, you would have done your best to annihilate your own relationship with your brother over some feelings you'd manufactured and convinced yourself that you'd had for me. You didn't want me, Jeremy. You just didn't want your brother to have me either. But I see you've rewritten a more convenient truth for yourself to live with."

Jeremy stepped toward her menacingly, his expression wounded. "That's just it, Laina. I did have feelings for you, and they had nothing to do with Patrick. I fought them for a long time before that night. When I came in, and you were crying, I couldn't help it. I was trying to comfort you. I didn't mean for Patrick to walk in and get the idea that he did. But I wasn't going to correct him either, especially after you left." Jeremy caught himself losing grip on his anger, so he unclenched his fists and took a step back from Laina, lighting a cigarette to buy some time. He took a long drag and looked back at her. "We eventually did mend our relationship the best we could, but he was never the same after that night. That's what I meant in my letter. The coroner may have called his death an overdose, but you and I both know my brother died from a broken heart." The smoke curled around his head as he lifted the cigarette back to his lips for another pull.

Laina was sobbing by the time Jeremy had finished. She knew he was right. She should have sought closure with Patrick while she'd had the chance. She wrapped her arms around herself in an effort to quit crying, but it didn't work. His words had hit the bull's-eye.

Jeremy watched her reaction, swearing under his breath. He flicked the cigarette to the ground. "Goddamnit, Laina. Even now, I'm still in love with you." He stepped toward her, pulling her close. "Maybe it was my fault too. But he's gone, and there's nothing either one of us can do about it now. I love you, Laina. Can't you just love me too?" His fingers dug into her arms as he spoke.

Laina winced, at the words and the bruises he was surely leaving behind. She snapped to her senses, unfolded her arms, and pushed him away, wiping her tears as she stepped out of his reach. "*No*, Jeremy. I don't love you, and I never will. I've finally given my heart to someone else. Someone who would never use his words or his family to hurt me. You need to leave and never come back. I'm not in love with you. Do you hear that? I'm in love with someone else."

She saw that Jeremy's gaze had traveled over her shoulder toward the house. Wondering what had caught his attention, Laina turned and saw Logan, standing in the open doorway listening to them, her mother's letter clutched in his hand, his eyes questioning.

"What the hell is this?"

CHAPTER
TWENTY

The surf had been powerful that morning, as Bo had predicted. They'd had a blast catching one big wave after another
until Logan rode one all the way in and stepped off his board
squarely onto one of the big rocks hidden by the high tide,
slicing his foot open. He could feel that the cut was deep,
so he carried his board out of the water to sit on the beach
momentarily in an attempt to stop the bleeding. When it
didn't stop, Logan knew that the wound must be impressive,
so he wrapped his foot in his shirt in order to limp back to the
house. Bo had drifted a few hundred yards over and was surfing in a different area, unaware that Logan had been injured.
Logan told a surfer headed out to the point to let Bo know
that he had gone back to the house for some first aid.

Logan had to wait for someone to leave through the
locked gate, since Bo was still wearing the beach key under
his wet suit. When someone finally left, Logan slipped out

behind them and hobbled up the path, leaving his board in the surf shack. By the time he'd made it to the backyard, he could see that his foot was swelling a bit. He wasn't sure whether the guest house had an ice maker, so he turned toward the main house instead. Logan figured that Laina and her mom would still be out on their errand, but he knocked on the sliding door to announce his arrival, just in case. When no one answered, he let himself into the kitchen, and using some paper towels, he finally managed to stanch the bleeding. He was looking for a ziplock bag for ice in a kitchen drawer when he spotted the note on the counter and read it, puzzled by the words. *Carina?* It must be for Laina from her mom. But what did it mean?

Logan was rereading the note when he heard a man's insistent voice coming from the front of the house. He limped into the foyer as fast as he could and opened the door. Laina was facing away from him, and had just pushed back from a stranger whom Logan instantly hated.

"No, Jeremy. I don't love you, and I never will. I've finally given my heart to someone else. Someone who would never use his words or his family to hurt me. You need to leave and never come back. I'm not in love with you. Do you hear that? I'm in love with someone else."

Logan froze, his mind unable to make sense of what he was seeing. *Jeremy? The Jeremy? What the hell was going on here?* Before he had a chance to move, Laina turned around and saw him standing there. He mumbled something he wouldn't remember later, and attempted to process the scene. Laina's hand covered her mouth in shock, and she started to cry, turning back around toward Jeremy.

"This is what you do, isn't it? You ruin people's lives." She sobbed into her hands, completely distraught.

That got Logan's attention. He looked at Jeremy, the pain in his foot forgotten. Stepping forward, he came within inches of the man's face. Close enough to see the hatred in his eyes. "You should leave. Now." They stood staring at each other for a long moment before Logan stepped back and took Laina by the shoulders. He folded her into his arms but never once took his eyes off Jeremy. "Don't make me tell you a second time." Laina shivered at his tone.

Jeremy was silent but continued looking at Logan. His hands were clenched into fists, and Logan sensed Jeremy was wondering whether to use them, before he ultimately decided it was a bad idea. "You know what? We were finished here anyway. For now, at least. I appreciate the brutal honesty, Laina. But, hey, that's how you do it, right? Quick and dirty." He looked at Logan again. "Be warned, asshole. Odds are, this won't end well for you." He sneered as he stepped back toward his motorcycle. "But, hey. There's a sucker born every minute."

Jeremy pulled on his helmet, threw his leg over his bike, and the engine roared to life. He was up and out of the driveway moments later, his tires screeching on his way down the street, leaving the mess he'd made behind him.

Laina had her head buried in Logan's chest, and neither of them moved or said a word as he comforted her, his hands rubbing her back.

Finally, Logan broke the silence. "What was Jeremy doing here, Laina? I don't know what I'm supposed to think. Please tell me there is a reasonable explanation here."

Laina sniffed, finally ready to face him. She looked up, and the hurt expression on his face almost broke her again.

"The band is performing in San Diego this weekend, and he reached out to my parents to ask them to intervene on his behalf. He's been texting me, trying to meet, but I wouldn't answer him, so he preyed upon my parents' kindness. I wanted to tell you, but we were having such an incredible weekend. I'll admit it: I chickened out. But I have nothing to hide from you, Logan. I should have told you the truth, and knowing that I dragged you into this mess and that you feel hurt by my indiscretion kills me."

Laina sighed and wiped her eyes with her shirt, certain she looked awful. "I would suspect that after what I told Jeremy, he's got no reason to see me again. Ever. I know he must have felt completely humiliated. It's not an emotion he understands well."

Logan nodded. "About that. I heard what you told him. Two things stood out to me. The first was that you've given your heart to someone else. The second was that you're in love." Logan bent his head down to look at her squarely in the eyes. "Did you mean those things, Laina, or did you just say them to get rid of Jeremy?"

Laina's face softened. "I meant them, Logan. I mean them." She leaned in close to brush her lips against his. Her voice came out in a whisper. "I'm so sorry. I love you. You do have my heart."

Logan's face was serious, although the faint look of hurt still lingered in his eyes. "Then promise me no more secrets. You can tell me anything, Laina. I'll always do my best not to judge or react too quickly. But that only works if we're completely honest with each other. OK?"

Laina nodded, looking down at her feet and wishing she'd done that in the first place.

Logan lifted her chin with his hand, bringing her eyes back to his. "One more thing. I'm ridiculously in love with you too. And I think you've had my heart since before you even knew you might want it." Their kiss was tender and thorough, saying all the things that words couldn't. Laina knew in that moment that she'd do anything for him. She would work hard to make the hurt he'd felt that day disappear.

They broke apart when they heard a car pulling into the drive and turned to see Laina's mother waving at them as she pulled around to the garage. Laina took Logan's hand, leading him inside the house. They walked into the kitchen, where Logan sat down and had started to tell Laina about his surf injury when her mother entered the house from the back hall, her keys still in hand.

Serena saw her daughter crouched down, examining Logan's foot, and gasped. "What happened? Logan, are you OK?" Serena furrowed her brow at Laina, worriedly searching her daughter's face for answers.

Laina stood up and exhaled. "It's fine, Mom. Logan cut his foot on a rock. He'll be OK. And he knows that Jeremy was here." Laina walked over to the sink to get some new paper towels to replace the ones she'd removed from Logan's foot. "Do we have any ointment or decent-size Band-Aids? His foot needs to be cleaned out, and I can do it if you have a first-aid kit here somewhere."

Logan looked up at Serena. "Your daughter loves me, Mrs. Ming. She told me so. Right out there in your driveway. And there are no take-backs. So she's taking care of me. That's the kind of thing that people who are in love do for each other." He smiled sweetly at Laina, who looked like she might faint. "Isn't that right, Carina?"

Laina's mother had her hand over her heart, her mouth open in surprise. "Oh, how wonderful! I had a feeling about this. I knew Logan was the one the moment I saw him."

Laina gripped the counter to steady herself. "Hold on, everyone. That might be a bit premature. Let's not give Logan any more confidence than he already has." She looked over at him and sighed. "But he's right. I do love him. And I suspected you and Dad would too. He's pretty darned lovable."

The three of them were laughing together when Bo rushed into the kitchen, looking for Logan. Laina was sitting on Logan's lap with her arm around his shoulders while Logan had his bandaged foot propped up on a kitchen chair opposite them. Serena was gathering up the collection of bloody paper towels and first-aid-kit items that they'd used to take care of his wound. Bo saw the mess and threw his hand up to his forehead.

"What happened here? Logan, are you all right? What did I miss?"

Laina answered, "Nothing, Dad."

"Everything!" Serena scoffed at her daughter's casual dismissal.

"I cut my foot open on a rock, and your daughter loves me, Mr. Ming." Logan wore the biggest smile of all.

Bo Ming dropped his hand in relief. "Oh good. I thought it was something serious. And who couldn't already see that for themselves?" He walked back out the patio door, leaving the three of them speechless.

🍓

They had a quiet dinner that night with her parents at home. They were all exhausted, so Logan and Laina said good night to her parents. They promised not to wake them the next morning when they left before dawn for their flight home to Colorado.

As they walked away from the main house and into the darkness of the backyard, Laina grabbed Logan's hand. "Do you have any desire to have a swim in the pool before we go to bed? I'm still kind of keyed up from today, and something about the water helps me relax. That's the reason I was down at the lake the night of the campout. I was all hot and bothered. And then to make it worse, you showed up."

Logan leaned in to bite her neck playfully, making her squeal and try to pull away from him. "I'll never forget when I turned the corner and saw you standing in that water. Talk about erotic." It reminded him of a secret he'd been keeping. "Can I admit something to you?"

They had reached the edge of the pool, and Laina stopped, turning to look at him. "What is it?"

Logan ran his fingers through his hair nervously before speaking. "You know how I went for my donations on Wednesday and Thursday this week? For Viv and Sienna?"

Laina nodded. "Yes, I distinctly remember some text messaging about that. You said everything came out OK, right?"

Logan exhaled. "You could say that. They put me in this sterile white room with a bunch of dirty magazines and a porn website, which, as I told you, isn't my thing." He scratched his head and bit his lip before continuing. "Instead, I made up my own little fantasy, starring you. In that lake. And it was pretty damned great. So good, I almost missed the cup."

Laina covered her mouth to stifle a laugh. "Well, I'm glad I could be of help to you, you big pervert. Please don't share that story with Viv and Sienna. Let's let them imagine that the whole process was very clinical."

Logan chuckled. "Good note." He turned back toward the house, confirming that all the lights had been shut off. "How about making some memories on our last night in Malibu? What do you say, girl who's given her heart to me? Are you up for a skinny-dip?"

Logan unbuttoned his jeans as he talked, letting them slide down his legs so he could step out of them, then lifted his shirt off over his head in one quick motion. "Last one in's paying for the wedding!"

Laina was laughing as he stepped out of his underwear and slipped silently into the deep end to wait for her.

"That's your loss, Laina. I'll have you know that I'm planning on having a huge ceremony. Lots of groomsmen. You'd better start saving."

She rolled her eyes at him but couldn't help feeling completely charmed. Laina untied the string of her halter dress, shimmied out of it, and let it gather around her feet before she stepped clear of it. To Logan's surprise, she wore nothing underneath.

"I guess that ruins my one last surprise for the weekend. Oh well. Maybe next time."

Laina let him absorb her words while she slid down into the pool next to Logan, who was busy picking his jaw up off the deep end.

"Hello, man who loves me ridiculously a lot." Laina kissed him before pushing off the side with her feet to lie on her back. "Come and float with me."

Logan watched for a moment. "If I'm floating with you, I'm not *looking* at you. That's no fun."

Laina poked her head up to roll her eyes at him again. "Come on. You'll love it. It's so soothing, and look"—she pointed skyward—"you can see the Big Dipper, right there."

Logan pushed away from the side to join her, and they held hands while floating under the starry sky together. When they drifted into the shallow end, Laina stood up and led Logan over to the hot tub. She slid over the wall, holding her hand out to him.

"Come on, let's warm up for a minute. It will make the dash into the guest house a lot more tolerable."

Logan got in and sat beside her. "Can I ask you something? Just so we can really put today behind us, for good?"

Laina turned to look at him. "Of course. I want that more than anything."

Logan rubbed his hair to remove the excess water. "Why did you agree to meet Jeremy? I mean, what did you think it would accomplish?"

Laina sighed in frustration. "Honestly? I was hoping it would give both of us a sense of finality. Closure. My parents are big believers in cleaning up the messes we make in life so we don't have to come back and relearn the lessons later. In other words, Karma. I just knew I wanted to be done with that part of my life, and that was my attempt at closing the book."

Logan watched as she talked. "Do you think you achieved that? And do you think Jeremy thinks he did?"

Laina shrugged her shoulders. "I can't speak for him. But if I had to guess, I'd say we both saw each other for who we are pretty clearly today. I still have to continue to process my own feelings about my role in Patrick's death. I know I could have made some better choices. Jeremy said some things to me today that stung because they were true. But he also really absorbed what I said to him. I could see it in his eyes." Laina shivered when she remembered the coldness she'd seen there. She turned back toward Logan. "And he saw you. And he heard what I said about you. My heart belongs to you, Logan. Today was just a part of the bigger plan the universe has to move us forward on our journey together. The hard stuff makes us better. I believe that's how it all works."

It was good enough for Logan. "Let's dry off, go inside, and light a fire."

Laina leaned in to kiss him. "Thank you for trusting me. You can, you know. Don't let Jeremy's parting blast get to you. His reality and ours are very different." She stepped out of the hot tub, reaching her hand back to Logan. They grabbed their discarded clothing and hustled over to the stack of towels that were piled next to the outdoor shower, grabbing two of them to dry off with.

Once inside, Logan stopped Laina in the living room. "Don't get dressed. Lay with me by the fire for a few minutes before we go to bed. I'm not ready for this weekend to end just yet."

Laina kissed him. "I'll be right back." She disappeared into the bedroom and returned a few moments later with two pillows, the duvet, and a sheet wrapped around her naked body. "How about we camp out here in the living room tonight, fireside? Here, help me scoot the coffee table out of the way."

They moved the furniture around and made space, and Laina unwrapped the sheet from her body, laying it down over the top of the plush sheepskin rug in front of the fire. She tossed the pillows at one end and lay down on her side, lifting the duvet to invite Logan in. She didn't have to ask twice.

"I'm having a very difficult time controlling myself, Laina. When I look at you, I morph right back into a teenage boy, with absolutely no willpower." He rubbed his calloused hand along the side of her body, down to her hip and back up again, before dipping his face to kiss her shoulder and breast. Laina took his face gently in her hands and guided it upward so that their faces were inches apart, his body pressed up against hers. She wanted him to feel her words at his center. "I love you, Logan Matthews. With all my heart." She watched him take it in, feeling his smile against her hands before he answered.

"That doesn't even begin to compare to how I feel about you, Laina. I want to protect you, keep you safe from hurt. I want to swim in a million lakes with you, and sit at your counter and watch your hands create art in the kitchen. But right now, I want to show you how much I love you too."

Their union that night was slow and purposeful, but when they'd finally reached the mountaintop, they were together again, crashing into each other with the sense that a certain fusion had taken place. Two very independent people had merged into something that would ultimately be better together.

CHAPTER
TWENTY-ONE

Their flight the next morning out of LAX had been delayed thanks to a wicked line of storms pummeling the Rockies, so by the time they finally touched down in Aspen, Laina was already running late for work. Logan encouraged her to jump into a cab and head directly for the restaurant, insisting he would wait for her luggage and drop it off at her house before heading home. Laina agreed she needed to hurry, but she'd had a hard time leaving Logan's arms when the taxi pulled up. Neither of them was ready for the weekend to be over. Laina inhaled the scent of Logan deeply before tilting her head up for one last kiss. She knew she'd never tire of the feel of his mouth against hers as she reluctantly pulled back and let him step forward to open the cab door for her.

"So, tonight, no sleepover. But I'm going to see you tomorrow?" They'd both agreed that they needed to catch up on their rest after the mostly sleepless weekend. Laina waited for

Logan to respond as she tucked her carry-on and herself into the back of the cab.

He nodded his head. "Absolutely. Do you want to come by the ranch in the morning? Have coffee with me in the barn while we decide what to do with our day?" He leaned into the cab and punctuated his question with one final kiss before standing up to shut her door, but not before she answered him.

"Sounds perfect. I love you, Logan."

Logan grinned. "I love you too, Carina."

It was the memory of that expression on Logan's face that made Laina stop and smile to herself an hour later as she worked in the restaurant kitchen, preparing a mirepoix for the Sunday dinner service. She was so distracted, she hadn't even heard Van come in.

"Well, I guess I don't need to ask how the weekend went." He paused, sizing Laina up. "That good, huh?"

Laina couldn't contain herself. "It was amazing. Why don't I listen to you more often?"

Van raised his eyebrows. "I ask myself that same question all the time. I'm very intuitive." He rolled up his sleeves and washed his hands. "Tell me three things I don't know."

Laina smiled. It was a little game they'd played for years. "OK. Let's see. First, my parents' wellness center is absolutely amazing. I can't wait for you to see it sometime." Laina scooped up the pile of onions she'd finished chopping and tossed them into a bubbling saucepan. "Second thing: Logan cut his foot pretty badly while learning to surf with my dad, but he's going to pull through. And number three: Logan loves me. And I love him. Any questions?" She peeked over her shoulder to see his reaction.

Van was grinning back at her. "Well, you certainly buried the lead. But I can't say I'm surprised. I had a feeling Logan was a match for you the minute I met him at the wedding. I just knew better than to meddle too much. It had to be your idea. I'm happy for you, Laina. You deserve this."

Laina stepped over to kiss Van on the cheek. "I'm working on believing that. He's incredible, Van. You don't know the half of it." She wiped her hands on a nearby towel and then leaned back against the counter. "Jeremy showed up in California."

Van's eyes narrowed. "What did that arsehole want? And how did he find you?"

Laina sighed and told Van the story, starting with the text exchange and ending with Logan asking Jeremy to leave her parents' driveway. "I don't think Jeremy was prepared to take no for an answer until Logan showed up. He was pretty angry when he left, but I think he's got it now."

Van blew out a breath in disgust. "He's lucky I wasn't there. That wanker isn't fit to lick your boots, so I don't know why he keeps trying. I'm glad Logan set him straight." He paused, considering her for a moment. "I'm hoping you've told Logan everything? About Patrick and Jeremy, I mean?"

Laina shook her head. "Yes. He knows. And it hardly fazed him. He's got such a confidence about who he is. It's refreshing. He reminds me of you, actually." Laina smiled and turned her attention back to the meals she'd been preparing.

Van chuckled. "Thanks. Now if I could just find someone stubborn and beautiful and full of sass, I'd be able to say I'd found your equivalent too. I'm not sure she exists, though. I took that woman from the yoga studio out for a drink Saturday after dinner service, and I almost fell asleep in my scotch. Why are all of the ladies I meet so pedestrian?"

Laina laughed. "You'll find the right person when you're least expecting it. Take it from me."

Van sighed. "It's probably better anyway. This isn't a good time for me to be meeting the future missus. I've got an opportunity that I wanted to discuss with you." Van set about deboning the fish they'd be using that evening. "My brothers Skyped with me this morning."

Laina raised her eyebrows in surprise. Van didn't talk about his family back in Oregon much, and she knew he wasn't in touch with them that often.

"Really? That *is* interesting. Is everything OK?" Laina couldn't see his face because he had his back to her while he was working, but she noticed his shoulders stiffen just slightly.

"My father has brain cancer. Won't be alive much longer, if what they say is true. My brothers called to talk to me about what to do with the family estate once he's gone. They want to turn it into some kind of income property—I guess to rent out—and they asked me to help them. They'll need to get appraisals, make improvements, hire staff, and such. Which means I'd have to go spend several weeks in Oregon in the spring, or next summer. Or whenever my father passes." His hands stayed busy the entire time he spoke, and Laina knew he was trying to control his emotions.

"Van. I'm so sorry."

He held up a hand to stop her, but he didn't turn around. "Please. He's a son of a bitch. Laid hands on my mum, even when she was sick. He'll get no sympathy from me." He set down the deboning knife and turned to look at Laina. "My brothers carried on a relationship with him after she died, which is why we haven't been close over the past ten years. They must have gotten the forgiving gene and I didn't. Anyway, I'm mulling it over, but I'm not sure it's great timing for me to be leaving you without help."

Laina stepped toward him and put her hands on his shoulders. "You will absolutely go, and you don't need to worry about me or House of Belonging. In fact, Logan and I were just discussing it on the plane this morning. We want to be able to spend time together and travel next summer. I've already decided to reach out to invite guest chefs to sub in for several weeks beginning after the New Year. That's been the idea behind this place all along. Everyone belongs, right? By next summer, the restaurant concept will be firmly established and I'll need a break, and so will you. I'm just wondering if you shouldn't go home sooner? Are you sure you don't want to try to get some closure with your father? Before it's too late?"

Van shook his head. "I've got all of the closure I need. He's been gone from my life so long, his physical death is just a formality at this point. I'll let my brothers be there for him. I'll go help them once he's gone. There is relationship work to be done among us brothers, for sure. If you're positive it's OK."

Laina hugged him close. "I'd be so upset if you didn't go. If you want me to come with you, I absolutely would, and so would Logan. We wouldn't have to stay with you, but we could be close by, just in case. Don't answer now, but I think you know that I've always wanted to visit the Willamette Valley anyway. I love you, Van. I'm here for you, always."

Van kissed the top of Laina's head and held her close. "Thanks, lass. I'll go to Oregon when the time is right, and you and Logan will always be welcome. But regardless of where I end up, I want you to know that I've got all the family I'll ever need, right here in Aspen."

Logan heard his phone chime in the cup holder as he pulled his Bronco into Laina's driveway. Picking it up, he read the text from Buck.

Buck: What time should I expect you?

Logan: I'm dropping something at Laina's now. Be there in twenty minutes. All ok?

Buck: Yes. See you soon. Welcome back.

Logan knew that Buck was a man of few words when it came to texting. It was unusual to get a text from him at all, so Logan hoped that everything really was OK back at the ranch. He got out of the truck and grabbed Laina's bag from the back seat. She'd told him where she hid her house key by the back door, so once he'd located it, he used it to unlock the kitchen door and lugged her suitcase inside. Logan debated about whether he should take the heavy bag up to her bedroom for her and then decided that it would be OK if he did. He hauled it upstairs so that Laina wouldn't have to and left it sitting in the hallway at the top of the landing.

On his way back down the steps, a framed pencil sketch on the wall caught his eye. He flipped on the light at the bottom of the stairs to get a better look. It was a very rough charcoal sketch of Laina, in profile, but the artist had captured her perfectly, even so. Logan peered closely at the signature.

DLaird. 2012

Van. Logan shook his head in amazement. He wondered what else he didn't yet know about his mysterious new friend.

Back in the kitchen, Logan left a quick note for Laina on a scratch pad near the fridge before locking up the house and replacing her hidden key. He shot off a text to his brother-in-law as he walked to the truck.

Logan: Quick beer tonight?

Garrett: Definitely. Come over whenever. We can hang on the porch.

Logan: Cool. See you around sunset.

Logan cranked the tunes on the short drive back to his ranch. His tires kicked up minimal dust when he pulled into the drive, thanks to the morning rains that had left everything looking extra lush and green. He smiled at the sight of the horses in the pasture, happy to be home where the animals outnumbered the people. California had been fun, but this was more his speed.

He carried his bag into the house and stopped to grab a bottled water from the fridge on his way out to the barn. He was crossing the yard when he noticed Buck coming out of the pasture, latching the gate behind him. Logan could tell as soon as he saw his friend's face that something was off.

"Buck? Everything OK?" Logan walked toward him, his brow furrowed. Buck removed his hat, wiping the sweat from his brow, his face pale underneath his whiskers despite his ever-present tan.

"Welcome home, son. Nothing's wrong with the horses or the ranch. Rest your mind. It's a personal problem I'm dealing with at the moment. And before you ask, my health's just fine, thank you." Buck hesitated, unsure if the timing was right to discuss his news with Logan.

"Do you have anywhere you have to be right now? I'd like to have a few minutes of your time if I might."

Logan nodded, gesturing toward his office in the barn. They entered together, and Logan sat down behind his desk while Buck settled into the overstuffed chair opposite him, fiddling nervously with the hat he still held in his gnarled hands.

Logan could feel the man's discomfort. "Buck, whatever it is, I can handle it, but you've got me worried. What's going on?" Logan waited for his friend to answer.

After a moment, Buck found the words. "Remember how I told you I've been seeing someone? Well, it's about that. I told you she was shy, which is why I haven't brought her around while you were home. Logan, we've only been dating a couple of months, but I've finally started to feel like I'm alive again, for the first time since I lost Annie, and it's because of her."

Logan smiled. "That doesn't sound so bad. I have to tell you, I've noticed the difference in you. So what's wrong?"

Buck sighed. "Well, earlier this week right after you left for California, I found out something about her, and we had a falling-out. I broke it off and convinced myself it was for the best. But these past few days have been hell. I haven't eaten or slept, and she's desperate to change my mind, despite this thing I know about her that I'm not sure we can overcome. God help me, Logan, I don't know if I can let her go."

Logan was puzzled. "I guess my advice to you would be to listen to your heart, Buck. If you feel like you can forgive her, and it's something from her past, that's all that matters, right? I've never seen you so happy, and I'd hate for you to throw that all away. People change. Is it possible she's better for what she's gone through?"

Buck stared at Logan before shaking his head slowly. "I knew you'd say something like that. Or I hoped you would." Buck stood and began to pace the office, running his hands through the thick silver and black hair on his head. "I want to believe she's a good person. I know she is. But she's done some things to people in her life—things she's fully admitted and talked to me about—that I'm not comfortable with. I know she's remorseful, and she wants to make amends. And I agree with you. People can change. I haven't known her long, but she's either a world-class actress, or she's a woman who wants to spend the time she has left in her life making up for her transgressions." Buck was fighting back tears. "And she also wants to spend that time with me, and I with her."

Logan sighed while standing up and walking toward his friend, then clasped him on the shoulder. "Sounds to me like you have your answer, Buck. Who among us hasn't deserved a second chance at some point?"

Buck blanched. "It's not that simple, Logan. There's something else, and I'm not sure how to tell you this."

Logan waited, the air in the room thick with anticipation.

"Her name is Jan. Janice Matthews, Logan. The woman I've been seeing. She admitted to me earlier this week that she's your mother."

Buck watched Logan's expression carefully, wishing he could spare him the pain that he knew was inevitable. Logan sat back down and looked like he might be sick. Buck hurried to explain.

"I want you to know that I had no idea who she was until this week. We met a couple of months ago at the bookstore in town and ended up having coffee together. She told me she'd moved to town to be near her son but that he was angry with her and didn't want anything to do with her. I've been trying to persuade her to reach out to him, but she told me their relationship was irreparable and that it was enough for her to live close to him, so I finally gave up. There is such a sadness in her eyes, Logan. She's like a wounded bird. I don't know what happened between you, but I do believe she loves you and only wants you to be happy. This week, she told me everything: that she'd found out that we worked together and that she'd purposely flirted with me at the bookstore that first afternoon. She admitted that she only went out with me at first so that she could find a way to be close to you. But we fell in love, Logan. This thing between us. It's real. My heart broke when she told me the truth, and what hurt the most was the look on her face when I broke it off. She knew I'd choose you, because she knows how good you are. People choose people like you, Logan. You're worthy, and she feels like she isn't. But she's wrong, Logan. She's worthy too, even though mistakes have been made. She told me that she's been writing to you for months but that you've hardened your heart against her. That doesn't sound like you at all. Is it too bold of me to ask you to meet with her? Do you think you could find it in your heart to hear what she has to say? For me?"

Logan sat perfectly still while he listened to what Buck was telling him, but he was having a hard time wrapping his brain around the information. *My mother is in Aspen? She knows where I live and infiltrated my life without me knowing for months?* The last time they'd spoken he'd lied and told her that Willow wasn't his biological sister after all and that he therefore had no claim to Willow's inheritance and neither did Janice. She'd faded away for the most part and hadn't tried to make physical contact with Logan in the year and a half since. He'd pushed that hurt from her rejection down deep and hadn't allowed himself to feel it since, but it all came rushing back with Buck's story.

Logan could see that his friend had been used, and that Buck was hurting too, so Logan chose his words carefully. "I wish I could tell you what you want to hear, Buck, but I'm in shock. I'm sorry you're in the middle of this, and if I could turn back the clock and change the course of history, I would. I need some time to process this situation, and I'm sure you do too. I can't promise you anything. There is a lot of history between us. I hope you understand." Logan stood up and took a deep breath. "Can we revisit this after I've had time to consider things?"

Buck nodded, dropping his gaze to the floor. "Of course. I'm so sorry, Logan. I know you just got back, but I couldn't keep it from you, even for a day. It was all I could do not to call you in California when I first found out, but I didn't want to ruin your trip."

Logan was quiet, not sure what to say, so Buck picked up his hat and set it on his head, turning to leave the office. Before he did, he had one piece of advice for the young man he'd come to love like his own.

"All I'm asking you is to think about the advice you gave me before you knew who she was. You are a rare person, Logan. Yours is a forgiving heart. Don't let the actions of someone else harden that part of you. You're family to me, son. Janice was right. If you ask me to, I'll choose you. But I hope it won't come to that. I love you both. So much." Buck nodded his head and turned to go, leaving Logan standing alone in his office, the life he'd just been so sure about in complete and utter chaos.

CHAPTER
TWENTY-TWO

Logan felt like he moved through the rest of the day in slow motion. Buck had taken their early-afternoon group out on a trail ride, leaving Logan behind with his thoughts. He led Diamond out into the paddock to graze and stood watching as the horse enjoyed the late-afternoon sun that glinted off his slick brown coat.

Logan had no idea what to do. He'd denied himself the desire for any kind of relationship with his mother after having not heard from her (besides the unopened letters) once she found out that Logan wasn't entitled to a big inheritance. He wondered if she'd somehow discovered that he was in fact Willow's brother and that Willow had split the money with Logan after all. *Is that why she'd come to town?* It was possible that she was after the money and not a relationship with Logan. He knew he had to tread carefully in order to find out whether his mother had ulterior motives. His phone buzzed in his pocket.

Laina: Hi

Logan: Hi.

Laina: I'm missing you already.

Logan: Me too. It was all I could do not to crawl into your bed and await your arrival.

Laina: You should have. How's your day going?

Logan: It's been interesting. I'll tell you all about it in the morning. 9?

Laina: If I can wait that long. Gotta run. Xoxo

Logan: xo

Logan stuffed the phone into his back pocket and checked his watch. He wanted to finish grooming Diamond and have his other barn chores done before Buck returned so that they could avoid an uncomfortable encounter until he'd had more time to think.

A couple of hours later, Logan had finished up and was about to walk down the road to Willow and Garrett's when he heard a car pull out of the driveway. He saw Buck's pickup turning out onto Maroon Creek Road, headed for town. Logan's stomach had been in knots all afternoon, knowing how the situation must have been weighing on Buck too.

Logan didn't want to see his friend gutted, but he didn't know the best way to prevent that from happening. He hoped that Garrett and Willow could give him some advice. He locked the door and headed down the steps toward his sister's house.

Garrett was already on the porch when Logan walked up the driveway. He reached down into a galvanized bucket where he'd iced down several bottles of beer and uncapped one for Logan, handing it to him once he'd climbed the front steps.

"Cheers, man. Glad to have you back. How was SoCal?" Garrett nodded toward the Adirondack chair next to him and Logan sat down, taking a long sip of the cold drink.

"It was amazing." He was about to go on, but they heard the screen door creak and looked up to see Willow poking her head out.

"You'd better not spill any details without me!" She leaned down to kiss her brother on the cheek before moving to perch on the arm of Garrett's chair. "So. How'd it go?"

Logan exhaled. "It went great, actually. Laina is everything I thought she was and then some. And her family is awesome. You can't believe the fancy party they put on for the opening of their wellness center. You would have loved it, Willow."

Willow smiled. "Full disclosure: I googled it. It looks like a cool place. Maybe Garrett and I need to take a trip to see it—for research, of course."

Garrett laughed. "I'm always up for a trip with you, babe. And if this guy's expression is any indication, I'm guessing it was pretty romantic?"

Logan raised his eyebrows. "That it was. Honestly, I'm not sure what I'm doing sitting here with the two of you. No offense, but I haven't been able to get her off my mind all day."

Willow clapped her hands together. "Oh, Logan. I can't tell you how happy that makes me to hear you say that. You deserve to be with someone interesting and smart and who might just challenge you a little bit."

Logan chuckled. "She's all that and more. I'm excited to see where this goes, and I can't tell you the last time I've felt that. If ever, really." His face grew serious, and he took another long drink before speaking. "There is something else I wanted to talk to you guys about, though."

Willow stood and pulled a third chair over to sit across from Logan. "What's up?"

Logan stared across the yard, watching the light from the fireflies flicker against the dusky evening sky. "My mom is here. In Aspen."

Logan heard Willow's sharp intake of breath and turned to see the shock on her face.

"Why? How?"

Logan shook his head. "You won't believe this. She's been seeing Buck for the past couple of months on the sly. He just told me this morning. He didn't know who she was until she admitted it to him earlier this week."

Willow was slack-jawed. "Oh my God, Logan. I don't even know what to say."

Logan set down his empty beer bottle and reached into the tub for a second one, the sound of the cap twisting off punctuating the silence.

"Honestly, I don't either. Buck thinks he's in love with her, and he's under the impression that she loves him too. Is that the craziest thing you've ever heard? You guys know Buck as well as I do. He doesn't suffer fools, so it's hard for me to imagine that he could have been so easily duped."

Logan filled them in on the rest of the story, then sat back drained, waiting to hear their thoughts.

Garrett was the first to speak. "Like you said. Buck isn't some gullible idiot. Do you think maybe she really has changed?" Garrett held up a hand against the look Willow shot him. "I know, it's hard to imagine. I was here too; I'm aware of what took place last year. But a lot can happen to a person in eighteen months. Is it possible that she had an epiphany? You're a pretty good dude, Logan. Could she have realized that a life without her son wasn't worth all of the money in the world?"

Logan pursed his lips. "You don't know how badly I want to believe that. It crushed me that she dropped off the face of the earth after I lied to her about the DNA results. Despite all of her faults and the mistakes she made when I was growing up, this is the first time she ever abandoned me. It showed me that I was worthless to her without the money. I don't know if I can get past that."

Willow reached over to take Logan's hands in hers. "You do what is best for you. Buck will just have to understand. If you aren't ready to have her in your life, that's your prerogative. We support you no matter what. *We* are your family, no matter what."

Logan squeezed his sister's hand. "Thanks. I know that, and I'm so lucky to have you. I'll give it a day or two to sink in and decide how to handle it. The last thing I want to do is make a snap decision when my friendship with Buck is on the line. Ironically he's the closest thing I've ever had to a father figure." He paused. "Which makes this whole thing that much weirder."

Garrett shook his head in disbelief. "You certainly have a few irons in the fire, my man. Take all the time you need. You'll make the right call. I'm sure of it."

Willow stood and kissed Logan on the cheek, leaving the men out on the porch to visit. By the time they'd finished talking, the moon was high in the sky and the air had cooled off considerably. Logan said good night to Garrett around midnight and started walking home. He pulled his phone from his pocket and was surprised to see several texts from Laina. Checking, he noticed that his phone had been on silent.

> Laina: Just got home. Thanks for lugging my suitcase upstairs.

> Laina: Just saw your note. For the record, you didn't forget to tell me. And I love you too.

> Laina: You must have crashed early. I'm exhausted too. Lights out. See you in the morning.

He'd started to answer her but saw that her last text had come through forty minutes earlier, so he decided to let her sleep. He'd get her opinion on things in the morning.

🍓

Laina's phone woke her up before seven. She blinked several times, trying to clear her cloudy vision, and reached toward the nightstand for her phone. Smiling, she read Logan's text, inviting her over for coffee later that morning. She couldn't wait to see him, and was about to get up and into the shower when she had an idea. She shot a quick text to Van.

> Laina: Could you drop something off at Logan's for me in a little while?

> Van: (this is me, still sleeping)

Laina: sorry! Nvm

Van: it's fine. I have to get up anyway. When does he need it by?

Laina: I'll leave it in a bag on the front seat of my car in the driveway. As long as you could get it there before 9? TY! I owe you one . . .

Van: You owe me three by my count, but it's too early to be splitting hairs.

A little before nine, Logan was finishing his morning to-do list when he heard tires on the gravel drive. He glanced out the front of the barn to see Van striding toward him, dark Ray-Bans covering his eyes. He looked like he belonged in a music video, and Logan marveled again at how this guy had remained single for so long.

"What's up, man? You lost?" Logan smiled as his new friend approached.

Van kept a straight face. "Very funny, lad. I don't get out of bed on my day off for many people, but Laina asked me to deliver this to you." He handed Logan a small backpack. "She said not to open it until she gets here. So that's a fun game for me to get to play on a Monday morning."

Van sized Logan up, lowering his glasses to get a better view while he did so. "I say, someone has the look of love. Laina said California went well. I'm glad." He studied Logan for a moment. "She told me about Jeremy showing up and how you handled the situation. I'm glad you were there. That guy is a total prick. I've been uneasy with Laina being around him since day one. Do you think he got the message?"

Logan considered the question. "It's hard for me to say. He wasn't very chatty. He tore out of there pretty quickly, but please know this: I wasn't Mr. Congeniality myself, so I don't think there's much of a chance that he'll mistake kindness for weakness."

Van nodded. "Good. He'd do well not to cross my path ever again, and despite the fact that we both know you've never been in an honest-to-goodness fistfight in your life, he doesn't have to know that. Let that punk believe there is a reason to be intimidated."

Logan choked back a laugh. "How do you know I've never . . . ? Actually, I'm not even going to dignify that comment with a response." He motioned over his shoulder. "You want to come in for a coffee real quick? I've got something for you anyway." He walked into his office, grabbing the small gift he'd picked up for Van off his desk.

Van called after him. "I can't. Laina will be here any minute, and I have a few things I need to accomplish this morning anyway." He waited for Logan to reappear, which he did, handing him a black baseball hat that said "Rip Curl" on the front.

Van shook his head. "Now I feel bad I didn't bring you something. Cool hat, thanks, man."

Logan laughed. "It's from a little surf and skate shop by Laina's parents' house. Just a small thank-you for letting me date your best friend and the coolest girl in the universe."

Van broke a little at that, the corner of his mouth twitching with the threat of a smile. "She is that, isn't she?"

As if on cue, Logan's attention was diverted to something over Van's shoulder. Turning to see what had distracted Logan, Van followed his gaze and watched as Laina ran up the driveway toward them, drenched in sweat and wearing a huge smile on her face.

She pinched Van on the arm as she slowed in front of them. "I knew I should have asked you to drop that bag by eight thirty." Turning to Logan, she smiled broadly, reaching for the backpack he'd slung over his arm and forgotten about. "I'll take that. It's my change of clothes. I decided I'd run over this morning. Check it off my list. You don't mind if I use your shower, do you?"

The air between them crackled with electricity, and Van stepped back as if struck by it.

"OK. On that note, I'll take my leave. You kids have fun today. Don't do anything I wouldn't do." He pulled the black ball cap Logan had given him onto his head and nodded good-bye to them, heading for his car. "I'll call you tomorrow, see if we can't set up a night to catch a Rockies game. I was thinking maybe this weekend? We could leave for Denver Saturday morning and come back either that night or Sunday morning, depending on how we feel. Think it over and shoot me a text."

Logan nodded. "Sure, sounds good. I'll call you." He hadn't taken his eyes off Laina, who was still smiling and blushing now.

Van pulled away, and Laina giggled, resisting Logan gently when he tried to kiss her. "Wow. I was feeling pretty grungy until you gave me that look. I'm so sweaty, though. Let me have a shower first. Then you'll have to beat me away with a riding crop."

Logan raised his eyebrows. "Not exactly what I had in mind, but I'm open-minded, I guess."

Laina swatted his arm playfully. "Come on. Show me which bathroom you want me to use. I'm excited to check out your bachelor pad." She studied the front of Logan's home, which was constructed from a warm brown barn wood and accented with a beefy stone chimney. He had two red swings suspended from the porch on either side of the front door. Laina loved how they complemented the hulking red barn that sat opposite the driveway at the foot of an expansive pasture.

They walked together up the front steps. "I haven't done too much to the house since I bought it, so it really is basic inside. Maybe you could give me some suggestions."

He held the door for her, letting Laina walk in ahead of him. She was surprised by how much light the space was getting. The entire rear of the house was covered in windows, letting in the dappled sunlight that filtered down through the grove of aspen trees in his backyard. Laina could see the kitchen off to the right, so she walked over to check out his setup.

"Wow, these appliances are actually pretty great. You've got a gas stove too, which is good. That could have been a deal breaker if it had been electric." She turned to smile at him. "Do you cook much?"

Logan shook his head. "I can make breakfast, and I grill out a decent amount. But that's about it. I did promise you a cup of coffee, though. Why don't I show you the bathroom, then I'll make us a pot while I wait for you?"

Laina followed him down the hall toward the end of the house, passing two bedrooms on the way. He had finished the rooms with the basics: beds, dressers, and lamps. But there was very little on any of the walls. Laina made a mental note to buy Logan a nice piece of art to start making his house feel more like a home. It had a ton of potential, and she was already charmed by the cozy layout.

They arrived at what she assumed was the master bedroom, a generous space with nothing but a giant king sleigh bed and two nightstands facing another wall of windows, these covered with blackout shades that were pulled closed.

Logan flipped the light switch in his bathroom and took a moment to put a few things away that he'd left out on the vanity. He reached under the cupboard to get Laina a towel and took a peek to make sure he'd left the shower in decent condition.

"OK. Holler if you need anything." He winked at her. "Anything at all." He was about to shut the door when Laina stopped him.

"Leave the door cracked in case you want to set my coffee in here on the counter. Now that you mention it, I'm craving a cup."

Logan gave her the thumbs-up and was headed into the kitchen when he realized he'd forgotten to ask her if it was OK that he didn't have almond milk. He walked back into the bedroom, surprised to see that the bathroom door was now open wide. He could hear the water running, and he was about to ask Laina if black coffee was OK when he was rendered mute.

From where Logan stood, he could see her clearly. He watched as she peeled her small black tank top up over her head, revealing her bare back to him as she dropped it to the floor. She ran her hands through her hair, smoothing it again before she reached for the waistband of her shorts, slipping them down over her hips, letting them fall around her feet before stepping clear of them.

She was incredible-looking, and Logan reached instinctively to adjust himself. There was a magnetic pull toward her that was hard to ignore, and he stood still for only a moment before deciding to say the hell with the coffee.

"Laina."

She didn't seem surprised to hear his voice at all, glancing slowly over her shoulder as she opened the shower door to step inside. "What took you so long?" She gave him a pointed look before disappearing into the steam, closing the door behind her.

Yeah. The fucking coffee would have to wait.

CHAPTER
TWENTY-THREE

Logan had never moved so fast in his natural born life. He stripped off his shirt and stepped out of his boots at the same time, almost falling over in the process. Leaving his clothes behind in a heap, he had the presence of mind to grab a second towel from under the sink to hang on top of Laina's towel that she'd dangled from the hook outside the shower. He'd been about to join her when he had another idea. Opening the top drawer, he pulled out a book of matches and lit the candle he kept on his counter before reaching over to flick off the bathroom light. The candlelight quivered, sending ripples of warmth dancing across the bathroom walls. Logan grabbed the handle of the shower door and stepped inside, closing it behind him.

Laina was standing under the water, her head back and eyes closed, a trail of suds sliding down her body toward the drain and the smell of Logan's bar soap hanging in the air. Logan moved toward her, unable and unwilling to wait a moment longer. Cupping the back of her head with his hands, he captured her mouth with his, taking what he wanted. The steam enveloped them as their bodies crushed together, and Laina's hands snaked around to grasp Logan's back before sliding lower to thrust him against her impatiently.

She tasted his moan in their kiss, and it emboldened her. Laina leaned back to look at him as her hand reached out for the cake of soap she'd rested on the shower ledge. Turning it over and over in her hands, she created a lather and set about enveloping his body with it. Logan closed his eyes in ecstasy, responding to the feeling of her slippery hands washing his arms, chest, back, and his other needier parts with a thoroughness that both impressed and disarmed him. She had him jelly-legged in no time.

"My turn."

Logan took the soap from her hands and set it back on the ledge, trading it for the shampoo. Turning Laina around, he stepped close behind her, squirting the product into his hands and working it into her hair slowly, methodically. He massaged her scalp, pausing only to kiss her neck and shoulders, provoking a gasp from her lips, before finally spinning her around and tilting her head back to rinse the soap out. With her head thrown back, Logan could pay closer attention to her breasts. She was exquisite, and for the thousandth time, he couldn't believe that she was his. Laina gasped when his lips found her nipples, one and then the other, and she put her hands out to brace herself against the walls as he teased her gently with his teeth.

"Logan. Oh God."

It was all he needed to hear. He reached back to shut the water off, stepping nearer to kiss her again but with a greater urgency. Logan pushed open the shower door, the towels that hung outside completely forgotten. He reached down and scooped Laina up into his arms and carried her toward his bedroom.

Laina wasn't sure if she'd shivered in response to the cool air in the room sweeping across her bare, wet skin, or because of the look in Logan's eye as he prepared to crawl toward where he'd deposited her on his bed. Likely it was a little bit of both, but in any case, the sensation was explosive. Logan's hand had barely grazed the top of her thigh when she threw her head back, overcome with desire.

Logan growled in response, unable to slow his pace. His own body was practically pulsing with desire as he poised himself above her, afraid to delay any longer. As he hovered at her entrance, he stopped and waited for her to look at him. Her eyes were shimmering when he spoke.

"I'm in this for the long haul, Laina. I have a craving too. For you. To be inside of you. Inside of and surrounded completely by the woman I love."

Laina was speechless, so she leaned up to kiss him, guiding him into her so that they could once again rise and fall together. She said his name and whispered things that lovers say, and before long they'd fused again, arriving at that place where they'd stopped being two halves and instead became a whole.

🍓

It was almost noon before they finally got dressed and headed into the kitchen to make coffee. Laina sat at the counter, watching Logan as he poured her a steaming cup.

"I could get used to this. Having my morning—or afternoon—coffee with you, I mean. This house feels so empty sometimes. I've spent more than a few nights wondering if I'd have been better off letting Walland House use this as a guest house and getting a smaller place in town for myself. I don't need all of this." He looked at Laina. "Do you ever get lonely out on your end of town?"

Laina sipped her coffee and considered the question. "I think I needed to be alone this last year, so it's hard to say. I adore my home. It's the most 'me' of any place I've ever lived. I love that it's close to town, but also remote, so that if I want to garden in my pj's, I don't have to worry about neighbors catching me." She leaned over to give Logan a slow kiss. "I could get used to this too, for the record."

Logan sighed, reluctant to spoil the perfect morning they'd been having with the thoughts that weighed heavy on his mind. He couldn't avoid it, though. "So, I told you yesterday that my day had been interesting. That was an understatement." He paced the kitchen, trying to find the right words.

Laina frowned. "What's wrong?" She flinched slightly, startled by Logan's cell phone ringing.

Logan debated letting it go to voice mail but decided to pick up when he saw who was calling him.

"Hi, Logan! Hope I'm catching you at an OK time?"

Logan covered the receiver with his hand and whispered to Laina, "It's Sienna." Turning his attention to the phone call, he assured her it was a good time to talk.

"Well, Viv and I had the procedure on Friday, and we just wanted to tell you that everything went beautifully. Thank you again for holding up your end of the bargain. There is no guarantee, but if we're extremely fortunate, this will be a one and done. Keep your fingers crossed."

Logan blew out his breath. "Whoa. No pressure. Swim, boys. Swim!"

Sienna laughed on the other end of the line. Logan mouthed to Laina, asking if she was free Monday early afternoon. She nodded her head yes. He turned his attention back to the phone call.

"I was going to get in touch with you today anyway. I think Van and I are heading to Denver on Saturday for a Rockies game, but let's hang out Monday afternoon, have lunch. And would it be OK if I brought Laina with me?"

"Of course! Bring Laina. And yes, Monday sounds great. How about noon? That's sort of the sweet spot between when I finish teaching my yoga classes and when Viv heads back into the office for the afternoon."

They chatted for a few more minutes before saying good-bye. Logan hung up and set his phone back down on the counter. "We're on for Monday at noon. I hope you're OK with coming with me? I feel like I should find out a little more about their expectations of me. And I want you to be a part of these conversations. This all feels very real all of a sudden."

Laina reached across the counter and took his hand. "Of course I'll be there for you. How are you feeling? Any regrets?"

Logan hesitated before shaking his head. "I wouldn't say that. I really hope we get good news in a couple of weeks, for their sake. I know how much they want this baby." He squeezed her hand. "I'm a little worried that I can't be what they need. Why did I promise what I did? I have no clue what it means to do 'dad stuff.' I didn't exactly have a prototype."

Laina smiled. "You're incredible, Logan Matthews. I have a feeling you'll be just right. But it couldn't hurt to share your feelings with them so everyone is on the same page." She stood, reaching up to kiss him. "Now, what were you about to tell me before Sienna called?"

Logan studied her for a moment. "You know what? Let's go for a ride. I'll tell you all about it on the trail."

Thirty minutes later, they'd finished saddling up two horses and were preparing to head out when they heard a commotion outside the barn. Buck was returning with a small group of riders, and he had just dismounted when he spotted Laina and Logan leading their horses out toward him.

Laina nodded hello at the handsome rancher, who was studying the couple with a quiet smile as they approached. "Hey, Buck. How was the ride?"

Buck looked past Laina toward his young friend. Logan shook his head almost imperceptibly, indicating he hadn't told Laina about Janice yet. Buck took the hint.

"Pretty day for a ride, that's for sure. You kids have a good time. Which direction are you headed?"

Logan cinched their saddles one final time to ensure that they were secure. "Thought we might head up toward Viv and Sienna's place. Maybe take a dip in the lake if we have time."

Laina turned to stare at him. She thought she saw his jaw twitch as he fought a smile.

Buck was pleased to see Logan happy. He'd watched him keep other women at arm's length in his persistent pursuit of Laina over the past year. It was satisfying to see that Logan's instincts had been spot-on. The spirited girl had obviously been worth the wait, if the current twinkle in his young friend's eye was any indication.

They said goodbye, and Logan and Laina headed up the hill toward the trailhead. They rode together in comfortable silence for the first few minutes, enjoying the peace and tranquility of the forest. The day was warm, but the lush canopy of trees provided a welcome relief from the beating hot sun. Laina loved the sharp, dusky smell of the aspen trees, mixed with the earthy aroma of the sagebrush underfoot. The sound of hooves beating against the dirt and the gentle way her horse carried her up the forest trail relaxed Laina, and she settled into the beast's rhythm as she followed Logan's lead. After a while, they came into a clearing and Logan motioned for her to ride alongside him. Laina did so, waiting for him to tell her about whatever was so clearly weighing on his mind.

Finally, he spoke. "So, I have some news. I'm sure you noticed that things were a little strained with Buck. He told me yesterday that he's been seeing my mother for the past couple of months." Logan saw the confusion on Laina's face. "Thing is, he didn't know she was my mom until she told him last week. Now Buck's convinced that he's in love with her and that she's changed. But I can't wrap my brain around why she kept her identity a secret from him for so long. Nothing good begins with a lie."

Laina was shocked. "Logan, I'm not sure what to say. And you haven't had any contact with your mom since you discovered Willow was your sister, right? Do you think she somehow found out? Is that what you're worried about? That she's after your money?"

Logan sighed. "Honestly? I don't know. But that's certainly not out of the realm of possibility. She's been sending me letters every few weeks for about a year, but I haven't read them. They're in a drawer in my kitchen." He smiled at her ruefully. "I guess we both keep our secrets in the kitchen drawer. Anyway, I'm not sure I want my mom back in my life. Why open myself up to the possibility of getting emotionally crushed by her again?"

Laina held the reins in one of her hands, reaching out to touch him on the shoulder. "I know we talked about this in California. Karma. At some point, you should do yourself the favor of dealing with this. When you're ready, obviously. It doesn't sound like she's going anywhere, and I know how important your relationship with Buck is to you. I'd hate to see this drive a wedge between you. What does he want you to do?"

"He's convinced she's changed. He practically begged me to give her a second chance, but he doesn't really grasp the history. I know I'm going to have to meet with her. I'm just not sure I'm ready yet. I'm inclined to tell Buck that I need some time before I can come face-to-face with her. Maybe I should start by reading the letters. Buck told me that if he had to choose between us, he'd choose me. Which only proves that his friendship is worth fighting for. But it also broke my heart a little bit. It might mean I have to suck it up and give their relationship a chance, regardless of whether or not I can have any kind of communication with my mother. I guess I need to have another conversation with Buck. I'll do it when we get back this afternoon."

They arrived at the clearing where they'd had the campout and then traveled single file the few hundred feet down the path through the woods to Lake Bonhomie. Logan climbed down off his horse onto the beach before helping Laina to dismount. He secured the horses to a fallen tree near the shore so the animals had access to the fresh, cool water and tall, wispy grasses that grew along the banks. Logan stretched his arms over his head, surveying the lake.

"It's really remarkable, isn't it?" He reached down to grab Laina's hand, bringing it up to his lips. "Swim?"

Laina laughed. "You know darn well I didn't bring my bathing suit."

The electricity crackled between them as Logan looked her up and down. "I'm more interested in your birthday suit, actually."

They spent the next hour thinking about nothing but each other, letting the bluebird skies and crisp lake water cleanse them of their worries.

It was late afternoon by the time they got back to Logan's place. Buck had just finished closing up the barn for the day and was walking across the gravel drive toward his truck.

"Go talk to him. Don't let this fester, Logan. I'll wait for you in the house." She halted her horse next to the hitching post and climbed off. Logan nodded, dismounting and taking the horses reins from her hand as she walked away.

"Buck! Hang on a minute." Logan tied the horses up and moved toward where the older man stood waiting for him.

"I've been thinking about everything you told me. I see how heavily this is weighing on you, and I would love to tell you that it's all going to work out. I need a little more time. That said, if you want to continue seeing my mother, I'm not going to stop you. I realize this means I'll eventually have to face her and hear what she has to say. But give me some time. I need to resolve some things within myself before I can do that. Fair enough?"

Buck inhaled deeply and shook his head. "Of course. I know how hard this is for you, son. And you telling me this shows me how much I mean to you. The feeling is mutual. I wouldn't be asking you to give her a chance if I thought there was even a possibility that she would hurt you again. You're like a son to me, Logan." He swallowed the lump in his throat before continuing. "Let her explain to you, Logan. Give her the opportunity to prove herself. When you're ready. I think she might surprise you."

Logan smiled wryly. "Well, it wouldn't be the first time."

The men embraced and said goodbye. As Logan turned to walk toward the house, his phone buzzed in his pocket.

> Van: We're all set for this weekend. Game tix? Check. Road snacks? Check. Oh, and you're driving.

Logan: Did you clear it with Laina?

Van: Just got off the phone with her. Figured if she put you in lockdown, I'd find a babe to take with me.

Logan: Wow. Glad I'm so replaceable.

Van: We leave Saturday morning. Game time 1:05. We can head back after the game or early Sunday so you can work.

Logan: It's a date.

Van: I'm not putting out.

Logan: I just threw up in my mouth.

Laina opened the front door as Logan climbed the steps. "How'd it go?"

Logan moved toward her, lifting her chin to kiss her softly. "We agreed to hold off on any meeting—for now. But Buck and me—we're going to be OK, no matter what." He kissed Laina again, more deeply. "I hear you've given me the green light to go to the Rockies game this Saturday with Van. Sick of me already?" Logan slid his arms around her, pulling her closer to him before lifting her shirt and grazing the skin on her back with his palms.

Laina shivered. "Never. I told Van not to make a habit of taking you away from me." She kissed Logan's neck lazily as she talked. "He needs this distraction. I know he needs to talk to someone, and it can't always be me. He's going through a difficult time too." She pulled back to look at him. "He can fill you in this weekend. I think you guys are good for each other. After what you've told me about your mom, maybe this trip is just the thing both of you need right now."

Logan reached down to scoop Laina up in his arms, striding through the front door and into the hall with her. "What I need right now is you. I'm not sure if I'll ever fully scratch this itch."

Despite his doubts, he spent the rest of the afternoon trying.

CHAPTER
TWENTY-FOUR

There wasn't much time that week for Logan to dwell on the situation with his mom. To Buck's credit, he carried on with their scheduled rides, keeping his interactions with Logan light and professional. Logan used the long summer days to get the barn cleaned out, pouring his nervous energy into the hard labor, turning things over in his mind as he worked. He hadn't been able to bring himself to read her stack of letters yet, but he had removed them from the drawer, and they now sat in a pile on the counter as a constant reminder that he'd have to deal with them sooner than later.

The busy week flew by, and Saturday morning dawned. Logan was looking forward to the chance to get out of town for the night with Van. He couldn't remember the last time he'd been to a Major League Baseball game, and both Colorado and the San Francisco Giants were in the playoff hunt that year, so the matchup promised to be a good one. He threw his overnight bag into the Bronco and set off toward town. Parking outside Van's town house, he took a moment to send a text to Laina. He'd spent the previous night with her but had gone home to shower and check in with Buck before he left for Denver.

> Logan: Waiting for Van. Missing you already.
>
> Laina: I'm still lying in bed. You've turned me into a lounger.
>
> Logan: Forget Van. I'll be right there.
>
> Laina: lol. You guys will have a great time. Don't worry about me . . . I'll work, come home, and binge on brownies and Netflix to cure my loneliness.
>
> Logan: We'll be back tomorrow morning before noon. You won't have time to miss me. Although I do look pretty sexy wearing my Rockies foam finger.
>
> Laina: God I love you.
>
> Logan: love u2

Logan watched Van lock his front door and make his way toward him, a black backpack slung over one shoulder, his signature Ray-Bans covering his eyes. He wore an unbuttoned Rockies jersey over his usual all-black ensemble. He opened the door and got into the truck next to Logan.

"Ready to rock. Sorry, I was finishing up a call with my brothers." He hesitated. "Long story."

Van buckled his seat belt and rolled down the window, setting his arm on the door.

Logan could tell he was preoccupied. "Well, we've got a long ride if it's something you want to talk about."

They headed east on CO-82, planning to take Independence Pass instead of going through Glenwood Springs, as it was faster and more scenic. They passed Laina's house a few minutes later, honking the horn as they drove by, but saw no signs of life.

Van broke the silence. "Has Laina told you about my family situation at all?" He glanced over at Logan, who was focused on the winding road ahead of them. Taking the pass was faster, but the drive wasn't for the faint of heart. Logan was used to mountain driving, but he still had a healthy respect for the hairpin turns that he was presently navigating.

"Honestly, she hasn't said much. She mentioned you're going through a rough spot, but I guess she figured you'd tell me about it if you wanted to."

Van stroked his blond goatee, pulling on it absentmind-edly. "Of course. She wouldn't. Laina is the most loyal lass you'll ever meet." He drummed his fingers against the side of the car, choosing his words carefully. "My family lives in Oregon. My parents moved there from Edinburgh, Scotland, when we were kids. I've got two younger brothers and a son-of-a-bitch father who I haven't seen in years. He's dying. Brain cancer. I have to say I'm surprised he's lived this long with his black heart. He's not a good man. My brothers have been calling me, trying to persuade me to come and see the old man before he dies, but I can't make myself warm to the idea. My relationship with Will and Ben has suffered because of the lines they chose to draw in the family sand a while back in support of my father. I could never get past him putting his hands on my mother. He was a nasty drunk, and she bore the brunt of his anger in order to protect the three of us. It's hard for me to understand how they could forgive him that despicable sin. And so we're at a bit of an impasse."

Logan exhaled sharply. "Damn. That's a lot to think about. Were you close with your brothers growing up?"

Van nodded. "Very close. We were best friends. Up until my mum died. I was twenty-four. Ben and Will were starting college at the time." He paused, lost in thought. "I don't know how they managed to rationalize things in order to maintain a relationship with our father. I'd seen and heard enough. I can still close my eyes and remember the sound of his meaty fist connecting with my mum's jaw. I wish I could forget. Some things aren't forgivable. Violence against a woman is one of those things."

Logan considered Van's words. *Was what Logan's mother had done worthy of forgiveness?* He wasn't sure he had an answer for that question yet, but he could feel the clock ticking up against his decision.

"Agreed. I think I might feel the same way if I were in your shoes. I grew up without a father, but there were a few guys that my mom brought around while I was young that weren't exactly upstanding citizens. I'll give her credit for one thing: she put up with a lot of shit, but not violence. One of her boyfriends took off his belt to whip me for breaking curfew, and my mom pulled a gun on him and told him that would be his last mistake. He left and never came back. She made a lot of mistakes, but she kept me safe and she made sure there was always food on our table. I can't imagine how it was for you not to feel safe in your own home."

Van sighed. "Yeah, it sucked. I remember counting the days until I was old enough to get the hell out of there. Problem is, I didn't leave right away. I felt too guilty leaving my brothers behind. I knew they'd be OK as long as my mum was there to be the buffer, but I couldn't make myself go. I stayed to protect them. Finally, after working my ass off in a mediocre restaurant in Portland for years, I was offered a full scholarship to the culinary institute thanks to an unexpected letter of recommendation from my boss. It was an opportunity to escape, one I couldn't pass up. My life finally began at twenty-four when I moved to New York. But it was the beginning of the end for my mum. Sometimes I think I let her down by leaving, even though she is the one that encouraged me to go."

Van looked out the window for a long time, lost in thought. "I miss them. My mum. And my brothers. I can't believe they've got me even considering going back to Oregon. But I am. If we stay divided, the old man wins. I have to figure out if I'm strong enough to forgive him and set myself free of the past in the process. Damn. It's hard to wrap my brain around the idea, though."

Logan felt something shift inside himself. If Van could even consider forgiving his father, Logan should make himself dig deep and find a way to do the same for his mother. Her only sins were lack and limitation. She'd done the best she could with him. She'd managed to simply survive. That was the instinct that had kicked in when she'd urged him to go after Willow's inheritance. Janice Matthews saw a way for her son to have long-term financial security, so she pressured him to capitalize on the opportunity. It didn't dawn on her that Logan would grow so fond of Willow and of Garrett in such a short time. Logan was sad that his mother had known so little about her own son that she'd thought him capable of such a grievous deception. But maybe that void in their relationship was partly his to own. Logan had distanced himself from her, moving to Colorado Springs to get as far from her as he could after he'd finished Ranger school. He tried to imagine now what a new-and-improved relationship with his mother could look like, daring to allow himself a small amount of hope in the process. He realized what he had to do. He'd talk to Buck when they got back and set up a time and place to meet. He'd go by feel.

Van reached over to turn the music up. "Enough of this heavy shit. Let's forget our troubles, lad. They'll keep. Right now, we have a baseball game to break down."

He reached down to grab the newspaper he'd brought with him from the floor, opening it to the sports page. "Who's pitching for our boys?"

The rest of that afternoon and evening revolved around beer, brats, and baseball. The game went into extras, with the Rockies winning on a walk-off homer in the eleventh. Van and Logan had stopped drinking early enough that they decided to start driving back, making it halfway before pulling into a hotel near Copper Mountain to crash for a few hours. Logan was jolted a few hours later from a deep sleep by a pounding on his door at four in the morning. It was Van, his face drained of all color.

"It's Laina. We've got to go."

House of Belonging was officially the hottest ticket in town. Laina had worked tirelessly beside her kitchen staff that Saturday night, finally leaving them around eleven to finish closing without her. She was usually the last one out each night, but she hadn't gotten much sleep all week, not that she was complaining. She figured she'd better take advantage of the boys being in Denver to catch up on some much-needed rest.

As she pulled up to her house, she noticed two trucks parked by the side of the road and wondered to herself if her neighbors had hosted a party earlier. Aspen was such a small town; it wasn't uncommon for people to walk home after having had too much to drink. Laina smiled to herself as she unlocked her front door, sliding her foot across the hardwood floor in front of her to clear any mail that might be lying on the floor. There wasn't any, though, which was strange, because she almost always got at least a couple of trade catalogs or bills each day. She set her messenger bag and the velvet bag that housed her knife set down on the hall table, and she was reaching for the light switch when she felt the hair rise up on the back of her neck.

She wasn't alone.

"You should be a little more creative about stashing your extra house key, Laina. A hide-a-key? Really?"

Jeremy.

Laina felt her legs start to give out. Her mind raced as she tried to figure out what to do next. *Her knives.* She felt in the dark, reaching into the velvet pouch to withdraw her butcher knife. She slid it out of the set, spinning around and holding it out in front of her in the direction of his voice.

"I don't know what you're doing here, Jeremy, but you should leave. Now."

The light flicked on, blinding her for a moment. It was just long enough for Jeremy to lunge toward her. He grabbed her wrist so hard, she winced, causing the knife to tumble from her hand and clatter across the floor, landing a few feet away in the living room.

"Relax, Laina. I just needed to talk to you. Alone. That's not easy to do, with your new cowboy friend always around. But now we've finally got some privacy. Indulge me, sweetheart."

She felt like she might vomit. She jerked her hand in an effort to get free, but Jeremy just squeezed harder, spinning her and pushing Laina up against the wall, with her arm twisted behind her back.

He stepped closer, whispering into her ear. "Play nice, Laina. You should stop resisting. I'm going to show you what you're missing."

She could smell the alcohol on his breath and felt his hips pressed up against her behind, the effect making her knees buckle again.

She knew she'd have to fight.

Laina threw her head back as hard as she could, landing a direct hit against Jeremy's nose, the sickening crack a prelude to his anguished cry.

It worked.

He'd released her, grabbing at his face in pain. Laina's eyes searched for the lost knife, finding it farther down the hall on the kitchen floor. She'd lunged for it, the handle within her reach, when Jeremy tackled her from behind, knocking her to the ground, and sending the knife scuttling farther out of reach. He viciously grabbed a handful of her hair, lifting her head and slamming it back down into the hardwood floor. Once. Twice.

Then darkness.

Time had passed—she wasn't sure how much.

Was it a nightmare?

Laina struggled to open her eyes, her head pounding, her face sticky with something she couldn't identify. Her mouth was gagged.

Blood. There's blood on my face.

She tried to move her hands but couldn't because they were tied behind her back. Her feet were bound at the ankles.

She wasn't wearing any clothing except her bra and underwear.

"Open your eyes, Laina. Quit being so dramatic. It didn't have to be like this."

She stifled the sob that tried to escape her throat at the sound of his voice. Her eyes fluttered open, taking a moment to adjust. She was on her living room couch, the only light in the room coming from candles he'd lit while she'd been unconscious. Jeremy pulled up a chair and sat close, watching her with a dark scowl. Laina closed her eyes, pinching them shut in an effort to lose consciousness again.

"Goddamnit, I said open your eyes."

His voice vibrated through her, and she did as she was told, tears spilling down her cheeks, her face pleading with him to stop.

"That's better. I know you don't want it to be this way either, baby. You've got to stop fighting this thing between us, Laina. We could be so good together. You just have to give me the chance to show you. Can you do that, Laina?" Jeremy's jaw twitched, his eyes wild and glassy as he stared at her, waiting for her response.

Drugs. I know that look.

Laina decided to try a different strategy. There would be no reasoning with him. She nodded, taking a deep breath to calm her pounding heart. She whimpered softly, raising her chin toward him.

He smiled darkly. "I know you want me to remove that gag, but I need to make sure you're going to be a good girl. Are you going to be a good girl, Laina?"

Jeremy ran his hand up her bare arm before tracing her breasts and letting his touch venture down along her stomach and toward her pantie line.

Laina willed herself to keep meeting his gaze, trying her best not to flinch at his vile touch.

"God, you've got me so hard right now. I can see that fire in your eyes. I'll take the gag out, but if you make so much as a sound, I'm going to have to silence you. Do you understand?"

Laina nodded, arching her body up in an effort to encourage him.

Jeremy chuckled. "OK, I can see you're coming around. I knew you'd be wild. That's why we're such a match, Laina. You may not realize it, but you need someone like me to keep you in line. That Logan guy is a pussy. I've been watching him with you. How could you pick someone so boring? Jesus. What a disappointment. I guess we all make mistakes."

He stood, reaching down to take the gag from her mouth. Laina gasped for breath, licking her lips in an effort to create some moisture. "Water. Please, Jeremy?"

She smiled meekly, praying he'd show her that small kindness. Laina knew she had to find a way to free her hands if she was going to have any chance at all. The only way that would happen was if she appeared cooperative.

Jeremy stood, walking toward her liquor cabinet, where he'd previously helped himself. There was an open bottle of whiskey and two glasses, one of which had already been used. He poured two fingers of the amber liquid into the empty glass, carrying it over to her.

"I've got something better. You need to relax." He lifted the crystal glass to her lips.

Laina let the sharp drink wet her lips, feeling the fiery path it burned as it slid down her throat. She coughed. Jeremy forced her to take a second sip, which she did, grateful for the almost-immediate numbing effect it had on her insides.

"That's it. Chill out. You don't know it yet, but we're both going to enjoy this." He set the glass down squarely on the end table. "Let me show you what you've been missing."

Jeremy eyed her crudely, lifting his shirt off to reveal his tattooed chest and arms. He slowly unbuttoned his jeans, pausing only when she spoke.

"Wouldn't it be better if you untied my hands? I'd like to touch you, if you'd let me." Laina conjured everything inside of her to put forth an alluring expression, despite the fact that she was fighting back internal hysterics.

Jeremy studied her for a moment. "I don't think you've earned that right yet. Show me you're capable of cooperating, and I'll think about it."

He lowered his pants, stepping out of them and moving to climb on top of Laina. Just before he lowered himself over her, she brought her knees up as hard as she could, connecting them with certainty against his groin. Jeremy howled in pain, rolling off her and falling onto the floor in front of the couch. Laina struggled to sit up, screaming as loudly as she could.

She knew no one would hear her, but her instincts wouldn't allow her to participate willingly any longer in Jeremy's assault. She'd never be able to live with herself. So she screamed. Over and over until Jeremy finally regained his composure.

"Shut the fuck up, you stupid bitch. I warned you." He stumbled into the kitchen, returning with the butcher knife that Laina loved so much clutched in his hand. "I warned you, and now you're going to understand me."

Laina shut her eyes and fell back on the couch, defeated.

"No, son. You're the one who's going to understand."

Laina's eyes snapped open at the sound of a shotgun.

CHAPTER
TWENTY-FIVE

Janice Matthews hadn't lived what anyone would have categorized as an easy life. She'd transitioned from a scrappy foster kid into an unwed teen mother in a matter of months, with no time left in between for living. She'd never for one moment considered giving up her son, not after her own experience in the system. Sure, the nurses had done their best to convince her that her baby would be adopted by a loving family, but she knew no one would protect and love her son the way she would. She'd needed Logan. He'd given her a reason to live. To work hard. She'd done whatever it took to make sure he was safe and cared for and had every chance that she'd always dreamed of but had never been offered.

It had been difficult. She was beautiful, and that had earned her the attention of men her whole life, both wanted and unwanted. She'd fought off the advances of more than one inappropriate foster care provider, but after she'd aged out of the system, she enjoyed the affection of some decent men, a few of them married, who'd offered to keep her and her son well cared for on the side, in exchange for her discretion. Janice's good looks were her capital, and she'd learned how to use them effectively over the years. When one source dried up, she'd fluff and primp and find her next victim. She'd do anything for Logan. The ends justified the means. She'd been too preoccupied to find love. Her job had been to acquire security. And she'd rarely failed. Money, she understood. Love—romantic love anyway—well, that was just some pie-in-the-sky idea she didn't have time to indulge in.

Meeting Buck Randolph had changed everything.

Janice had done her homework before coming to Aspen. She'd been clean and sober for over a year, having finally hit rock bottom after her falling-out with Logan over his sister's inheritance. She'd already known with certainty that Willow was his sister. She hadn't needed to wait for the DNA test to confirm it. The test was for Logan's benefit. Janice knew her straight-and-narrow son would need that assurance. He was the one thing she hadn't screwed up. She was shocked when he'd lied to her about the results. She'd traveled to Aspen almost immediately to talk some sense into him, but had found out about Willow's accident and Logan's organ donation from the local paper.

The news had hit her like a punch in the gut.

Her son was protecting his sister. From Janice. His own mother.

She was toxic to Logan, and she'd realized it fully in that moment. It had sucked the will to live right out of her. She'd flown back east, and after a few months of feeling sorry for herself and indulging in more self-destructive behavior, she finally checked herself into a rehab facility and committed to do the work it took to start her life over again.

After nine months of sobriety, she'd been convinced she could have that life she'd always wanted. She'd written to her son monthly, apologizing for hurting him like she had, but he'd never responded. Her heart ached, not having a relationship with Logan, so she'd decided to pack up her life and move west. Even if Logan shunned her, Janice knew it would be enough for her to live closer to him. She needed to make sure he was all right.

She'd rented a small apartment and taken a job in the local bookstore. She kept mostly to herself, but any chance she got, she'd ask around town for information about Logan. She'd heard he'd purchased a ranch near his sister, which was how she'd found out about his new business partner.

Janice had recognized Buck immediately when he'd walked into the bookstore that afternoon a few months earlier. She'd already seen him from afar, but he was even more handsome up close, and Janice found herself flirting out of habit. She hadn't lost her touch, and Buck asked her out after a few minutes of chatting. They began dating, and she'd started to feel hopeful about life again. Janice was still consumed by thoughts of a reconciliation with Logan, but she'd also started allowing herself to explore her growing feelings for Buck, and she wondered what kind of a future they could have together.

Three weeks earlier, they'd finally admitted that they loved each other, and while Janice had never been happier, she'd also been forced to acknowledge her rising panic. She'd known she'd have to find a way to tell Buck who she was, and why she was in Aspen. If she'd learned anything in recovery, it was that she had to start operating from a more genuine place in her life. She needed to be honest with Buck if they were going to have any chance at happiness.

When she'd admitted to him who she really was, Buck had been stunned, and it had broken her heart to know she'd hurt him. She'd considered running again, leaving Colorado before she could cause any more pain. She'd sat at a bar in Glenwood Springs for two and a half hours, staring at a glass of wine before she made herself get up and walk out without taking a sip. When she'd gotten home that evening, Buck had been waiting for her. They'd agreed that he would tell Logan and let the boy decide how they should handle things. Buck loved her, and it meant the world to Janice that he'd been willing to go to bat for her.

Logan hadn't been immediately receptive to the idea of a reconciliation, but he'd told Buck that he'd take some time to think about it, which was more than she could have hoped for. She knew he was in a new relationship, and she hadn't been able to help herself from asking around about Laina. She was a bit of a mystery to most folks, but from what Janice had been able to gather and from what Buck had said, Laina made Logan happy. Still, Janice had wanted to see for herself.

She'd slipped out that Saturday evening after Buck had fallen asleep, borrowing his truck to drive toward the east end of town. The street outside Laina's house was quiet, so Janice parked along the road and turned the car off to wait. She wasn't sure she'd be brave enough to knock on the door. As she sat contemplating, a second truck turned into Laina's driveway before backing out and parking in front of her. She'd slouched down in the driver's seat, watching as a dark-haired man got out of the pickup and walked around toward the back of Laina's house. Janice watched as he disappeared into darkness, wondering who he was and what he was up to. She'd almost decided to get out and follow him when a small sports car pulled into the drive, and Laina climbed out, headed for her front porch.

The girl was beautiful: exotic-looking, with her short black hair and slender frame. Janice watched curiously as she unlocked the front door and stepped inside. The house remained dark for a bit before the light turned on, and Janice could see the male figure standing with his back to the front window. After a moment, he stepped quickly away and out of sight. *Is it possible Laina is meeting another man while Logan is out of town?* Buck had mentioned that her son was in Denver for a Rockies game with his and Laina's friend Van, so she knew it couldn't be him. Janice bristled at the idea that the girl was being duplicitous.

She'd been about to pull away a few minutes later, her mind convinced of what she'd seen, when she noticed the man carrying Laina in his arms, placing her gently on the couch in front of a large picture window.

So Laina is cheating on my son.

Janice's hands gripped the steering wheel tightly, and she reached to turn the key halfway in the ignition, rolling down the window to get a better look. The front room was dimly lit, so she couldn't see very well. It occurred to Janice that she should try to get some photographic evidence, in case Logan needed convincing. She grabbed her cell phone and opened the camera app before climbing out of the truck, closing the door softly behind her. She slipped up the front steps, peering into the window while she raised her phone to snap a photo.

That's when she noticed that Laina was bound. And gagged.

Janice felt the rage bubble up inside her almost instantly. She ducked down, rushing back toward the truck to call 911, when she remembered that Buck kept an old shotgun in the tool chest in the bed of his truck. She prayed it was loaded, and she was checking to make sure that it was when she heard Laina let out a blood-curdling scream.

Janice cocked the rifle and took the porch steps two at a time. She tried the front door, which mercifully was unlocked, and stepped inside just in time to see the intruder walking toward Laina with a butcher knife in his hand.

"I warned you, and now you're going to understand me." The man took another step toward the couch at the same time Janice raised the rifle.

"No, son. You're the one who's going to understand."

Janice aimed the gun as best she could, closed her eyes, and pulled the trigger.

The police arrived and took their statements, deciding pretty quickly that the shooting could be justified as self-defense. The ambulance had already taken Jeremy to the hospital, where he'd begin a long recovery, trying to figure out how he would live a life in prison with no recognizable genitalia left to work with. Considering it was the first time she'd ever shot a gun, Janice had hit the veritable bull's-eye, rendering Jeremy a eunuch. It was a small consolation.

Laina was taken to the hospital too, as a precaution, and Janice rode along in the ambulance, still in shock. She'd told the girl she was Logan's mother in the moments immediately following the shooting, but Laina had only nodded, shaking so violently that Janice had rushed to call the authorities before cutting the poor girl loose, sitting with her and holding her in her arms until the police arrived. They'd watched together in horror as Jeremy writhed on the floor in pain before finally passing out from excessive blood loss.

Once at the hospital, Janice paced in the waiting room, unsure of what to do. Should she call Buck? He'd know how to reach Logan. She wasn't sure. She'd finally decided she wanted to talk to Laina first, to find out how she wanted to handle things, when the hospital doors whooshed open and Buck came rushing toward her, his eyes frantic.

"What in the hell happened, Jan? Are you OK? The sheriff called. Said my shotgun was used to shoot someone out at Laina's place. I reached Logan on the way here, but he didn't know anything about it. He and Van are rushing back from Denver now. What happened? What were you doing at Laina's house in the middle of the night?"

She told him everything, and to Buck's credit, he sat and listened quietly, without interrupting her. When she'd finished, he took her into his arms, holding her against his chest. No one was more surprised than Jan when she started to sob uncontrollably. She hadn't realized how scared she'd been. She'd acted on pure instinct, just as she'd had to do so many other times in her life. But unlike those other times, now she had someone to hold her and tell her it was all going to be OK.

"I love you, Jan, God help me. I love Logan too, but if I have to, I'll choose you. Driving over here, I wasn't sure who'd been shot. All I knew was that both you and my truck had gone missing. The thought of something happening to you tore me up. Don't do that again, OK? Don't leave me. Stay with me. Be mine." He rubbed her back with his strong hands, holding her close.

Janice tried to steady her racking sobs, but it took some time. Buck's words washed over her like a balm, erasing the evidence of the neglect and longing she'd been molded by her entire life. Finally exhausted, she surrendered, allowing herself to fully absorb his affection.

"I love you too, Buck. I'll stay with you as long as you'll have me."

They held on to each other until the nurse interrupted them some time later.

"Excuse me, Ms. Matthews? Ms. Ming has asked to see you. You can come with me."

Janice nodded, wiping her eyes and looking questioningly at Buck.

"It's OK, honey. Go to Laina. She'll need you to talk her through what happened. She'll want to understand why you were there. She's an amazing girl, Jan. If you get to know her, you'll see why your son loves her so much."

Janice considered his words as she made her way down the hall toward Laina's room.

Laina had her head turned, staring out the window, when Janice paused at the door, knocking softly on the open threshold. Laina turned, giving Janice a meek smile before bursting into tears once again.

Janice rushed forward to grab her hand. "Oh, honey. I'm so sorry for what you went through. I hope what I've done hasn't traumatized you even more." She waited for Laina to stop crying, squeezing her hand in support.

Laina was incredulous. "You saved my life! He was going to rape me. And who knows what after that? I'm not sure how to thank you." Laina studied Logan's mother, who'd clearly been crying herself. "Logan looks so much like you. He has your eyes. Your coloring." Laina's voice quaked. "How is he going to feel about me after this?"

Janice huffed. "Don't you think like that. This wasn't your fault. Damn that animal. If you start to let what he tried to do to you—and failed to do—change you, then he wins. You won't let him win, will you?"

Laina shook her head, closing her eyes.

"Good. Then it's settled. You fought back the best you could. It's not a fair fight when it's man versus woman. The rotten ones know that. It's why they do these things when they have no other way to feel powerful against us. It's really just a sign of their own weakness."

Laina wondered if Logan's mother was speaking from personal experience, but she sensed it wasn't the right time to ask. Instead, she had another question. "Why were you at my house?" Laina studied Jan's face as she considered her answer.

"Honestly? I'm not sure. I wanted to know more about you, since Buck says my son is hopelessly in love with you. I don't know what I thought to gain by my visit. I doubt I would have been able to muster up the courage to knock on your door if I hadn't seen what was happening."

Laina sighed. "Thank God you were there. It doesn't matter why. You were my angel tonight. I'll never be able to repay you."

Janice smiled. "Are they taking good care of you here?" She poured Laina a glass of water from the pink plastic pitcher on her tray, handing it to her so she could take a sip.

"Yes. They want to keep me for the night for observation until my blood work comes back from the lab in the morning. Standard procedure, I guess, since I suffered a concussion." Laina took another sip of her water. "Would you mind staying with me? Just until Logan arrives. I don't want to be alone right now."

Janice stepped into the hall to send word with the nurse to Buck that she'd be waiting with Laina, and by the time she got back, the girl was curled up in the fetal position, sleeping peacefully. Janice dragged the padded chair over next to Laina's hospital bed and reclined herself, but not before taking the girl's hand in her own.

That's exactly how Logan found them when he arrived a short time later.

Buck had already explained everything after Logan and Van had arrived at the hospital to find him fast asleep in the waiting room. The drive had been intense, as their imaginations ran fast and loose with the few details they'd been given. Buck had tried to call them back after he'd talked to Janice, but both of their phones had died, dumping him directly into voice mail.

Van agreed to wait in the lobby with Buck, allowing Logan to see Laina privately first.

Logan stood in the doorway of Laina's hospital room, watching the two women sleep, listening to the faint beep of the machine monitoring Laina's vital signs. He'd never felt so relieved in all his life, and in that moment, he felt his heart crack wide open. There was still love there for the woman who'd raised him. She'd done her best, and yes—she'd failed. Often. But what she'd done for him that night would make up for a thousand disasters. His future lay in that hospital bed, holding hands with his past. It was a beautiful, powerfully complex moment, one Logan would never forget.

Janice opened her eyes as if she'd sensed his presence. Her voice cracked when she spoke. "Son. I'm so sorry." She didn't move, not sure what he was thinking.

Logan walked over to where she sat, reaching for her hand and pulling her up into his embrace. They stood that way for a long time, not speaking. Logan could feel his mother's sobs as he fought back tears of his own. Life was too precious. Too short not to move forward. Nothing would be gained by looking back.

"Logan."

They stepped apart at the sound of Laina's voice. She'd been watching them, her own cheeks wet. Logan rushed to sit next to her, brushing the hair off her forehead to place a kiss there where the skin had been split open from the force of Jeremy's blow.

"My God, Laina. I'm so sorry I wasn't there to protect you from that animal. I promise you he will never hurt you again."

Laina shook her head. "He won't hurt anyone again, thanks to your mom. She's got incredible aim. She showed up just in time. Another minute and . . ."

She couldn't finish, the lump in her throat getting in the way of verbalizing what could have been.

Van appeared in the doorway, with Buck behind him. Laina smiled meekly, motioning for them to come in. Buck stood by Janice, taking her hand in his, while Van bent over Laina, kissing her cheek before standing up to study her.

"That daft prick should have known better than to mess with you ladies. Now he'll spend the rest of his days as a nutless wonder in prison. Serves him right." He turned to Janice. "Donovan Laird, ma'am. But please call me Van. All my friends do. After what you did for our lass tonight, I'd say you fall in that category."

Janice smiled, glancing nervously at Logan before dropping her eyes to the floor. "Thank you, Van. My son is a lucky man to have such loyal friends."

Logan looked around the room at each of them, overcome by emotion, relief, and exhaustion all at the same time. "I'd say we're all lucky. To have each other."

EPILOGUE

April

The call came in the middle of the night. It had been snowing heavily when they'd gone to bed, and a quick peek out the bedroom window told Logan that the spring storm hadn't let up. It was a real-life snow globe, with the absence of wind having allowed the huge white flakes to accumulate with impressive fluffiness.

Laina groaned and rubbed her swollen belly, wondering how she was going to make herself get up. It was getting harder to sleep each night, what with the foot or elbow or whatever other body part was jutting up into her ribs. She didn't have to struggle long because Logan had heard her from their bathroom and came rushing out to help. His face was still dotted with shaving cream, his hips wrapped in a white towel.

"Here, love, let me help you." He sat beside Laina, wrapping one arm behind her back and using his hand to help her sit up. "If you want to stay here, I can go to the hospital by myself. It's pretty snowy out there. I don't want you out on the roads if you don't have to be."

Laina swung her legs over the side of the bed, letting her swollen feet gratefully touch the cool floor. She'd been about to speak when she'd gotten confirmation of what she'd suspected all night long. "Logan, you know I wouldn't miss the birth of your first child for anything. Anything that is, except for the birth of *our* first child."

Laina grimaced, disappointed by the poor timing. They'd gotten the call just fifteen minutes before from Sienna, telling them that Viv had been admitted to the hospital, and that she was already pretty deep into her labor. Sienna suggested that if Logan still wanted to be there, he'd better head to the hospital to join them before dawn.

Logan studied Laina with a concerned look on his face. "Are you OK, Carina?" He got off the bed and squatted down in front of her, looking worriedly into her eyes. "Is it the baby?"

Laina exhaled slowly, smiling at Logan while she reached to wipe the remaining bits of shaving cream off his cheeks with her fingertips. "Oh, it's most definitely the baby. Either your children are coming into this world already very in tune with each other, or they are racing to see who can be the first to be born." She winced, taking another slow breath before continuing. "Vivian may have a slight lead, but the way these pains are starting to intensify now that I'm sitting up, I'd say I'll be catching up pretty quickly. For a guy who wasn't sure he wanted to be a dad a year ago, you're about to have your hands full."

Logan's heart raced, and he stood up, looking around the bedroom in a panic. "I'll get dressed right now. Oh my God. I can't believe this is happening." He leaned in to kiss Laina before rushing to throw on a pair of jeans and an old sweater he'd just unpacked that afternoon.

Logan rushed down the stairs to make Laina a cup of hot tea for the ride while she finished getting dressed.

Glancing outside the kitchen window at the swirling snow, Logan was relieved once more that he'd been able to persuade Laina to move into town instead of continuing to live at the ranch. He knew that, in this weather, the roads beyond Walland House were likely impassable by now. They'd found out about her pregnancy the morning after her attack, when the blood work results came back, but Logan and Laina had initially kept the news to themselves until they'd had time to get over the shock. Laina hadn't been able to go back to her old place after what had happened with Jeremy, so they'd sold it almost immediately. She'd been staying with Logan at the ranch house until the week before when they'd finally closed on this home they'd bought together in the West End.

They'd had some work done to the new house, and managed to integrate their styles in a way that made the new place feel like it belonged to both of them. The kitchen was Logan's favorite, anchored by antique hardwood floors and the beautiful mint-green vintage appliances they'd ordered to offset the wood beams on the ceiling and the hand-scraped white brick walls.

As he slid his boots and coat on, Logan paused to smile at their wedding picture, which sat framed on the bookcase next to the front door. He'd surprised her with the trip to Nepal in August, and he'd both proposed to and married her in the city where her parents had first found her. Logan had called her father to ask for her hand, surprised when Bo and Serena offered to fly over and attend the ceremony. The framed photograph was of the four of them, standing outside of the airport in Kathmandu, a tiny bouquet of flowers in Laina's hand. It wasn't the most romantic setting, but it had been special to them, as evidenced by the smiles on their faces. They'd thrown a huge party at Walland House and renewed their vows in front of family and friends a week after they'd returned. They shared the news that they were expecting that same evening, much to everyone's delight. Thinking back now, Logan couldn't imagine a time when he'd questioned his desire to be a father. But as he rushed outside to start the truck, he was acutely aware that the fear that Rex had warned him about had slowly crept in. The fear of loving something so deeply, he was terrified to lose it. That's how he felt about his life now. He had a wife he adored, and within the next few hours, he'd have two babies to worry about. He knew his life was about to change forever.

Logan had just come back inside from shoveling the walk when he heard Laina call to him from the top of the stairs.

"OK, look out below. Here I come . . ."

Logan laughed, admiring his gorgeous wife as she descended the stairs toward him. She was exaggerating her physical presence, as usual. Logan thought he'd never seen her look more beautiful than she did that morning, with no makeup and a nervous look of expectancy on her face, one hand resting on her tummy as she walked. She stood on the landing and held Logan's face in her hands before giving him a tender kiss. "Well, Daddy. We'd better get moving if you don't want to have to build a roadside igloo to deliver your baby. Also, did you text our parents?"

Logan helped her down the final step and held the front door open for her as she stepped outside onto the porch. "Yep. Mine and yours. Your dad said they'd catch the first flight here and asked me to keep them posted. Mom and Buck will probably beat us to the hospital. And yes, your bag is already in the back seat." He turned the key to lock the front door, taking Laina's hand in his. "The next time we walk into this house together, we're going to be someone's mom and dad. Then it's really going to start to feel like home."

Laina turned to kiss him one more time before letting him help her into the passenger seat of the Bronco, snowflakes catching on her eyelashes as she looked at him. "My home is wherever you are. And it always will be."

"Buck, be careful. We want to make sure we get there in one piece to meet those grandbabies."

Janice still wasn't used to the epic snowfall in the mountains, and she was very glad she hadn't had to drive in it. She and Buck had been inseparable, especially since they'd moved in together in the fall. Janice still woke up most days feeling the need to pinch herself to make sure it wasn't all one big dream. Logan had made huge strides in trusting her, and they'd worked hard at healing their fractured relationship. It helped that Janice was also determined to repair any damage she'd done with Willow. Janice worked with Buck part-time, helping him run the office out at the ranch, so she was around Walland House often enough that she'd been able to put forth an honest effort to get to know Logan's sister, whom he adored. Janice was happy that their children would likely grow up together too; Willow and Garrett had just announced at Christmas that they, too, were expecting their first child together that summer.

Buck winked at her as he steered the truck through the unplowed streets, turning into the hospital parking lot. "I promised I'd get you here in one piece, honey, and here we are." He pulled underneath the overhang to let her out at the front doors before parking his truck nearby to join Janice in the lobby where she stood waiting. Van rushed in just as they'd gotten directions to the family waiting area from a passing doctor, so they rode the elevator upstairs together.

"Hell of a night for a party. I guess these babies are going to have minds of their own, just like their parents." Van raked a hand through his hair, squinting in an effort to wake up. "Let's find a coffee maker and see if we can't get some news out of one of these nurses."

The only information that they were able to get was that there was no word yet about either couple. Their labors were progressing, but the nurses couldn't say much more than that until either Sienna or Logan came out to share more. The first hour crept by, then the second. Morning dawned, but it was difficult to tell since the snow continued to fall, covering the world in white. Willow and Garrett arrived around seven, bringing with them a bag full of homemade breakfast sandwiches. Garrett walked up behind Van but stopped short when he saw that he was talking on the phone.

Van held up a finger as he finished his conversation before hanging up his cell phone in frustration. "Sorry. It's this hotshot director who is going to be using our property in Oregon for a movie shoot this summer. I'm starting to wonder why I let my brothers talk me into this. We should have just started in on the renovations right away, but the price the studio offered us was too damned irresistible. And they wanted the place as is." Van sighed. "They're there scouting the location this weekend, and I'm getting calls every couple of hours with loads of questions." He glanced at his watch. "I guess starting time is six a.m., West Coast. I keep saying I'll be back on Monday, but you know these Hollywood types. They want their needs met yesterday."

Garrett chuckled. "Are you regretting leaving already? Maybe you should keep your place here. Just in case."

Van shook his head. "Nah. I'm not attached to it. I'm not sure I'm coming back here to live anytime soon. I moved here in the first place to support Laina, and I suppose that worked out just fine. But now that she's settled, it's time for me to figure out what the hell I want to do when I grow up. Maybe this project in Oregon is just the thing that will get me pointed in the right direction. If not, I can always come back when the renovations are finished." He clasped Garrett by the arm, gesturing toward the man's pregnant wife. "Besides, I've got to get out of Aspen. There seems to be something in the water."

In the end, it was almost nine before the friends got the news. The snow had stopped falling, and, as was not uncommon after a Colorado storm, the sun prevailed in the bluebird sky, her warm rays slanting in through the windows of the waiting room, bathing them all in welcomed light.

The double doors leading from the birthing wing finally opened with a loud click, getting everyone's attention.

Logan and Sienna walked toward their friends and family together, holding hands. Each of them wore huge smiles but looked exhausted. Sienna spoke first.

"Our girls were amazing. I have a whole new respect for Vivian, for Laina, and for women everywhere. I just experienced an absolute miracle. Viv and I are the proud mommies of a beautiful baby girl, gifted to us by this incredible man standing here." She paused to squeeze Logan's hand and brush away her own tears. "Shanti Matthews Livingston joined our family this morning at eight forty-five. Seven pounds, four ounces of absolute perfection. She barely even cried."

Logan grinned, bursting with news of his own. "And in true big-brother form, Oliver Ming Matthews beat his little sister to the finish line by exactly one minute and almost two pounds, weighing in at a svelte nine pounds two ounces. God bless my wife. She did it without any drugs. I'm not worthy."

As everyone cheered and congratulated them, Logan couldn't help feeling that, somehow, he really was worthy of it all. He knew in that moment, surrounded by the people that he loved the most, that he'd work every day to make sure he earned the privilege.

The privilege of belonging to the family he'd been born into, and to the family that he'd managed to create for himself, all at the same time.

ACKNOWLEDGMENTS

"Each friend represents a world in us, a world
possibly not born until they arrive, and it is only by
this meeting that a new world is born."
—Anaïs Nin

Truer words were never spoken. Midway through this third and final book in the Hesse Creek Series, it finally clicked. The overarching theme of *Walland*, *Seeds of Intention*, and *House of Belonging* is about distinguishing the difference between the family we're born into and the tribe we cobble together for ourselves over the course of a lifetime. I've moved a lot since I was a child, but I've managed to weave together a beautiful tapestry of people whom I hold so dear. Many of them don't live near me but that doesn't mean that if push came to shove, we wouldn't be there for each other in a heartbeat. I've made my share of mistakes in life, but one thing I've done well is choose amazing friends. Some have been around for a season; a few have been here for a reason, but a precious few will last for a lifetime. I'm grateful for all of them, and for the lessons they've taught me—and continue to teach—about life and about myself.

To my merry band of friend-editors: Lisa Salyers, Terri Carrick, Kara Clarke, Lekshmi Nair, Dawn Wood, Shannon Murante, Erin Doppke, Trish Alikhan, Mim (Aunt Merilynn), and my sweet cousin Gina Tolomeo. You have no idea how it makes my heart sing to be able to send you my unpolished pages, knowing that I can trust you and that you'll be honest but kind about the art that I've created. There is no one else I'd be able to be so vulnerable with. Thank you for your gentleness. Thank you to my dear friend Julie Burns for your friendship and support, and for sharing my books with so many of your friends and contacts. And thanks to Patra Dunn for making sure my books were so well traveled.

Mim: You deserve a special shout-out for always being so willing to go the extra mile to share my books with the world. Whether it's schlepping copies to libraries all over Michigan (and Ohio!) or hand delivering them to anyone you might meet along your travels. Thank you for being such a cheerleader for me. I love you.

To my mom's cousin (and mine), Kim Frum. Thank you for so willingly importing the Hesse Creek Series to your friends in West Virginia. I hope I'll get to meet them all in person during this next book tour.

I wouldn't have a beautiful book to show the world if it weren't for the amazing team at Girl Friday Productions: Christina Henry de Tessan, Nicole Burns-Ascue, Meghan Harvey, Rachel Marek, Paul Barrett, Stefanie Hargreaves, Michelle Hope Anderson, and Carrie Wicks. Thank you for the thoughtful feedback, the extensive editing, the beautiful cover design, my gorgeous website, and so much more. The GF team is the absolute best. If I could do a free commercial for you, I would. I hope my books make you as proud as they make me, since they were a complete and total team effort.

I've had so many lovely bookstore author events and media opportunities thanks to the hard work of my publicists at JKS Communications. Angelle Barbazon, Ellen Whitfield, Marissa DeCuir, and Sydney Mathieu, along with the rest of your incredible team—what would I do without you? Thanks for not only coordinating my bookstore events but also making sure that local media knows I'm coming, and that I'm always supported in every way. You've been instrumental in connecting me with book bloggers, whose efforts have been so critical to my success. Thank you to author Susan Alexander for all of your help and guidance as I dipped my toe into the world of online advertising. What a difference that has made! Thank you to my friend and local publicist Stephanie Krol of SKPR for all of your help with the local Chicago media opportunities—I'm so lucky to have met you at the beginning of my writing career.

ATTENTION, BOOK BLOGGERS: I say prayers of thanksgiving for you every single night. I've been blessed to receive good feedback about my Hesse Creek Series from some incredible bloggers. Thank you in particular to those that both reviewed and took time to post those reviews on either Amazon or Goodreads for me: *Publishers Weekly*; *NDP Book Review*; Barbara Bos from *Women Writers, Women's Books*; *A Beautiful Book Blog*; *Happy Ever After Blog—USA TODAY*; *RT Book Reviews*; Susan at *The Book Bag* blog; Dianne at *Tome Tender*; Kristen Kranz at *Hypable*; Kandice Cole at *Windy City Reviews*; *NY Literary Magazine*; Kristina Hickey; Jennifer at *Bookish Devices*; *The SubClub Books*; *The Book Bellas*; *Kelly's Thoughts on Things*; *Traveling with T*; *Reviews by Crystal*; *Cristina Reads*; *The Blabbing Bibliophile*; *Stranded in Books*; *The Bandar Blog*; *Sweet Book Obsession*; *Katy's Library Blog*; *Everlasting Charm*; *Cleveland Scene*; Bookishamanda; librarycutie; books_on_books; bookwormeverlasting; lifeinlit;

thebookgawker; booknerdnative; readingbringsjoy; and so many more. (This goes to print early, so if I missed you this time around, I'll certainly thank you in the next book! Please know how grateful I am to all bloggers who show such wonderful support for authors.)

I really love visiting with book clubs. It's so fun to be surrounded by smart, funny, welcoming women talking about our mutual love of reading. Dee Bauer—thank you for not only hosting one of my first book clubs, but for hosting a second, and also for urging people who liked my books to follow up with reviews, which you know are so important for up-and-coming authors like myself. I am grateful for your friendship and support, and take much inspiration from the way you live your life, giving back to others. Our HJWC book club is such a blessing in my life. I love all of you ladies so much, and can't wait to spend more time together in the future. Alison Peters—I'm so excited to be connected with such an amazing writer—thanks for your support. And to Jeannie Stawoiak—a special thank-you for hosting my very first book club for *Walland*. They say you'll never forget your first.

One of the coolest experiences I've had has been hearing my books come to life. I'm blessed to have Marnye Young as the voice of the entire Hesse Creek Series. I cannot imagine anyone else having voiced my beloved characters so perfectly. And thanks, too, for the introduction to the supremely talented voice artist, Sean Patrick Hopkins, who joins us in voicing the men of *House of Belonging*. I have a feeling this is just the beginning of a dynamic working relationship going forward. You're an amazing talent, Marnye. Thank you.

The book tour for *Seeds of Intention* was an absolute blast. I'm humbled by the willingness of bookstores and booksellers to go out on a limb to support up-and-coming authors. Thank you to all of you who chose to say *yes*!

In Chicago, thank you to Georgette at Barbara's Bookstore in Burr Ridge for coordinating and hosting my launch event for *Seeds of Intention*, and to all the family and friends who came out to support me. I loved my humble event at Garfield Ridge Library, too. Thank you to Mina for hosting me and passing my books along to your book club. And thanks to Paula Wilding at Prairie Path Books in Wheaton for hosting me for a lovely author talk and signing. And special thanks to Michelle Rollins for connecting us in the first place! Special thanks to Scott Jonlich and Rosie Conway for the generous cover story in the February issue of *Hinsdale Magazine*. I fully expect to see Rosie's book on the shelves one day soon. Gratitude to a friend I met thanks to our mutual love of books and baseball (and the White Sox!): Michealene Redemske— it's been such a pleasure getting to know you better.

In Cleveland, thanks to Fireside Book Shop for hosting my signing, and to the *Chagrin Valley Today* for the lovely preview piece letting people know I was coming. Roxanne Washington at the *(Cleveland) Plain Dealer*, thank you for helping me get the word out once again. It's always fun to talk with you. And special thanks to Colleen Smitek at *Cleveland Magazine* for writing such a nice article and for the opportunity to grace your December cover with my sweet husband. Mark Nolan—thanks for always letting us crash your various hosting duties when we're in town. It's so fun to visit with old friends at WOIO, and to spend the morning with you and Jimmy Malone and Tracey Carroll at WMJI. Thanks to Margaret Daykin, Stefani Schaefer, and our friends at the WJW Fox 8 in the *Morning Show* for having us back again to talk books and baseball. (And *Outlander* :) Thank you to the ladies at the Chagrin Valley Woman's Club for inviting me to be their guest author and keynote speaker. It's a delight to be able to help support students from one of my very favorite cities in the world.

In my husband's hometown of Peoria, Illinois: Thank you once again to Bonnie at Barnes and Noble for always welcoming us with open arms. It's a treat to visit with you each and every time. In you, I've found a kindred spirit. I'm blown away by the support of our family, friends, and even strangers who embrace us every time we visit Peoria. Many thanks to both WMBD-TV and WEEK-TV, along with the *(Peoria) Journal Star*, for featuring my work in advance of my author event. Stacy Litersky—thank you for your support and friendship for all of these years.

In Aspen, Colorado, thank you to Margaret, Mark, and Katelyn at Explore Booksellers for hosting my friends at a lovely event in mid-September. You've shot up the list to become one of my all-time favorite bookstores. I look forward to the chance to return as soon as possible. To the girlfriends who made that trip so special: Natalia Alem, Sondra Fowler, Monique Thanos, Jacquie Parrillo, Kelly Milne, Erin Doppke, Dawn Wood, Tifani O'Rourke, Dee Bauer, Cindy Short, Katie Mueller, Kara Clarke, and Karen Wooley Hood. I love you all, and I'll cherish the memories of that trip forever.

We are one of the lucky families that had the chance to live in the Twin Cities for a while, which is why I was so excited to return for an author event at Subtext Books, one of the best independent bookstores around. Thanks to Mary Ann Grossmann at *Pioneer Press*, who wrote the nicest article, spreading the word about my visit, and thank you to Sue Zumberge and Matt Keliher at Subtext for organizing my visit and being such gracious hosts. Leslie Bergstrom—thank you for coming and spreading the word about my books. You're an amazing friend. And what a wonderful opportunity to see and spend time with my baby brother. I love you, Nick.

I had the remarkable opportunity to share the stage as a fiction panelist with some amazing authors at the Southern Independent Booksellers Alliance (SIBA) convention in New Orleans. Thank you to Wanda Jewell and everyone at SIBA for putting on such a lovely event, and for connecting authors and booksellers from across the South. I was so grateful for that special opportunity.

Carole Sullivan and the folks at *Today in Nashville*: thanks for having me visit one of my favorite cities to talk about books with you! I'm grateful for how readily you've opened your arms to me.

Laurie Kirby from "Women's Watch" on WBZ/CBS Boston—thank you for having me on the airwaves! And a big thank-you to *Southern Distinction Magazine* in Atlanta for featuring my work.

Thanks to my fellow Woman's Board members at Children's Home and Aid in Chicago for asking me to emcee their gala last September. What an honor it was to play a small part in helping to raise funds for families and children in crisis.

Suzy Sparacio: you're our angel. We couldn't love you any more if you were actually related to us. Thanks to both you and Michael for allowing us to travel, knowing that our kiddos are in the very best care in our absence. We love you, and can't wait to share in the evolution of your own personal love story this year.

Thank you to Paula and Chris Murphy for all of your help last summer, allowing me generous amounts of time to write *House of Belonging* while in California. I'm grateful to you both and wish you love and light always.

Sean Finnegan, you must be properly thanked for paving the way for me to join Soho House. It's been such a blessing to have a quiet (and super-cool) place to write when I need it.

Thanks to Jerry Azumah and Brenda Robinson for vouching for me as well.

Thank you to my friend Sonia of Sonia Mani-Joseph Photography and Nicee Martin of Miss Motley Photography for the lovely head shots and fabulous pictures from my launch party. I love knowing such amazing women who can take kick-ass pictures the way the two of you can! Remember: you must try your very best to make me look young and skinny! And Heather Ann Thomas—you'll always be the one who first inspired me.

Sally Gries, Ed Bell, and Brent Ballard: we couldn't do anything without you. The words "thank you" will never be enough. Pam Ziegan and Shannon Gallagher: you've each saved us a time or two—or fifty. Thanks for your friendship and continued support.

To everyone who took the time to come out to one of my author events, read my books, post words of encouragement to me, or just send good vibes when I needed them most: thank you so very much. I love being a writer, and it means the world to me to know that my work is helping to connect with others in some small way.

The hardest part of writing acknowledgments is the feeling that I'm leaving someone out. If I have, please know it wasn't intentional. Every single person who passes through my life leaves footprints on my heart. I'm a lucky girl, and I know it.

I have the best family in the world.

Dad, thank you for teaching me to say yes . . . and for always being willing to jump in and help us out. We couldn't do it without you, and I love you so much. (Wear your helmet!)

Lila and Landon: I couldn't imagine my life without you. You've both grown into lovely human beings, always ready with a kind word for others and a hug for your tired mom when she needs it. You're my everything, and I'm so proud of you both.

Finally, to my husband, Jim. You are a Hall of Fame human being, and there is no one else that makes me laugh like you do. I love the fact that after twenty years of marriage, you still grab my hand when we're walking beside each other. Thank you for loving me and supporting me and letting me sneak away to my "writing retreats" when needed. What a gift to get to live with my best friend every single day. I feel very lucky that our kids have you as their dad.

OK. Time to get to work on the next series. Who's ready to head to the Pacific Northwest?

(Prepare yourselves to meet three remarkable brothers. I can't wait to introduce them to you.)

In the meantime . . .

Remember, whenever possible, be kind.

(And it's always possible.)

Until next time . . .

Andrea

ABOUT THE AUTHOR

Andrea Thome is a former broadcast journalist, having covered both sports and news during her career. In her novels, Andrea explores some of her favorite travel destinations, from the foothills of the Smoky Mountains to the Colorado Rockies, painting rich backdrops that become characters themselves. Thome lives in Chicago with her husband (a retired professional baseball player) and their two children. She spends her spare time traveling and pursuing her other passion—photography. You can see a sampling of her photography and learn more about her books at www.andreathome .com. *House of Belonging* follows *Seeds of Intention* and *Walland* in the award-winning Hesse Creek Series.

CPSIA information can be obtained
at www.ICGtesting.com
Printed in the USA
FFOW02n0521310518
46937967-49184FF